The Box of Bones

A Skye Cree Novel

VICKIE McKEEHAN

beachdevils
PRESS

The Box of Bones
A Skye Cree Novel

Published by Beachdevils Press
Copyright © 2014 Vickie McKeehan
All rights reserved.

The Box of Bones
A Skye Cree Novel
Copyright © 2014 Vickie McKeehan

Published by
beachdevils
PRESS
ISBN-10: 0692207279
ISBN-13: 978-0692207277
Printed in the USA

Cover design by Vanessa Mendozzi
Wolf designed by Jess Johnson

Visit Vickie at:
http://www.vickiemckeehan.com
http://vickiemckeehan.wordpress.com/
http://www.facebook.com/VickieMcKeehan
www.twitter.com/VickieMcKeehan

Don't miss these other exciting titles by bestselling author
Vickie McKeehan

ACKNOWLEDGMENTS
To Rich, for all things cop.
To Jess, for graphics that really pop.
To Kristi, for all the social media help.
To Dana, for all the corrections and catches.
As always, any mistakes belong to me.

For my family and friends.
It's you guys who keep me going.

"We serial killers are your sons,
we are your husbands,
we are everywhere."
Ted Bundy

The Box of Bones

A Skye Cree Novel

VICKIE McKEEHAN

Prologue

Twenty years earlier
Fort Lewis, Washington

"**Y**ou made soup for dinner? What kind of an idiot woman thinks a man can make a meal outta soup?"

Black-haired beauty Trisha Danes, barely out of her teens, had only been married to the twenty-two-year-old army corporal for six months. But Trisha had already decided it had been the worst time of her life. How was she supposed to know that Milo got pissed off about everything *before* he'd slipped a twenty-dollar ring on her finger? That's what she got for marrying somebody she'd only known a short two months.

She trembled a little at the sound of Milo's angry tone. Lately he always seemed to be mad about something. And tonight was no exception.

In her best Carolina drawl, she tried to pacify him. "It's…not…soup, honey. It's stew. And dontcha know, it has lots of meat and veggies like potatoes and carrots and onions, just like you like," Trisha went on to point out.

"Well, whatever it is, you made it so damn watery that it looks like soup to me. I can see the bottom of the damn pan," Milo grumbled.

That was because she'd tried to stretch all the ingredients. But she didn't say this to Milo. Instead she did her best to appease him again and offered, "Okay, okay, no need to get upset. How about I fix you a nice grilled cheese instead? You like those. You can eat it with the…soup."

"I'm not eating a damned sandwich. A man wants a real meal when he gets home from working a ten-hour shift, not a bunch of cheese on toast."

Trisha sucked in a nervous breath. It might be different if Milo had an exhausting job loading trucks for the army from six in the morning until four in the afternoon. But he didn't. What Milo did was sit on his ass at a desk inputting data into a computer all day, keeping track of shipments coming onto and going off the base. Not exactly grueling work in Trisha's mind. But she didn't dare mention that at the moment. She didn't want to fight. And because of that she went to the refrigerator and dug out the carton of eggs. "How about I scramble you up some of these?"

"Damn it, woman! That's breakfast food. I want you to fix me supper. What about that don't you understand?"

Now was probably not a good time to remind Milo that they still had another week to go till payday. He could eat a cheese sandwich, or the two scrambled eggs or the watery stew. Honestly though, Trisha was getting mighty tired of Milo's temper flaring like a volcano over the least little thing like what he had for dinner. Trisha backed away from the fridge as Milo stormed over to the same appliance and yanked the door open to see for himself what was inside.

Trisha wasn't taking any chances. She moved three feet away to the counter.

"There's nothing in here but some ketchup, mustard and mayo. We don't even have a hotdog to throw on the stove. Where the hell is the food?"

It wasn't like she'd eaten it up herself. Beginning to shake now with fear that he might take it up a notch, which she'd seen him do lately, she did her best to remind him of their situation. "We have seven dollars in our checking account, Milo. It's gotta last at least another six days before I can go to the PX. We've used up our allotment for food. Look, I've got a can of beans in the pantry I can throw in and add it to the stew. That'll make it a lot thicker."

But when Milo slammed the ice-box door shut and wheeled around with fire in his eyes, Trisha knew she was in trouble. "Don't you dare hit me again! I didn't move three thousand miles all the way across the country to a place where all it does is rain all the damned time for you to use me as a punching bag every single time you get mad about something! I'm not putting up with you hitting me anymore, Milo."

"Oh yeah? Then leave. Get out of my face *and* my house. What good are you anyway? Can't even fix a damn meal the right way," he groused.

But when she reached for the keys on the counter to the only vehicle they owned, Milo's truck, he slapped her hand away. "You ain't takin' my pickup. You wanna get out of here? Fine, you walk. You leave with what's on your back."

"That's not right."

"Yeah, well neither is me coming home and finding a crappy meal on the stove." With that, he shoved her through the back door. "Now get your ass out of my sight before I decide to smack you."

"Where am I supposed to go, Milo?"

"Hey, you wanna leave? What the hell do I care where you go?" He pushed her onto the narrow porch and then slammed the door shut in her face.

The minute she heard the lock turn on the other side, Trisha's shoulders slumped. What was she supposed to do now? She took two steps and started pounding on the door. "At least give me my purse. Come on, Milo. I need my wallet! It has my ID in it."

When the door cracked open slightly, she had hope. But then Milo tossed her handbag over her head and it landed on the wet patch of dirt and weedy grass behind her.

"There. Satisfied now? By the way, I took the checkbook out of it, too. I don't want you writing hot paper all over town that I'll have to cover. Now get out of my sight! You knock on this door again and I'll bash your face in."

Knowing he would do it, Trisha backed down the steps and ran over to retrieve her pocketbook. She brushed off the tan faux leather grain hoping all the grime came off.

It was beginning to get dark and already chilly for October. The sun dipped in the west over the tips of the evergreens as she made her way through the complex heading to the nearest pay phone, a good half mile away.

She didn't even have her jacket. Asshole Milo, she thought, as she tromped off in the direction of the PX. What she had ever seen in the piece of shit, she could only wonder now.

It was time to call her stepmom, Brandy Sue Grainger, collect back in Charlotte. Trisha hoped the woman accepted the charges. After all, it was her stepmother who had tried to warn her about marrying Milo. She wished now she'd listened to Brandy. Not only that, Trisha hoped she could talk Brandy Sue into sending her bus fare to get back home. If that didn't happen, she'd have to hitchhike her way clear across the country. But first, she'd have to wait for Milo to go to work in the morning to go back to the apartment to get her clothes.

As Trisha contemplated where she planned to sleep that night, a Jeep pulled alongside her with the windows rolled down. That seemed odd to Trisha because she'd been here two months and not a single soul had gone out of their way to be friendly to her.

When the man behind the wheel brought the car to the side of the road and came to a stop, Trisha stopped walking.

"You need a ride, honey? It's awful cold out here and you don't even have a coat on."

He seemed nice enough and wow was he ever cute all that dark hair and all. Maybe her luck in the man department had turned.

As she opened the passenger door and hopped into the front seat, Trisha had no way of knowing it was the last ride she would ever take.

Chapter One

Present day
Seattle, Washington

For a woman who'd never traveled farther south than the state of California, jetting to St. Kitts for her honeymoon in the middle of winter had been nothing short of heaven.

Skye Cree didn't jet-set. She didn't consider herself a fan of the glitzy or the privileged. She wasn't particularly materialistic or fashionable. But when it came to touching down on the lush island surrounded by sparkling blue water, she'd been captivated by all the trappings that went with a luxurious resort hotel. She'd even taken advantage of the spa where some guy named Javier had given her a massage that made her feel like she could float on air.

After all, even the most dogged hunter needed to get away, needed to take a break from chasing down scum once in a while. Maybe that's why she'd reveled in the trip. And not for the obvious reasons a new bride might have, who itched to get the man she loved all to herself for two weeks in a tropical setting. That was a bonus. The fact that she'd rarely gone anywhere in her life before meeting Josh Ander left her wanting to see places she'd only dreamed or read about.

So she'd taken advantage of every minute there. She'd used her camera like a pro, filling up the disc with no less than two hundred pictures. The trip had yielded plenty of things to check out, to explore, new things to experience.

But like any other newlywed couple, she and Josh had rarely left their hotel room, opting instead to spend their nights languishing in bed, their days not that much different.

When they had ventured out, they'd acted like typical tourists. They'd sipped on fruity exotic drinks made with pineapple and mango and rum and topped with those little paper umbrellas. They'd danced to the sounds of acoustic guitars and ukuleles and drummers keeping the beat with their steelpans.

They hadn't wanted any of it to end, not the twenty-four-hour room service nor the brilliant sunrises and sunsets that came with it.

They'd flown out of SeaTac with a cold wind breathing down their backs. Eight hours later they'd landed among bright green rolling hills, warm crystal blue water slapping at white sand, sand that glistened as though slivers of diamonds were lining the shores. With temperatures reaching the high eighties every day, their fourteen glorious days in the Caribbean flew by. The tranquil time had flown by way too fast.

She supposed there were rules to getting back into the swing of things. But it had ended and now, here she was back dealing with Seattle's winter.

Temps had fallen overnight to a chilly record low of twenty-seven degrees. A light drizzle spat down from above as she blew into the lobby of the gleaming Breslin Building.

Taking a deep breath, she prepared to step back into her role at the Artemis Foundation, the Foundation that located missing children.

When the polished steel doors opened to the elevator, she dashed into the car and punched the button for three. As it began its upward motion, she had to admit she'd missed her little office on the third floor. Okay, truth be told, she couldn't wait to get back into the swing of things.

She'd gotten a late start though. She'd lingered over her toast and jam and her second cup of coffee too long while her husband of sixteen days had headed out the door for work.

She knew Josh had a brutal software schedule to keep. With his job as the CEO at Ander All Games he was often behind at work. Even before their wedding, he'd struggled to keep up. In fact, since his transformation he often had to play catch-up. She worried he didn't get enough sleep. There never seemed to be enough hours in the day or night, especially that time after midnight when they searched Seattle's streets. They'd negotiated the hours, times they'd set aside for themselves and compromised on everything else. Teamwork, he called it.

But it didn't matter if they'd reached an agreement. Skye still felt responsible for the crazy workload he had. It was a waste of time to talk herself out of it. Wasn't it her fault? All of it.

Native American blood coursing through her veins might make her susceptible to its folklore but it was her Nez Perce spirit guide, a silver wolf named Kiya, that made her a believer. If not for Kiya, she would never have escaped from Ronnie Whitfield at the age of twelve.

That was long before she and Josh wound up in the woods outside Whitfield's cabin. Long before Kiya had saved Josh. That day, her mystical wolf—her protector, her guardian, had come through again by merging her life forces with Josh's to save them both.

Such drastic measures had come at a steep price and changed Josh forever. But they would never have been there in the first place if not for her obsession, her stubborn refusal to stop looking for the man she felt had gotten away with a slap on the wrist. Her fixation on Whitfield had almost gotten both of them killed.

She had to take responsibility for that.

Unlocking the door to the office suite, Skye stepped inside as the silver wolf nipped at her heels. These days, Kiya went everywhere with her—too many crazies out there not to. It had taken the wolf months to regain strength, to adjust to the cells from Josh so that she could fully make use of the human traits she'd acquired in the merge.

As the wolf prowled the suite, checking out every corner, Skye had to concede Josh acted much the same way at times. Amused at her own wit, she understood the analogy. Even though Josh didn't actually walk around on all fours, he did prowl and pace. Often. Plus his persistent, stubborn ways could get annoying at times. Since taking on Kiya's qualities, his dogged pursuit was one of the qualities she most admired, while at the same time accepting blame for that, too. He certainly wasn't the same man she'd met that night in a dark alleyway.

If he were standing here, he'd no doubt argue that those differences made him a better man, improved him as a team player, someone she could count on in a fight. Lately, Josh tossed out the word "team" a lot. It could be maddening at times. After all, he was now more skilled at tracking than she was. Thanks to a keen sense of smell and the wolf blood that ran through his veins, his strength was a hundred times what it had been before the merge. But no matter how much his abilities had improved, Skye still hoarded a major chunk of guilt. There was no way around it. She didn't think it was likely to go away any time soon. She'd carry that burden of guilt for years to come.

But not today. Today she had to dig in, get a ton of things done to catch up.

She took a moment to glance at the huge map hanging on the back wall, the best place to keep track of all child abductions that had taken place in the Pacific Northwest. Most were teenagers. Colored pushpins and photos indicated where each had been last seen. Recently she'd started including the disappearances of males and females gone missing in British Columbia. Since the area was less than a hundred miles to the north it seemed practical to cover Canada as well, or at least that little part of it.

She stared at the snapshots tacked around the map, at the fresh faces. A reminder to her or anyone else who walked through the door of what the Artemis Foundation was all about—finding those who'd vanished without a trace, who'd left behind heartbroken loved ones without a word, families that still didn't know what had happened to their children.

She knew some of them had invariably ended up in the human trafficking trade, shipped out like cargo, destined for other parts of the world where no one could trace their movements. She'd vowed to find them, every last one, even if it took her years to do so. In their spare time, she and Josh had already spent hours going over manifests. So far, their efforts had not turned up a single missing teen.

But that didn't mean she'd give up. In fact, her latest project was making sure the kids and teens were all listed in every available national databases and agency that allowed her to add them.

She looked around the office and recognized she was stalling—nothing like coming back from a long vacation and stepping back into a mess. She could barely see the top of the makeshift folding-table she used as her desk, cluttered with an assortment of cards and letters. The floor was littered with boxes stacked in hap-hazard fashion, no doubt wedding gifts still pouring in from well-wishers.

As she set her bag down she realized the first order of business had to be catching up on all the messages left on the office phone. The voice bank was full. After listening to some thirty calls, most were goodwill wishes. She jotted down names and numbers on a legal pad to get back to them later.

But one warranted another listen and an immediate response.

Skye could tell even over the phone that Karen Houston was frantic and worried. Karen was the mother of Shawna Langley, a teen who'd gone missing while they'd been out of town making Shawna's case the most recent. It seemed on the first day of school after Christmas break, the fifteen-year-old had boarded her regular bus that morning and headed for class. According to her mother, the teen never made it inside the building. Somewhere between getting off that bus and her first-period math class, Shawna Langley had disappeared.

As Mrs. Houston explained in her message, she hadn't discovered her daughter missing until five-thirty that evening when she'd gotten home from work. With the house empty and no sign of Shawna, she'd called all Shawna's friends and learned they hadn't seen their classmate at school that day. After that, Mrs. Houston had checked her answering machine. One of the messages had been from the vice principal telling her that Shawna had been marked absent from all her classes. That's when Karen had panicked and called the police.

Skye listened to the woman's detailed message a couple of times, and heard the voice of a mother in agony, worrying and frantic with fear. Since the time stamp on Mrs. Houston's message was from two days ago, that meant Shawna might still be missing.

Before dialing the number, Skye took several deep breaths, steeled herself to cope with another missing child.

As soon as Mrs. Houston picked up, Skye identified herself and began with an explanation of sorts. "I'm sorry for the delay in returning your call. But I've been out of town for two weeks and just got your message this morning."

"Call me Karen, please. I remember seeing you on the news. The news anchor reported you'd gotten married. But you had to come back eventually. And when you did, I wanted Shawna to be the first one you helped."

"Then why don't you tell me more about your daughter's disappearance?"

Karen went into the fine points and ticked off specifics while Skye continued to make notations on the legal pad.

"The cops think she ran away. Shawna wouldn't do that," Karen urged.

"That seems to be a very typical response from law enforcement."

"I didn't appreciate being told that. I tried to tell them Shawna loved school, that she was a member of the honor society. She had tons of friends. She was active in numerous social events. She had cheerleading practice the afternoon she went missing. Why would she run away from all that? She had no reason to."

Unfortunately, Skye had heard it all too often before—popular teenage girl with a routine life vanishes without a trace.

"Let me ask you this. Do you know if the police questioned the bus driver?"

"Yes, they did. And I called her myself. Her name's Lori Denny. She's fifty-seven, a grandmother who picks up extra money by driving the bus. Lori says she watched Shawna exit the bus that morning like everyone else did."

"Okay, did they check video of the kids entering the school? Because most high schools these days have security cameras installed."

"You're good, very thorough. I knew you would be. I like that. But the police told me they did look through surveillance tapes which covered the hallways. Look, I want to hire you to find my daughter."

"It doesn't work that way, Karen. I'm not for hire."

"Then I'll make a donation to the Artemis Foundation. I want to do something."

"A donation to the Foundation is fine. How about this? I'll follow up, make some calls to law enforcement myself and see what turns up. I won't give up."

Karen sighed. "I was hoping you'd say that."

After assuring Karen she'd do everything she could, Skye ended the call on a depressing note. Would children ever be safe to walk down their own streets, live their lives without fear of being snatched? It was a sobering thought.

With that, she booted up her laptop. For thirty minutes she perused the over one hundred and eighty emails sitting in her inbox. Getting rid of the obvious spam first, she opened each one in methodical fashion, reading, and then replying to those requiring a response.

Suddenly the smell of caffeine drifting from another office on the same floor got to her. She remembered she needed coffee. She pushed to her feet, went into the little kitchenette to start a pot of strong java. As it brewed she attacked the mound of cards and letters stacked on her desk. The pile was so high she couldn't see around the twelve-inch mountain of paper.

After sorting through and opening the obvious cards from supporters, strangers really, who'd read about their nuptials in the newspaper and taken the time to write, she spent another hour reading through the stack of mail. She set the cards aside in their own batch so she could write each one a personal note later.

By the time she poured her third cup of coffee, she decided to tackle opening the boxes. Skye couldn't believe people would actually take the time to shop for wedding gifts—especially during the holiday season—for a couple they'd only seen on the news. But while she and Josh had bathed themselves in suntan oil and sunshine, it seemed the packages from strangers kept coming.

Her father, Travis Nakota, had dropped by every other day to deal with the deliveries, the ones dropped off by FedEx or UPS or the mailman, or to collect what managed to slide through the slot, only to heap all of them underneath the metal table.

By one o'clock that afternoon, she'd opened up a dozen cartons containing stuff like a shiny new toaster, crocheted doilies—the lacy things made by a little old lady in Aberdeen who wanted to give them something homemade—along with a varied collection of recipe books. Somehow it had gotten out that Skye Cree liked to cook. Because of that, the citizens of Seattle had taken it upon themselves to make sure their heroine had the means to prepare the best dishes—whether it was linguine or coq au vin or good ol' Southern-fried chicken—and they'd sent her a wide range of cookbooks. She browsed through page after page wondering if she could find something unique to fix tonight, their first full night back home.

The next parcel that caught her eye was a long, brown rectangular cardboard box. Its size alone caught her attention—a good eighteen inches wide and two feet long—it had a depth of at least ten inches, which made it the largest gift by far. As soon as she picked it up, she heard Kiya's warning yip and growl. It was about the same time that she realized whatever was inside rattled, as if something had broken into bits and pieces. Whatever delicate item was inside had cracked, she decided. Whatever it was had obviously met a bad fate. But she didn't understand why that would send Kiya into howling-mode.

She sighed a little at the notion that someone's generosity had ended in a bad way with a careless shipper. Despite images of delivery drivers slamming packages against doors and tossing them on concrete, she held the box up to give it another shake. The contents definitely clattered around inside. Skye decided she'd have to send them a thank-you anyway. But when she looked for a return address in the upper left-hand corner she noticed it had been left blank. She turned the box on its end to check the bottom side. But there was no shipper info at all.

She picked up the scissors she'd been using to breach the other cartons and slid the sharp edge across the tape. Throwing back the cardboard panels, she pried the lids back to reach inside. Instead of the pretty, delicate, tissue paper she'd found in the other gifts, her eyes landed on old newsprint. The sender had used it to buffer whatever rested within. Unlike all the other presents she'd opened so far, this one held an odor so strong it made her want to gag. Kiya's yowling got louder. Because of that, she almost missed the date on the yellowish copy of the *Seattle Times*. 1992.

As she peeled back the sheets of paper, a funny feeling hit her. That feeling began to climb up her backbone all the way to her neck. By the time she'd unwrapped the layers of newsprint, the core of it began to sink in.

From the center of the box a skull stared back at her, the shape and form unmistakable. It lay nestled among an assortment of bones, a femur, a tibia, and what looked like a patella, or kneecap. The leg bones were complete but there was no foot.

Underneath them all was a typewritten note.

Skye looked around for anything she could use to pick up the paper. Knowing the police would want to know if she'd handled anything inside the box, her eyes landed on one of the already-opened wedding gifts, a set of kitchen gadgets that included a pair of metal tongs.

With unsteady hands, she used the tongs to grab for the note to angle it out of the box. In spite of how careful she was though, the back of her hand brushed up against some of the bones. The contact caused her to shiver. That's why it took three tries before she was able to lift out the message without tearing the paper. Carefully she placed it onto the newly-cleared surface of the desk so she could read the words.

> *The media says Skye Cree is the greatest hunter. They say you love to track down really bad guys. I'm a really bad guy. I'm sending you this box of bones. See if you can find out who this woman is. I don't exactly remember her name. It's been too long. Maybe Julie? Janie? These few bones were all I could stuff into the box. See if you can use what's left of her to catch me because I took her life. I'll give you a clue. I killed her with my own hands. To be honest, I've killed others since this one.*

But you probably won't be able to find any of them because after all this time no one else seems to care. I'm not even 100% sure anyone ever looked. Let's see if what they say is true. Let's see how great you really are. Because somewhere out there families wait for answers that never came. Are you the one good enough to find them answers? We'll see. Because I'll be watching you.

Skye's jaw dropped open. She reread it again and then a third time before she reached for the desk phone.

"Josh, you'd better get down here. I don't know if this is a sick prank or if it's real. But I've never seen anything like it. You have to get down here, see this box of bones for yourself."

Chapter Two

It took the founder of Ander All Games ten minutes to make it downstairs from his cushy office on the twentieth floor. Mainly because once Josh left his office, after being away for two weeks, people kept coming up to him wanting to make small talk. What had the weather been like in St. Kitts? How did it feel to be a married man again? And when was he planning to tackle those latest bugs in the software updates. He didn't mind the questions or the interest in his personal life because he liked to think the people at Ander All Games were like his extended family. Widely known for treating his employees well and paying competitive salaries, it was one reason his company maintained their edge in the marketplace. Josh liked to think he offered them more than a great benefits package and regular bonuses. For the most part, the work environment was relaxed. He believed in teamwork and always encouraged communication between departments. Employees knew they could come to him with work-related issues, hopefully nipping festering resentments in the bud before they could built into full blown grudges. That's one reason, his door was usually open.

He'd found a deepening friendship in his business partner, Todd Graham, as well as the rest of his team. Maybe not as much as he once had, but he still liked to think he'd formed a bond with most of them. Lately life had created new opportunities. That's what he chose to think anyway at the turn in the road his life had taken—

ever since that night he'd met a certain Native American woman with violet eyes.

By the time Josh reached suite three hundred, his curiosity had reached new heights.

When he opened the door, their eyes met—his gray, almost silver—hers the deepest blue. His heart practically stuttered in his chest at her narrow Native American face with its high cheekbones and the long, raven hair.

Since meeting Skye in that dark alleyway almost a year earlier he'd felt like he'd tapped into the mother-lode. That hadn't changed since tying the knot.

At the sight of her, his lips curved up.

Skye tilted her head and met a smile with a smile. For that brief moment, she stopped thinking about death and appreciated what was right in front of her. Not in a million years would she have ever believed this man would be such an integral part of her life now.

His black hair fell gently around his shoulders. Its length didn't detract from the man's shrewd sense of business or his ability to dress the part of a man in charge, a man who ran a successful gaming empire. There was no doubt he'd made some bucks over the years. But Skye knew he was as down to earth as a guy could get.

"I got here as soon as I could."

Skye's face told him what he already knew. Not two hours earlier he'd left her in a perfect state after they'd made love. And now, someone had put an end to that blissful scene by sending her remains.

He took another look around the small office knowing full well his wife wasn't prone to exaggeration or posturing to get a reaction. He met her in front of the folding table and took a stance beside her at the box peering inside. His recently acquired wolf instincts kicked into overdrive. "This is no joke, Skye. Those are definitely human bones."

"I figured as much. That's why I've already called Harry. After I calmed down a little and bothered to go through the box for a closer inspection, I determined that for myself."

Josh nodded and began to scan the note, then read it through a second time. "Welcome back to the ugly world we left. Looks like, our vacation is officially over and you've been challenged."

"Looks like I have. That old copy of the *Seattle Times* you see is dated 1992. I didn't want to handle it too much but…it's the classified section, help wanted ads, a few personals, a whole lot of used cars for sale. You know what it means though? We'll have to check every missing teen or woman in the area from that general timeframe to get a bead on this guy."

"The newspaper might not even be a viable clue as to the date of the bones. Simply put, it could be nothing more than a false lead."

"I thought of that. But that's why we'll have to eliminate it first. There's no other way. If it turns out the paper is in anyway a reference to the year Julie or Janie died, it means the killer's been at this for a very long time. There's no other conclusion, Josh. It's a morbid thought. The idea that this woman's remains aren't even complete is just…sad. Do you think he kept the rest?"

"Oh yeah. I think he would. Don't you?"

"I do. It means he has a trophy room somewhere and at least a twenty-year head start."

"I don't like the sound of that."

The voice came from the open doorway where Harry Drummond stood. The look on his face was that of a beleaguered homicide detective. A uniformed cop trailed Harry while a crime scene technician followed behind the patrolman. The tech carried a camera and a metal briefcase containing his equipment. The new triad immediately clustered around the desk and the box. It didn't take long for the small space to feel cramped.

Bobbing his head in Skye's direction, Harry wanted to know, "You touch anything?"

She sent him a roll of her eyes. "You know me better than that. I used those tongs there to pick up the note and the newsprint"

Harry shook his head. "You attract some crazies, Skye. You know that?"

"Seems there's nothing I can do about that. Take a look. It's the damnedest thing I've ever seen. And I've seen some pretty weird stuff. I want to know who these bones belong to. Was she someone's daughter? Was she a mother who left children behind? Was she a sister? Are they still actively looking for her? What were the circumstances where she ended up in a cardboard box? And how did her remains get here, specifically to me, to my office?"

"All reasonable questions," Harry remarked.

"There's a trail and we need to follow it," Skye asserted.

"Read the note," Josh prompted. "The person who sent the package obviously kept up with current events, knew Skye's tie-in with the Artemis Foundation."

"Why make his sins public now? Why write about them now? Why contact me like this at all?"

Harry scratched his head. "I'm no profiler but… I'd say he has some terminal disease and he thinks the clock is ticking or he wants attention or could be both. If it's for the attention he probably thinks the spotlight has somehow escaped him."

"He wants his fifteen minutes of fame," Josh concluded. "On that we all seem to agree."

"I know one thing. He knew Skye was out of town," Harry proposed after skimming the message. "Knew the box would likely sit here until she came back to deal with it herself. Who gathered your mail while you were gone?"

"Travis. He came by every other day. But I only talked to him once in two weeks." Her cheeks got a little pink at that, remembering she'd been absorbed in other things, too busy to do much else, other than enjoy the island and Josh.

"At the time Travis mentioned that quite a bit of mail had piled up. I thought he was exaggerating." She threw her arms out wide. "Obviously he wasn't."

Josh frowned. "If this guy knew we were away, then he's probably staked out this place at one time or another, maybe even staked it out today to watch you guys show up here."

Harry thought about that then leveled Josh with a stare. "Is it too early to ask if you're getting anything from the note, the bones? Point me in a direction, Josh."

Josh ignored the astonished looks from the police officer and the crime scene tech. "Not a thing, other than the fact they're human bones. Female." He waited a beat before adding, "She died violently. That's implied, of course. But I think she was strangled. Sorry, I can't do any better than that."

"Isn't that unusual in light of recent events?" Skye prompted, meeting Josh's eyes. "I mean, I thought you'd pick up on...a lot more than that."

Josh lifted a shoulder in a shrug as his lips spread into a wide grin. "Maybe I've lost it. Maybe spending two weeks in the tropics drummed it out of me."

"Or maybe the bones are just too old or more like we're witnessing a shield of some kind that combats your special powers. Ever think of that?" Skye returned in a teasing tone.

"Maybe. But I want to go on record as saying I didn't handle these bones up close so I'll reserve the right to add any additional info I obtain from said special powers in the immediate future."

"That's convenient," Skye quipped. "Admit it. You've lost your touch."

Harry shook his head at their back-and-forth banter. "I've got a dead woman's bones in a box and you two are squabbling about what I find very weird in the first place."

"Weird is the new vogue," Josh tossed back.

"Good thing, too. Because weird is the staple around here and right now, that's all we've got," Skye retorted as she watched the tech take possession of the box destined for the medical examiner's office and—what she hoped most—answers.

Chapter Three

Weird lapped over into dinner that night at their stylish loft, located in Seattle's upscale Pike Tri area where Skye played hostess to their family. Along with Travis Nakota, Doug and Phyllis Ander gathered around the dining room table waiting for a nervous Skye to take the roast out of the oven—a tasty pork and pineapple recipe she'd found in one of the new cookbooks she'd gotten.

When she did finally make her way through the swinging door from kitchen to dining room, she glanced around the open layout. The polished wood floors might gleam but right this minute she regretted not having taken the time to put her own touches on the place. She should have. The condo still felt like it belonged solely to Josh. Her fault, she knew. Even though she'd hoped to make it feel more like her home by bringing over her clothes and a few knickknacks, she still felt Annabelle's presence. After all, the woman had died here. That fact alone had to be weighing on Josh, too. Maybe it was time to get serious about a new address instead of buying new pillows or a bucket of paint.

But it was too late now to worry about things like color schemes. She had hungry guests to feed.

Josh nudged her into a chair and whispered, "Stop worrying. The table's beautiful. You're beautiful. And I love you."

She took a deep breath, let it out one layer at a time and dropped into the chair.

Over slow-cooked pork tenderloin, rice and asparagus tips, Skye looked around the table and picked up her glass of wine. "So how many serial killers do you suppose work an area at any given time? I mean, we've had our share in Seattle over the years but how many do you think are active here?"

"I've read the numbers, the studies," Josh said, taking a sip of the Cabernet. "Some have estimated there are between thirty-five and three hundred active serials around the world. I'd say locally there could be as many as ten and as few as four at any one time working the area along the I-5 from Canada down to the California border."

"Those numbers sound awfully high to me," Doug interjected.

But about that time Skye caught the appalled look on Phyllis's face. She quickly apologized. "Oh, sorry. I guess this isn't the usual conversation you're used to having over supper. We've gotten into several bad habits lately, talking about murders is par for the course."

Phyllis bristled at getting caught and cleared her throat. "I'm not without a sense that such subject matter takes place in this house of late, but I'd rather not discuss morbid things like that at the dinner table."

"You're right," Skye said.

"No, she isn't," Josh imparted. "Sorry, Mom, that you're uncomfortable. But I'd like to point out predators count on people like you to avoid conversations like this one. Let me ask you something. What if you knew someone who was a victim? What if it was one of your loved ones? What if you knew your daughter or son was out there somewhere, missing, taken by an unknown assailant? What if the police decided they'd left on their own though? What if you didn't buy that theory? So now, you're stuck, in a black hole because you're never quite sure what happened to them. You have no answers, no clues. The reality is there are families out there exactly like that. They're left wondering what happened to a son or a daughter. If we can't have a dialogue about predators like this who grab strangers off the streets, then what's the point? Part of working to find the bastards who do this type of thing is to make people aware—even if it is over pineapple pork and rice."

Doug put his hand on his wife's wrist. "You know, Phyllis, Josh is right. It's one thing to avoid the topic entirely but if a conversation helps figure out who's responsible for sending Skye that box of bones, and ultimately finding out the identity of the victim, then so be it."

Chastised, Phyllis glanced at her husband, her son, at Travis and finally her eyes settled on Skye. "I can't imagine what you went through as a child." Her voice faltered, flattened. "I don't know how you ever get over something like that. But to think you've gone on to do incredibly brave things for victims... I admire what it is you do. You know I support your efforts."

Skye smiled and reached across the table, squeezed Phyllis's hand. "I know that. I also know that just because you feel that way doesn't give me the right to discuss such things at dinner. I forget sometimes that most people aren't geared to hearing about society's dregs or the horrors they bring to people. Not everyone needs to have it shoved in their face over a meal."

Determined to change the subject and put her guests more at ease, Skye turned to Travis. "How's that roast?"

Travis's eyes met his daughter's. Understanding his role in getting the subject turned to a more favorable topic, he replied, "It's delicious. I never would have thought putting pincapple on top of a pork roast could be so flavorful."

"Stop that," Phyllis finally said. "It's okay. You don't have to make small talk on my account. My son and I often don't see eye to eye on things and tonight is no exception. Although I do think he could've set me straight in a less overt way."

"I suppose I should have. Those bones got to me, got to Skye," Josh admitted. "I apologize."

Phyllis tilted her head, stared into the eyes of her son. "You've changed these past months. At first I attributed that to finding new love. Now, I'm not so certain."

Josh sipped his wine again, picked up his wife's hand. "I'm learning there's magic in finding the right woman."

"I can attest to that," Doug agreed. "But I wouldn't mind getting back to this serial killer thing." He ignored the look of disgust from his wife. "What kind of guy boxes up bones from his victim and sends them through the mail?"

"One who wants attention. Badly," Skye offered. "He's tired of being ignored. He wants an adversary so that he can show off his kills."

"Exactly," Josh stated.

"But why Skye? Why not just contact the cops? Why get you involved at all?" Travis wondered. "There's no excuse for that. I know you made headlines taking down Frank De Palo but that doesn't explain why this man has picked you to reach out to. I don't like it."

Skye looked sideways at her father. "For one thing, I'm female. He probably sees me as an inferior opponent. Add to that, I'm getting more press than he is. Someone with his ego doesn't like that."

"I'm impressed with that assessment," Doug added as he speared another tasty bite of meat. "She's good."

"Thank you. But don't be so impressed. I've spent years studying this type of human behavior. This package is only the tip of the iceberg. There'll be others."

"Other packages?" Travis asked, clearly upset. "You're saying this monster will continue to contact you? I don't like it," Travis said again. "I want this guy caught."

This time Skye smiled at him. They were just getting used to feeling more at ease with each other. She liked this overprotective side to him—most times. "We'll see what we can do about making your wish come true."

About that time the buzzer sounded from downstairs. Josh got up, went to the control panel to press the button. "Yes?"

"Mr. Ander, this is Selma Tolliver in five-forty-four. I was headed out for the evening and noticed someone had left a package by the front door addressed to Skye Cree. I'm sure they meant to put her married name on the address."

But Josh thought otherwise. "Thanks, Mrs. Tolliver, I'll be down to pick it up." He turned to look at his wife. "Call Harry."

"But it might be nothing more than a wedding gift, Josh," Skye reasoned. "Calling Harry if someone boxed up a blender hardly seems reasonable to me."

"I don't think it's a blender, Skye. Call Harry," Josh repeated, hitting the button on the loft's private elevator to head down.

"Okay, but I'm coming with you."

"Then let's go," Josh said, sending a quick wave to his parents, to Travis, before hopping on the elevator. "We'll be back. Don't move. Keep eating. Give us twenty minutes."

When they got to the lobby, Selma greeted them with a big smile. Without warning the attractive dark-haired tenant shoved the parcel into Skye's hands.

"My date's waiting in the car outside. I could've just left the gift on the hall table there where you'd likely see it, but I wanted to take this opportunity to tell you both congratulations. I'm so glad Josh found someone special. I've heard all about you, Skye. You're our local crime fighter, but still such a regular-type person. And now you live in *my* building!" Selma declared, leaning in so she could give Skye a quick hug, again without much notice. "You keep up the good work."

Before Skye could do any more than hug the woman back, Selma dashed out the door.

Josh gave Skye a twisted smile, cocked a brow. "Selma's obviously a big fan."

"Oh, shut up. Where do we do this? I'm not sure your mother could handle seeing a set of bones crammed into another box." She eyed the package she held—much smaller than the one that had arrived at the office earlier, and added, "Let's hope this is an omelet pan. We could use one."

"We can hope." He took the carton out of Skye's hands, flipped it to read their address. It had been handwritten in blue ink. He looked around the lobby, decided on the mahogany sofa table. "What about here?"

"Fine. I opened the first, how about you open this one?"

"Sure. Let's see what we've got." He took out a pocket knife, ripped open the tape, pulled back the flaps. This time the note rested on top. It was a couple of lines, much shorter than the first.

> *I thought you were the best. That's what they said on the news. They were wrong. You missed my message. It was so obvious. How could you have missed it? And they said you were the best. I'm so disappointed.*

"What's he talking about? We got his message, loud and clear, read it over several times," Josh pointed out.

"Maybe the note isn't it. Maybe there's a clue in that newspaper. I didn't even think to read it all the way through. You know, peruse the personals."

"The personals? Could that be it?"

Skye started to pace, nibbling on her thumbnail. "I don't know, Josh. If it isn't that then there's something else, something I missed entirely."

"Skye, the only things in that box were the bones, the note, and the newspaper. Harry has the evidence. The coroner has the bones. If the medical examiner had come up with anything else, Harry would've told you by now."

She shook her head. "Maybe, maybe not. What if Bayliss didn't get to it yet? What if the bones are still just sitting there waiting for tomorrow's time in the queue? Besides, how did this guy know I didn't find his message? How did he know to send me a follow-up package already?"

Skye surveyed the outside of the box. "And there's no postage on this, Josh. Someone delivered this within the hour. Personally. Otherwise, Travis or your parents would've noticed it when they got here. I'm afraid to ask, but, what's underneath the note this time?" She looked in, sucked in a breath. A mummified hand stared back at her. Each nail still bore a faint trace of pink polish. "This guy's sick."

At that moment, her cell phone dinged, signaling Harry had returned her call. "I got another package. This time at home." Without bothering with a greeting, Skye gave Harry the lowdown. She went on to explain the note and the hand. "Is there any way you can get us inside the coroner's office?"

"Right this minute? Not a chance. And you know that's highly irregular. The box of bones is scheduled for Bayliss tomorrow. And you know he's difficult enough to deal with as it is without asking for favors."

"Yeah? Well so is a crazy bastard who claims to be a serial killer and gets his jollies by cutting off body parts."

"Okay, okay. I'll find a way. I'm coming for that box, Skye. Give me thirty minutes."

"Fine. But whatever you have to do, get us inside the coroner's office. We need to reexamine that box, those bones, for ourselves in case we missed anything. And Harry?"

"Yeah?"

"You need to get a court order so you can go through surveillance tapes for the building just in case he delivered this package personally."

"Hey, who's the cop here? I'm on it," Harry griped. "But surely you don't think he'd be that stupid, do you?"

"You never know. After all, he's the one who started this thing. Stupid? I don't think he's that, but he does want attention."

After she ended the call, Josh took her chin. "You didn't miss anything, Skye."

"We'll see," Skye muttered as she stared down at the mummified hand, studied it closer in greater detail. "Harry'll be here soon to collect the box. By any chance are you picking up anything from this?"

"I don't think this hand belongs to the bones that showed up this morning."

Skye rocked back on her heels, nodded in agreement. "I was afraid of that. But right now, we're in a holding pattern until the medical examiner makes his determination, which if we're lucky we'll get to be a part of. But right this minute, we need to get back to our guests. I'm not letting this asshole ruin what's left of our evening, especially the dinner I slaved over any more than he already has."

"Then we'll wait for Harry and get back to them soon."

But it took longer than they'd planned for Harry to drive across town and take possession of the box. By the time they got back upstairs the food was cold and it didn't take long for the obvious questions to start. Was it from the killer? What was in the package? How did the person know where you lived?

Travis pressed her for more details which Skye managed to sidestep during the rest of the meal. But with dinner over, Travis followed her into the kitchen where the talk turned to warnings and cautionary tactics.

"This is tantamount to invading your personal space. You said this asshole would send another package which means his ramping up is just getting started. Now that he's made contact, he'll keep up the full court press until he shows up. Do you plan to live here or look for another house? I thought you guys wanted a nice place out of Seattle. Now might be the perfect time to move. This guy obviously knows where you live now."

"Settle down. Take a breath for God's sake. The loft is easy enough to find. I'm not hiding or moving just because some nutcase decides to send me notes. We don't even know yet if those bones are the real deal."

But Travis wasn't that naïve. He didn't buy her bravado or defiance. "What exactly was in that package downstairs?"

She could see the determination in his eyes, so there was no point in evasion or trying to bluff. She let out a sigh. "A mummified hand, complete with pink nail polish."

Travis ran a hand through his hair about the time Josh came through the swinging door carrying more plates. "So we have a killer who dismembers?" He aimed his frustration at Josh. "What exactly do you intend to do about this?"

"Ah, so you've heard about his latest offering," Josh assessed. "I won't let the bastard anywhere near Skye, if that's what you mean."

"It wouldn't hurt to take Skye house-hunting this weekend," Travis suggested.

"I hadn't thought of that," Josh said, sarcasm dripping from his tone. "Since we've been back a full day I'll get right on that." He slapped Travis on the back. "Seriously though, after what happened downstairs, finding a place in the country sounds ideal. The glut in the housing market right now might make it the best time to look."

"You're both overreacting," Skye stated, annoyed with both of them.

"Don't tell me you aren't concerned about this guy, Skye," Travis tossed back. "You certainly know better than to underestimate an adversary like this one."

"I'd be an idiot to take this guy lightly on many levels. So yes, I take him seriously. I'm on the receiving end of his depravity. His sending me remains in a box twice in one day—delivered to my home no less—creeps me out. It implies a disturbed individual, perhaps even one harboring some sort of deep psychosis. I know that."

"I rest my case," Travis concluded. "Promise me you'll think about getting out of the city, out of this loft and get a new place of residence, the sooner the better."

"You forget the city is my hunting ground. Always has been."

"But perverts don't limit themselves to a specific area, Skye," Josh reasoned. "This guy could very well have set up shop to work in the pristine countryside. For years."

"That's my point," Skye shot back, glaring at Travis. "That's why I'm not running off to live life as a Martha Stewart clone in some remote part of the Northwest to sit around waiting for seeds to sprout. My life is here." She wheeled around to Josh. "You know that's true. My heart is here."

Josh took her hand. "I'm beginning to see that. Let's slow down a minute. We'll take the path that works the best for both of us. It won't hurt to look. When it comes to a new place, no one's suggesting you give up the hunt. Compromise is the key."

After their guests left, Skye changed clothes and noted the time on the clock. Turning to Josh, she said, "You look tired. Why don't you sit this one out?"

Josh perused his wife up and down. Dressed in black and leather, she looked like a fierce warrior prepared to do battle at a moment's notice. All she needed to complete the image was a weapon, maybe a shiny, steel sword she could brandish in a fight. He supposed it was the gamer in him that saw her as a skilled combatant.

She carried no gun, but kept a nightstick hidden under her long coat along with a knife and another blade tucked inside her boot just in case.

There was no doubt in his mind she could take care of herself or handle a tough situation. She'd proved herself time and time again. But every now and then a guy had to remind her they were a team. "We've been all through this before. I'm not letting you go out on the streets alone. Besides, you're out of practice."

She narrowed her eyes. "I most certainly am not."

"You haven't walked Seattle's streets in over two weeks," Josh pointed out in challenge. "Eighteen days to be exact. Last time you went out you had a wedding on your mind. You're rusty."

Skye rolled her eyes, knowing exactly what he was doing. She shook her head. What was the point in arguing back and forth when she'd just end up giving in anyway? "Okay, okay, but if you're going with me, move your ass. The clock's ticking and neither one of us is getting any younger."

He bumped her shoulder. "That's what I like to hear. Compromise. That's what a good team does," he said by way of a too familiar refrain.

"This team could use a little less jawing and a lot more moving. You change clothes while I go make sandwiches."

"Sandwiches? No thanks, I'm still full from dinner."

She cast him a long glance, narrowed her gaze. Sometimes his naivety reared its ugly head and surprised her. Now was one of those times. "You want information from people living on the street, you offer something in exchange. It's either money or something to fill their hungry bellies."

"Ah, sorry. I wasn't thinking."

"It's okay. It's hard to imagine sleeping in a doorway when you've got a comfy bed each night. People tend to forget not everyone is as fortunate."

Thirty minutes later, after stuffing baloney and cheese sandwiches and all the apples they had on hand into a backpack, they headed out the door. As they walked toward Atlanta Street and Fulton Avenue, Josh turned to his new bride, noted her calm demeanor. "The wolf is ever patient and always on the hunt."

"Poet and philosopher, I married a man who does both with equal ease, I think." Now was the perfect time to tell him about the missing teen, Shawna Langley. She hit the highs and lows, went back over the conversation with Karen Houston.

"So we're on a mission tonight?"

"We're always on a mission. Shawna's the latest one. Her mother dropped by this afternoon after our phone conversation to give me Shawna's most recent school picture and some leftover flyers she had printed up. Tonight we're going to ask around about Shawna, hand out a little food, and hopefully get a few answers in the process."

They drifted past a rundown motel, long abandoned, its architecture unremarkable, its roof used by advertisers to hold their billboards. "You know, I was thinking. What if we took a piece of property like this and remodeled it to give some of these homeless families a chance at a new start?"

Skye stopped walking and turned to stare at Josh. "What? How would building another homeless shelter help?"

"It wouldn't really be a shelter. Not as I see it anyway, but more like individual little studio apartments, complete with a small kitchen, a bed, a bathroom, enough to feel like they have something."

"You're kidding? Is that even doable?" she asked, surveying the ancient building.

"I think it is. Gear it to the homeless who are trying to better themselves, or the working poor. Rent's expensive around here. Of course, they'd have to sign an agreement stating there would be no criminal activity in their unit. And to agree in writing that if they don't have a job, they'll look for one, or they'd be willing to enter some type of job skill program to change directions, attend classes, and actively keep their unit up."

"How much would a project like that cost? Renovating an old motel would mean spending some major bucks. Anyone else you know attempted such a thing?"

"There's one in Utah. The state offers a 'no strings attached' apartment program for people who remain habitually homeless. And there's an artist in Oakland who makes tiny homes out of stuff he finds on the street."

"Really? That is…so cool. Could we actually do something like that right here with an old motel?"

Even in the dark, Josh picked up on the sparkle in Skye's eyes at the prospect of it becoming a reality. "Sure, why not? Stranger things have happened. After all, who would ever think someone like me could be part wolf, part spirit guide?"

"You know you aren't part wolf. Travis went over all that with you. And since you aren't Nez Perce, you can't be an official spirit guide either, more like honorary. Look, she's leading the pack now because she's on the hunt."

"You're such a buzzkill. But I love you anyway. What does it hurt if I consider the possibilities?" At that, he turned his head to the sky and let out a yowling moan that had Kiya doing the same.

When a few onlookers milling about on the other side of the street turned to look at the crazy man howling at the moon, Skye let out a huge sigh. "Stop that. It's embarrassing. You're a bad influence on Kiya." But even as she said it, she burst out laughing. "Oh my God, I'm married to a total nutcase. You do realize this makes you a few fries short of a Happy Meal."

About that time someone began yelling her name from down the block. "Skye! Skye! Skye Cree! It's me, Jade Rain."

"Who's that?" Josh asked, staring at the scantily clad woman, dressed in a miniskirt and tank top, teetering on rhinestone high heels that sparkled in the dim street light, he watched as the woman, who had to be at least forty-five, kept waving her arms.

"A hooker, homegrown. They call her 'mother' behind her back 'cause she kinda looks out for all the young girls coming up. Jade's been strolling the streets for as long as I've been doing this. Come on," Skye urged as she darted across traffic toward Jade.

"What you doin' down here, girl? Last time I saw you, you was lookin' for that missing redhead. Found her, too, as I recall," Jade said, between puffs on a just-lit Camel.

"Always lookin' for somebody, Jade. You know that."

"Don't I, though." Jade looked Josh up and down, blew out a long trail of cigarette smoke through her nose. "Who's this fine lookin' man you got followin' you?"

"This is the hubby."

"No shit. Well, you picked a handsome one, I'll say that. Just look at all that long, dark hair."

Skye pulled out the photo of Shawna. "Any chance you've seen her?"

Jade took the picture, studied the girl with the long brown hair, then looked up again. "Cute little thing. You think she's one of those girls somebody snatched to live out there in the sex trade?"

"Maybe. I don't know. She's been gone now a little over a week. She's only fifteen, Jade. Have you seen her?" Skye repeated.

"Not me. But maybe Sadie has." Jade put her fingers between her teeth and gave out a loud whistle. "That's our signal to come on the QT. Don't worry, she's just down the corner. She's the only girl who hasn't got picked up tonight. But she will."

Skye glanced around, spotted a skinny girl of about nineteen heading toward them from the corner. Sadie was doing her best to sprint along the sidewalk in what looked like, five-inch bright yellow plastic heels.

"Here's my baby girl now." The minute Sadie reached them, huffing the whole way, Jade handed her the photo.

Crushing out her filtered Camel under the toe of her pump, Jade blew out smoke from between her lips. "Skye wants to know if you've seen this girl, Sadie."

Sadie shook her head as she tried to catch her breath. "Nope. She looks young, too. She a runaway, Skye?"

"I don't think so. How about if I leave a flyer with both of you. That way, if you see her, you can give me a call. My number's at the bottom."

"You got it, Skye. Good luck finding her."

"You guys take care," Skye said as she pushed a twenty into Jade's palm. "Watch out for yourself, Jade."

Josh watched the women go, then grabbed Skye's arm, guiding her toward Sylvan Street. "We need to go this way."

Noting his jovial demeanor had morphed into a more serious attitude in a matter of minutes, Skye veered off down an alleyway behind him. She caught sight of Kiya a good twenty yards up ahead. "She's onto something." A sidelong glance at Josh told her they both were.

They turned the corner into a back street near the waterfront seawall and restoration project. Huge cranes and several dump trucks had been parked overnight in a vacant lot. After another twenty minutes, Skye wasn't sure whether she was following the wolf's instincts or Josh's.

They walked past more equipment, meandered through the massive construction area around the Alaskan Way Viaduct, crossed another dark lot. They passed in front of an old abandoned church where the homeless had carved out a place on the sidewalk to sleep for the night. People slept under cardboard boxes, tattered sleeping bags, blankets, and even old pieces of carpet, anything that would protect them from the cold and the hardness of the cement. Shopping carts filled with their worldly possessions lined the walkway.

They crawled over a divider that separated the staging area for the backhoes and haulers from a woody hillside. They made their way between two concrete pillars, dropped down into a larger encampment hidden behind a line of evergreens. Someone had built up a fire where a group of men and women huddled around it for warmth and camaraderie.

Approaching the campfire with caution, Josh and Skye geared themselves for a hostile welcome. This time, Skye decided to let Josh take the lead. She pulled out several baggies of food from her knapsack and held them out for inspection.

"How's it going?" Josh said. "We brought some sandwiches, some fruit, thought maybe we could exchange them for information."

"Let's have the food first," one of the men groused. "What kind of information?"

Josh handed the man a bag along with Shawna's photo. "We'd like to know if any of you have seen this girl."

Another man stared at Skye then at Josh. "You two cops?"

"No. This girl went missing a week ago. We're trying to find her." Josh watched while they passed around the picture, each one taking the time to stare at the girl's image. Halfway around the circle, a woman in her fifties looked up and said, "I saw this girl at the burger joint over on Third and Simonton."

Josh frowned, waited a beat. "You mean Pete's Grill?"

"That's the one. Went down there for one of those breakfast tacos they make, tasty way to eat eggs. And after midnight they reduce the price to just a buck."

"They serve cheap burgers, too, if you don't add cheese," said another man who sat off to the side in the shadows.

One of the other women put in, "The doughnut shop over on Twelfth gets rid of the day-old stuff for the taking around two in the morning, just tosses it out in the Dumpster."

"Let's get back to what happened when you saw the girl," Josh prompted.

"Okay. Anyway, the manager, he had to call the paramedics 'cause that girl you're looking for fainted right there on the floor in front of us." The woman turned to the man sitting next to her, elbowed him in the ribs. "You were there, Joe. Take a look at her picture. It's the same girl, right?"

Joe considered the photograph, held it closer to the light. "Damn it, Molly, you know I don't like getting involved. We don't even know these people."

But Molly would hear none of that. "She's got family worried about her, Joe. You back me up here and tell them what they want to know."

Joe grunted, made a menacing sound in his throat. "Might as well, you won't leave me alone 'til I do." He studied the photo, grunted again. "That's the same girl that fainted, all right, just like Molly said. She was standing in line right in front of us. She swayed on her feet, went down in a heap on the sidewalk. We hadn't made it inside yet, 'cause there's always a line out the door 'round midnight for breakfast tacos." Joe handed the picture back to Molly, who gave it back to Josh. "Satisfied now?"

By way of answer, Molly grinned showing her yellow teeth in need of a dentist.

"When was this?" Skye asked, stepping out of the shadows into the flickering firelight.

"Hmm, that would be two nights ago. The girl was all bruised up, like she'd taken a tumble or something. Her eyes looked all glazed over like she was on drugs," Molly added.

Josh and Skye exchanged looks.

"Any reason you remember this so clearly?" Skye wanted to know.

"Poor thing looked out of place, like she didn't belong in our neck of the woods."

"Why do you say that?"

"She had on a pair of those fancy jeans and no coat like she wasn't supposed to be outside."

"You wouldn't happen to know where the paramedics took her, would you?"

"No clue," Molly said, taking a deep drag on her cigarette.

After handing out all the sandwiches to Molly and Joe and their companions as a way to say thank-you, they followed the same path as before. When they reached the viaduct, Skye said to Josh, "Pete's is one of those places open twenty-four-seven, like Country Kitchen. I'll call and ask if anyone there remembers the paramedics taking a teenager to the hospital. In the meantime, you check which hospital is closest. I'll Google the number for Pete's Grill."

With that, they both took out their cell phones and began separate online searches.

"Closest hospital to Pete's Grill is Harborview."

"How many blocks is that?" Skye muttered as she punched in the number for the burger joint.

"From here? I'd say about six."

As soon as someone answered the phone down at Pete's, Skye relayed the situation, but got nowhere. It seems a different manager had been on duty two nights earlier. Ending the call in frustration, Skye's temper flared. "Damn it, this is exactly how kids fall through the system. No one gives a damn about a girl who keels over in a dive in the middle of the night obviously sick and injured. We should just head to Harborview."

"Do you honestly think they'll give out personal info on a patient, let alone one who is underage, to two people who aren't related, to strangers who walk through the door and start asking questions? We don't even know for sure it's Shawna. We don't even know if they kept her there. They could've released her by now and she's out wandering—"

"Don't say it!" Skye aimed her lethal glare at Josh. "You know as well as I do, it's her and she's still there. I feel it."

"Okay, but why didn't the hospital personnel notify her mother? Tell me that."

"Oh I don't know," Skye shot back. "Maybe because she had no ID on her at the time, no coat in the cold and she's been out of it for two days. I don't know. Okay?"

"Try not to jump down my throat. Okay? Try to remember, I'm on your side."

"Sorry," she mumbled as they made their way back through the waterfront along the seawall. Her shoulders slumped. "Sometimes this gets old, you know? I get so fed up at all this. I think I know why I loved getting away for two weeks." She spread her arms wide. "I got away from this, from stories like Shawna's."

He gripped her hand. "I know it's infuriating to have so many kids on the streets and not be able to help each one. Do you think Shawna ran away after all?"

"Honestly, I don't know what to think. Karen, her mother, was so sure her kid wouldn't bolt."

"Like that's the first time a parent's been wrong about their child. We have to ask ourselves how certain we are that this is Shawna. What's your gut telling you?"

"Before I answer that, what led you straight to that homeless camp tonight? Was it just following Kiya or something else inside you?" She tapped his chest for emphasis. "Because you went there without hesitation, Josh, something led you there other than Kiya."

Josh breathed in the night air, looked up at the dark sky. "Okay. Then I guess we do this and see how good we really are. We'll reserve judgment as to why Shawna was at that greasy spoon until we get some solid answers."

Chapter Four

Just shy of two a.m. they walked into one of the largest and busiest public hospitals in King County. Harborview treated hundreds of patients a day. The crowded waiting room was evidence of that. It brimmed with people in dire need of medical attention—everything from knife wounds to raging fevers.

Skye strolled up to the front desk with the flyer in her hand. As soon as the woman behind the counter turned around, she wasted no time getting to the point.

"Look, I know you're busy with a line of patients waiting, but my name is Skye Cree. Hear me out. That's all I'm asking. I'm looking for this fifteen-year-old girl." She held up the flyer and the photograph. "Her name is Shawna Langley. She went missing eight days ago. Today would make it nine. There's a mother back home frantic to locate her daughter. We have reason to believe that she's here. Paramedics picked up a girl fitting Shawna's description two nights ago at Pete's Grill over on Third—"

The woman held up a hand to stop, nudged her coworker in the arm. "It's Skye Cree. Skye Cree is looking for a missing girl."

"In our hospital?"

Skye blurted out, "That's right. Apparently they brought her to Harborview after she fainted. Witnesses said she also looked bruised and beaten, maybe even on some type of drugs or meds. Maybe if you pass around her picture to the ER staff, someone might recognize her, remember working on her."

"Wait. What about that girl on three? She looks a little like that photo, hard to tell though since her face is still swollen, black and blue, too. Let me call upstairs and verify the day she was brought in. Be right back."

The other woman added, "You know we won't be able to give you anything more than that, not without a court order, right?"

"I know that," Skye said glancing at Josh. "What's her condition now? If you could just tell me that in a vague and general way I could convey that to her mother."

When the first admitting clerk hung up the phone she turned to Josh and Skye. "I talked to the nurse upstairs. The date fits. The girl's been a Jane Doe since she was admitted. She was in and out of it and then lost consciousness altogether. She hasn't been awake at all. You really think our Jane Doe might be your missing girl?"

"How about we call her mother and let her take a look at your Jane Doe?" Josh said, holding up his cell phone over Skye's shoulder.

"But it's after two in the morning," the clerk pointed out.

"Trust me. The girl's mother won't mind getting this kind of news in the middle of the night."

Two hours after getting approval from the hospital staff, Karen Houston positively identified the girl who'd passed out in Pete's Grill as her daughter.

Skye and Josh lingered in Shawna's darkened room while Karen sat stoically beside the girl's bed, clutching Shawna's pale hand in hers. Finally Karen asked, "What do you suppose happened to her the morning she went missing?"

Skye shook her head. "I have no idea. We'll have to ask her when she wakes up."

Tears streamed down Karen's face. "Do you think she will? Wake up, that is."

"Yes, I do. You heard the doctor say that she likely hit her head but that her brain scan looked good. And her tox screen came back clean."

"Which means she didn't faint because she was on drugs," Josh added. "Right now, Shawna's brain is resting, getting stronger so that when she does wake up, she'll be able to tell us what happened."

"You really think so?" Karen looked from Josh to Skye. "How in the world did you two find her? You're both incredible people. You did what the cops were unable to do. Thank you. I'll never be able to repay either one of you. I'm so glad I got in touch with you, Skye. I almost didn't."

"Why's that?"

"Because Bob, that's my husband and Shawna's stepfather, told me it was a waste of time and not to bother."

"Bob discouraged you from doing everything you could to locate your daughter?" Josh snorted, bewildered at the notion. He met Skye's furious eyes. Like two mobile devices syncing up, their signals linked in a like mindset.

But when Josh opened his mouth to explore that line of questioning further, Skye shook her head and mouthed the words "not now."

Stymied, Josh did his best to sound light and casual as if making small talk when he asked instead, "How long exactly have you and your husband been married?"

"Two years last November."

"Ah, that almost qualifies as newlyweds," Skye proffered.

Karen blew her nose into a Kleenex, tightened her grip on Shawna's fingers to keep that fragile bond intact. "If only that were true. The last two years have been rather rocky between us. There's been a lot of tension in the house."

"How so? Some relationships just take more work than others," Josh tossed out, hoping Karen took the bait. But when she sat there stoic, he simply said, "It's a shame Bob didn't come down here with you tonight."

"He's out of town. He travels quite a bit. I called him though. I guess he had that 'do not disturb' feature on. It went straight to voicemail."

"So he might not know yet that Shawna's been found?"

"Not yet."

"Look, Karen, Josh and I should get out of your way and leave you alone with your daughter. Be sure to keep us updated on Shawna's progress, will you?"

"Oh, I will," Karen said, dabbing at her eyes. "If not for you two, I wouldn't be sitting here with her. I'll call you the minute she wakes up."

Out in the hallway, Josh turned to Skye. "Okay, that isn't like you to drop a hot topic and run. The stepfather knows more than he's saying."

"Of course, he does. But it wasn't the right time to confront Karen. We woke her up. She's raw and vulnerable right this minute. If we go into grilling mode about Bob, she'd likely jump to her husband's defense. What good would that do us? Besides, without Shawna's input, we have nothing but a wolf's instinct and a strong suspicion. I'm betting Karen had no idea the stepfather had the hots for her daughter. So as soon as Shawna regains consciousness, we'll be back here to talk to her. That's the best time to enter the fray."

"But we can't give Bob time to show up here and let Shawna wake up to her stepfather standing at her bedside," Josh argued.

"We won't. Let's go talk to the nurse. If we have to, we'll get Shawna's attending physician involved."

"Then it's time to call Harry."

"Yep. Harry's on speed dial."

"Do you think the hospital did a rape kit when Shawna was brought in?"

"We're about to find out."

Harry was more than willing to confront Karen Houston about her husband. That's why around nine o'clock that morning he guided her into one of the offices on the first floor of the medical center. There, he asked her point-blank about Bob Houston.

"Where was he the morning Shawna went missing?"

As Skye predicted, Karen became defensive. "You aren't suggesting Bob did this, are you? Lord knows, he has his faults, but he wouldn't do something like this to my daughter."

"Then tell me where he was."

"He'd gone to work."

"So he wasn't out of town?"

"Not then, no."

For the next forty-five minutes, Harry put Karen through a series of questions. But Shawna's mother stuck to the same refrain.

Before Harry finally let Karen go back to Shawna's room, he left her with one thought. "When Shawna passed out that night, the paramedics couldn't have brought her to a better medical facility. They took a rape kit, which is standard procedure. Be sure to mention that to your husband when he comes back into town. As soon as your daughter wakes up, as soon as she's well enough to talk to me, I'll be here. In the meantime, I'm leaving orders with the staff that her stepfather is to be kept out of her room."

"You can't do that," Karen argued. "Bob cares for her, too."

"That may be true. You have my permission to tell him that we'll be formally requesting a swab for his DNA to clear him of any wrongdoing. At this point, it's standard procedure. If he so chooses, Mr. Houston can certainly sit with you at the hospital in the waiting room. But until Shawna wakes up, Bob Houston will not be allowed in her room until I get answers from your daughter. Are we clear on that?"

Karen nodded and Harry watched the woman storm out. He checked the time on his watch. If he hurried, he just might be on time for the meeting with the medical examiner at the morgue where Skye and Josh were no doubt already waiting.

Chapter Five

At ten-thirty the next morning on less than four hours sleep, Josh and Skye were still mulling over the mystery of Shawna as they dragged themselves out of the car and into the morgue.

While Skye watched the fifty-six-year-old medical examiner, Roger Bayliss, get ready for their meeting, she decided everything she'd heard about the man was true. Dressed in blue scrubs, Bayliss wasn't exactly the welcoming sort.

All business, gruff and surly at times, the no-nonsense, board-certified coroner had been at his job for a quarter of a century. Before that, his goal had been what most med students hope for, to open his own practice. But that all changed after Bayliss realized meeting people on a daily basis might not be his forte. His patients complained that his bedside manner bordered on abrupt and rude, and that was on a good day.

Giving up his private practice forced Bayliss to apply for a job at the county. He soon discovered the medical examiner's office was a much better fit. Unlike his former patients, these people didn't seem offended with every churlish word that flowed out of his mouth.

With all his years on the job, the man had his autopsies down pat. The weighing of organs, the measuring of bones, the taking of photos—even speaking into a recorder to note the particulars of a case in his gravelly voice usually took him no more than an hour at most to complete.

But today his reputation as a grouch was evident.

Skye noted the man's irritation at having outsiders taking up space in what he considered his domain. Skye already knew Bayliss didn't like onlookers or a crowded work space. It was widely known that dealing with either one made him testy. Today the man had to contend with both.

The room was fairly large, but with four extra people lurking around Bayliss, it got crowded pretty quick. Joining Skye and Josh, were Harry and a forensic anthropologist named Dawson Hennings. They all stood like statues doing their best not to make any unnecessary movements as they waited for the first directive from Bayliss. Surely he wouldn't throw out the people who'd driven across town to observe. Observe what, Skye wasn't exactly sure. All she knew was she had to be here.

She knew that going in Bayliss didn't have a lot to work with, in fact, none of them did. Because of that Skye didn't think Bayliss would let them stay for too long. That's why she intended to make her time here count.

She watched as Bayliss began to spread out the bones. He set the skull down first, then the femur, the tibia came next, along with the patella. Last, he placed the mummified hand down on the exam table.

The sparse number of bones laid out on the stainless steel made for an eerie, yet incomplete sight.

She turned to Harry. "According to your message this morning there were no fingerprints lifted from the note accompanying the first set of bones and none found anywhere on the box, right?"

"That's right. The lab already went over the newspaper tucked inside and found it didn't yield a single clue, not even under ultraviolet light. This morning three detectives went over last night's surveillance tape of the building. On my way over, they called to say the tape shows a messenger service dropped off that second box. They're checking now on who placed the order."

"It won't lead back to him," Josh said with some confidence. "Any bets on whether or not he used a phony name?"

"Probably."

"If we could just cut the chatter," Bayliss protested. He glanced around the room to make sure the intruders had put on their latex gloves. Satisfied, Bayliss kicked the ball to the opposition. "What exactly are you hoping for here, Drummond?" he barked. "A cause of death?" Bayliss shook his head. "You won't get that from me, not today. Whoever boxed these up and sent them to you knew exactly what he was doing, knew these particular bones of this particular victim wouldn't give up how they died. He gave you just enough to pique your interest and mine, but not enough to tell us much else."

"Then give us what you have got," Harry urged.

"Not much. As you can see there is no outward damage to the skull, no visible fractures, not even a hairline crack in any of the bones. The rest of the skeletal remains would be necessary to determine a cause of death, if then. No tissue to deal with means this victim could have died in any number of ways. Natural causes, possibly asphyxiated, could have been stabbed in the heart without nicking any bones. See, not a single nick on any of these. Unfortunately for us, in this case, the bones don't give up much. I have no hyoid bone and so far nothing to indicate a violent death. But since your sender sent bones in the first place, their showing up like they have, it does open up a whole list of possibilities as to how this person could've died. Are we all on the same page here so far?"

When everyone nodded Bayliss continued. "As to identity, there's hope there, thanks to the genetics expert I've brought in. Hennings here is the best. Old human remains are his specialty. Hopefully he'll get lucky and ID this victim by getting DNA out of the teeth in the skull.

The bones themselves might eventually yield DNA. Patience is key here. In turn, Hennings will extract DNA and run it through CODIS."

Skye interrupted him. "But traveling down that road, obtaining an ID by that means, would depend on whether or not the victim's family actually took the time to submit to DNA screening at some point."

Bayliss stared at the striking woman with the violet eyes. "You are indeed correct. Not all families with a missing loved one take that extra step. Which brings us back to square one. So I'll ask again, what do you expect me to do here today, Drummond? After all, we don't even have a pelvis to indicate whether we have a male or a female."

"The note said it was female so we're assuming—" Harry began but was interrupted by Bayliss, who simply gave him a withering stare and continued.

"I'm not here to assume, detective."

Just as stubborn, Harry snapped back. "There's pink nail polish on that hand. I'd say it belongs to a female."

Bayliss squawked back, "Or a transvestite. Did you consider that? If I may continue. With such little to go on we don't even know if the hand belongs with the bones that were mailed first. The hand could belong to another person entirely. That's mainly why I called in Hennings here. His lab is state-of-the-art and at this stage will likely be able to help you a good deal more than mine." Bayliss glowered at the younger man, an overt indication to take his cue from that and run with it.

In response, the forty-year-old Dawson Hennings cleared his throat. "The remaining teeth in the skull tell me it's more than likely from a young adult, between the ages of sixteen and twenty-four. I say that because there's no indication the wisdom teeth came in before the time of death. And see the cranial sutures in the skull? They aren't yet fully closed. Another indication the victim was young."

Skye winced just a little as she watched Dawson pick up the head to show the others what he meant. "Like Dr. Bayliss pointed out, it would be great if we had a pelvis to indicate male or female, but since we don't, I'll extract DNA, send it to the clearinghouse and as he said, we could get lucky with a match. If not, at least we'll know gender."

"What if you can't get DNA from these bones?" Skye wondered.

"It's rare that we get no usable DNA whatsoever from teeth, but I won't lie, it is a possibility. Bones in water for too long or exposed to the environment may not respond well to testing the nucleus."

"If that happens, then perhaps we could find a forensic artist to do a facial reconstruction for a missing person flyer. Maybe identify her that way," Skye suggested. "If we get no DNA match we should at least try to find out who she is."

Hennings nodded. "If that turns out to be the case, then I know an excellent one we could use. Only problem is she's in Hawaii."

"What about the hand?" Skye persisted. "It seems to me that it's been kept in a different kind of environment entirely than the other bones."

Hennings's eyebrows darted up. "Why do you say that?"

"Because there's no dirt on the hand like there is on the rest." Skye reached in her pocket for a ballpoint pen, used it as a pointer. "You can see the dirt around the eye socket and the femur. Plus, I think the hand indicates our killer must've parted with a treasured trophy to make his point. It was never buried."

Clearly impressed, Hennings said, "Very observant." He moved over to a forensic compound microscope, an ultraviolet light where he could inspect the skull even further. He adjusted the lens, punched in several strings on a keyboard so that the image appeared on a digital monitor for everyone to see.

"Why use the ultraviolet light?" Josh asked.

"So we pick up any other type of matter clinging to the bone. As Skye's already pointed out there is no flesh left on the skull, just dirt, no skin or tissue. Proof that at one time there was a major difference in where the bones from the first box were kept versus where the hand was stored. See the dirt particles embedded in the teeth. Your sender didn't bother to clean the skull up too well before he packed it inside the box. It definitely shows that at one time the bones he mailed spent time underground. We might be able to do a study of the soil found on them, but we'll save that for later."

Hennings picked up the mummified hand, slid it under the light. "As you can see there are no particles like that on the hand. In that regard, it's fairly pristine for a macerated specimen. Using this, we can also detect skin or hair or other matter more readily under ultraviolet light and get DNA from it. And see, right here is a piece of skin tissue. This'll make an excellent source to find usable DNA. Let me show you what I mean."

Hennings picked up another bone, this time the femur. "I've already measured the thigh bone. The length is forty-one centimeters or a little over sixteen inches. Because of the size, I'd say this person was no more than five feet, four inches in height. Now in the event the femur and the hand are from two different victims, I can take a small sample of bone from the femur, grind it to a powder, extract DNA and try to piece together as much as I can from this person's genetic profile."

Hennings scanned the femur under the light. "See how thin the bone is. I'm going out on a limb here and say female. Males tend to have thicker thigh bones than this." Just as he was about to remove it from under the microscope and pick up the tibia, something on the bone caught his eye. "This is highly irregular."

"What's that?" Skye asked. Focusing on the area in question, she stared up at the magnified image on the screen overhead. "Wait. It looks like there's something crudely etched into the bone. Any chance of making that area in the middle any larger?"

Hennings nodded and then complied by magnifying the small area until the numbers and words jumped off the monitor.

5/8/93 #1 Catch me or let me continue to walk free.

Skye exchanged looks with Josh. "This is what he wanted me to see," Skye reasoned.

"Gotta be the date of the first victim," Josh said half aloud. "I don't see it as anything else."

"That's my guess, too. Busy boy. If his first victim was 1993 then we're looking at over two decades worth of victims. How many do you suppose, Harry?"

"I'm getting too old for this," Harry groaned in frustration. "Come on, Hennings. Let's see if this bastard left us anything else."

As instructed, Hennings began to inspect the rest of the bones under the ultraviolet light. After several minutes, he uttered, "There's nothing here."

"Sure there is," Skye determined.

Josh nodded. "He wants Skye to know that he's able to pick and choose. Dr. Bayliss already addressed the fact he sent specific bones of one victim he knew wouldn't yield a cause of death, and the hand of another. This guy is far from stupid."

"He's gone all this time flying below anyone's radar. He used the hand for shock value, nothing more. Since it's likely from another victim it tells us there are more out there, which is why he sent it. He's showing off," Skye muttered.

"So what have we got other than the fact he's a serial *and* he dismembers his victims?" Harry asked.

Dawson cleared his throat again. "But you're under a misconception, detective. Your killer didn't dismember the first bones he sent Skye."

Skye's smile faded. "He didn't?"

"No. He simply waited until the bones had been in the ground long enough for the soft tissue to breakdown and decomposition was complete. The bones were all he has left of this victim. He simply utilized what he had on hand."

"But I thought…we all assumed…"

"Now the hand, the hand was dismembered from the arm. See the cut marks. He nicked the wrist bone, here."

There wasn't a lot of room to pace, but Skye did her best. She turned to the high bank of windows, walked there and back again and retraced her steps.

"Okay, so he keeps them for a period of time, days or perhaps weeks, tortures them while he has them bound and at his mercy before he decides to end their life," Skye advised. "At some point, depending on his mood, he cuts them up or not. Is that about right?"

Hennings nodded. "He wanted to show you the disparity from one victim to the other."

"Sick bastard," Josh muttered. "Could I touch one of the bones? Anyone of them will do."

"Sure, you have your gloves on so it should be okay," Hennings agreed, handing Josh the shinbone.

The minute Josh held it in his hand, the montage of images blitzed through his head. "He doesn't live alone. He has family, has people close to him. His personal torture chamber is isolated which means he probably has access to a second home."

"You mean like a cabin with a cellar, or something like that?" Skye asked.

Josh shook his head. "I don't know, not exactly. I don't know," he repeated. "But something major has recently triggered his need for attention. Whether it was something he saw in the news or something else, he's blown away by the fact that he's never gotten his just due. He's fed up at the cops for not connecting his numbers. For some reason he's decided his ego needs stroking. He wants to play."

"BTK did that. It'll be his downfall," Skye surmised.

"Let's hope," Josh sent a distressed look at Harry. "In your favor, the cops may never have connected his victims because he may not have left many in a location where you could easily find them. Plus, he grabs them from various jurisdictions. The good guys don't connect the dots and he keeps doing what he does best. And if he ever did leave a victim where she could be found, it had to be in the early years. He's kept on killing and evolved. But now I think he'll change his method."

"You mean abandon his own special place, his own dumping ground for high visibility, start leaving his victims where he wants them found? He wants his numbers to go up."

"Exactly."

The banter went on. As everyone in the room picked up on the dialogue, between Skye and Josh that showed an unmistakable intuitive insight into the killer, almost paranormal.

"Will all this unconventional stuff help catch this guy?" Hennings wondered to Harry.

"Sometimes with no crime scenes it all comes down to this. Law enforcement has to rely on the unconventional. And these two are about as unconventional as you could get."

Chapter Six

That weekend the unconventional pair contacted a realtor and went looking for a house.

Behind the wheel of his Ford Fusion, Josh angled his way in and out of traffic on the I-5 under foggy conditions. So far the heavy pea soup prevented any real buildup of speed. That's why they sat back and made the most of their morning together and the prospect of going on the hunt for the perfect house.

"I'm not sure I want out of the city. I like the loft," Skye admitted. When she noted the beginnings of a smile form at the corner of his mouth, she added, "Believe it or not, it's grown on me, although I do draw the line at liking that French provincial crap in the lobby."

He picked up her hand, turned it over to kiss the palm. "I knew it would if I gave you enough time. Think of it this way, if we find a new place we both like, I guarantee you won't have to put up with that French provincial crap at all."

"Hmm, not having to look at those marble-topped tables with the ornate gold legs might be worth it."

"So no furniture with cabriole legs? Got it."

"I don't mind the look of country French but all that gold crap is just ugly."

"Somewhere I'm sure Louis the Fourteenth is heartbroken to hear that."

Skye put her hand over her mouth to muffle the snicker.

Josh cut his eyes to hers in an amused look while watching the Dodge truck in front of him. "A place in a nice wooded area similar to what Travis owns would be great, something with an acre or two of land to go with it. That way you'd get to putter in a real garden of your own."

"The idea of replanting my little garden balcony into a real plot of ground is…tempting. But I don't really spend that much time 'puttering' as you so aptly put it. In case you haven't noticed I usually stay busy with Foundation stuff. Your fault," she reminded. "And now with this butcher roaming around our little enclave snatching women at will, I'll be hard pressed to find any time to putter."

"Protest all you want, but going on the hunt for a child creates tremendous tension. You do it every single night. Even cops are sometimes forced to take downtime. Face it. You need a place to unwind when things get stressful. Tending to your herbs and flowers is a big part of what you do to relax."

When he said it like that, it did make sense. "Josh, what I do isn't a formal job but more like a—"

"Don't you dare compare what you do to a hobby. It's much more than that. As it is, you don't get paid for Foundation stuff because you refuse to take any of the money. But that doesn't make it a hobby. The very least you should do is get to putter and dig in the dirt whenever you want."

"Taking money doesn't feel right to me, Josh. Besides, it leaves more in the bank to go for more important things like essential state-of-the-art equipment I can use to track predators better. Cracking databases make it a tad easier if I have the right software, the right hardware, and the right access. That all takes major bucks."

"Does Harry know you have military-grade, night-vision goggles?"

"No. And Harry doesn't need to know my complete inventory list. In fact, no one needs to." She looked east toward the Cascade Mountains in the distance. "Where are we going? Any particular reason we're headed south instead of north?"

"I thought we'd use today to do some exploring, take a little time to see some different neighborhoods from those we already know about."

"Ah, so we're researching our options? Great idea."

They came out of the Rainier Valley, passed Sea-Tac Airport to the right and watched for the first time since they'd left the loft as the marine layer began to burn off. Streams of sunlight burst through the low-hanging clouds, enough that she could almost see across the choppy waters of Puget Sound to the tips of Quartermaster Harbor. The scenery changed from inlets and islands to the distinct area around Commencement Bay and the Port of Tacoma.

Josh drove past commercial docks, past downtown in the distance, and the busy railroad yards.

By the time they reached the turnoff for Lakewold Gardens with its Georgian-style mansion and stately Japanese maples, Skye began to feel ill.

She suddenly felt a chill move down her spine. Looking to the left, she spotted the line of vehicles waiting to get into what was now, Joint Base Lewis-McChord. A sense of déjà vu hit her so strong it caused her breath to hitch, her pulse to race. Her heart seemed as if it stuttered in her chest.

"I know this area around Fort Lewis," she blurted out.

From the driver's seat, Josh's instincts kicked in. He could hear her heartbeat quicken, picked up on the fear emanating from her body. "What's the matter, Skye? You look pale. Are you okay?"

"No. This is the same way I felt every time I'd come out here to look for Ronny Whitfield in Tacoma." She flipped down the visor, studied her reflection in the mirror, felt her own forehead. "Just look at me. My face is white as a sheet. All of a sudden I'm perspiring like I ran up four flights of stairs. My palms are even clammy."

"Skye, there's no reason to be alarmed, nothing to be afraid of. Ronny Whitfield's dead. He can't hurt you," Josh reminded her.

"I know that. I'm not a child," she snapped. "But she had to admit she was reacting like one—more specifically, a five-year-old scared of the dark. "There's something here, Josh, something malevolent maybe. Don't you feel it, too? It's a feeling of old souls and they're pissed off about—not being around anymore."

Josh frowned and shook his head. "Most of this land used to belong to the Nisqually Indian tribe. Eminent domain confiscated more than three thousand acres in 1917 for the military installation, which turned into Fort Lewis. Over the years the place has seen a lot of soldiers come through its gates. It has a lot of history, which I'm sure includes violent deaths over the years. So yeah, I guess it could feel like old souls wanting a few answers."

She wasn't sure the way she felt now could be attributed to anything that took place a hundred years in the past. "My father spent years working here as a civilian contractor. He had an apartment near here. I used to go there to visit him on weekends. Sometimes there was a woman with him. They might've been living together."

"You act as though you just thought of that, like a childhood memory or something."

"It's so vivid. The picture of the apartment, the two of them like a couple. A childhood memory, huh? Yes, that's exactly what it seems like. Strange."

"How so?"

"That I would feel this strongly about something so insignificant from that time of my life when I'd never thought of it before today. Why do I remember it in such detail?"

"You want to talk about it?"

"She was the woman my father spent time with after he and my mother separated, after he found out about her affair with Travis."

"Why would you remember that now, today?"

"I have no idea. Now you tell me something. Why are we really out here driving around the military base? We didn't drive all this way past Tacoma to look for the perfect home in the country."

"I keep getting pulled here, Skye. Since the day you received that box of bones I keep getting images from right here. Since this is the only base in the area, and since you're getting weird vibes from the past, too, we might have a link to this place—you and I. Put it all together—I think there's a chance you might have a connection to this guy. What exactly it is, I don't know, could be nothing."

"Interesting. What kinds of images? What kind of connection?"

"Images of soldiers on maneuvers, typical training exercises that sort of thing. They may not mean much at all. As to the link, I'm picking up on ties through your father."

"So the way I'm feeling right now might be an indication I sense this tie to our killer. Is that what you're saying?"

"There is one thing about the images."

"What's that?"

"They're from a long time ago. Circa early nineties."

"The same timeframe as our killer," Skye determined. As they passed the base, she studied the terrain, the barracks, even the chapel, trying to pick up on anything else. But when she tried, she got a blank.

"Exactly. I'm not sure what I thought I'd accomplish coming out here today. We can't even get on base. How about we try this another day? Go look at those houses."

"You said it yourself. This area has a colorful history, soldiers passed through here in droves. Next time, how about we do our research first before we decide to storm the gates?"

Josh found a place to turn the car around to head north again as Skye's phone dinged with a text message. "Is that from Harry?"

"Yes and it's just as we guessed, the guy used a phony name to place the delivery order. But I doubt the killer takes a chance like that again. Even though I don't think he's particularly tech savvy."

"Why do you say that?"

"He printed the address on the packages in his own hand."

"Or got someone to do it for him."

Skye frowned. "Anything's possible. Anyway, my point is that while the address might be handwritten, the note itself was typed. Apparently he used an old Optima typewriter so the note was not computer generated. Harry told me that much."

"So they have a starting point."

"Only if we find this guy and end up comparing the note to the typewriter."

"What's troubling you then?"

"Other than the obvious murderer we have on the loose?" She sighed into her hands then rubbed at her temple. "Do you realize how many people go missing without a trace every single year? Just up and vanish?"

"No, but hopefully you're planning to tell me."

She grinned. "Sure. I won't even make you guess. It's in the neighborhood of six-hundred-and-seventy-thousand who go missing each year."

Josh's mouth dropped open. "You're kidding?"

"Nope. The majority of that number is resolved, of course. But of those that haven't ended with a resolution, the number is staggering. It still leaves about three thousand cases across the country."

"A huge chunk."

"You bet. One is too many, especially when they're here one day and…gone the next. I won't lie. Those are the cases that drive me crazy. They still can't locate all the victims of the Green River killer."

"And what about all the remains that are found but aren't identified?"

"Those are tough because there are probably forty thousand remains that no one is able to put a name to."

"Sad but true. That's a lot of families without answers."

"Look, you okay with having dinner at Lena's tonight?"

"Sure. Why wouldn't I be?"

"No reason. Unless you count the crush Zoe has on you."

"Not me. Not anymore. Zoe's transferred whatever she felt for me and is now fully locked into the hero worship stage. Haven't you heard? She wants to be just like Skye Cree."

The look on Skye's face said it all. Her forehead wrinkled in concentration. "When did that happen?"

"I don't know. Could be after you kicked Frank De Palo's ass. Could be after we tied the knot and she saw how beautiful you looked at the wedding. Either way, Zoe's moved on from me and that's a relief."

Hearing Josh was uncomfortable as Zoe's heartthrob made her laugh. "She's waiting for you to make that job in testing a reality. Teenagers and games, they just seem to go together."

"And she'll get her chance come summer. I want to see how she does in her first full year of eighth grade first with no distractions. I told her that at the reception because she had some major catching up to do in school."

"That she did. But she seems to be doing so much better living with Lena than we ever thought possible."

"No question Lena's provided the stability Zoe needed. Taking in a kid like that, Lena Bowers is *my* hero."

"Yeah. Mine, too."

In her fifty years Lena Bowers had known loss. Ten years earlier her husband of eighteen years had succumbed to pancreatic cancer. Upon high school graduation, her oldest son, Jason, had joined the military and was promptly shipped to Afghanistan to serve his country. He never made it back.

Her youngest son, Jarod, had his own life in California attending San Jose State—which meant she rarely saw him mostly during holidays—the last time, four days at Christmas. At the time, Jarod hadn't been overjoyed about his mother taking on a former runaway, a street kid by the name of Zoe Hollister. But Zoe had filled a void in Lena's life. And now that the courts had let Lena become Zoe's foster mother, the bond between the two had only gotten stronger.

She had experience raising boys. Zoe, however, came with a different zeal for life that made Lena grateful she'd offered her home to the young teen.

For one thing, despite the girl's protests about going to school, the fourteen-year-old eighth grader had discovered she actually enjoyed learning. Zoe especially loved English class. Her love for reading rivaled Lena's. They spent hours discussing the suspense of *Hunger Games*, all the while dealing with the knowledge District 13 hadn't been destroyed in the first rebellion—or rehashing Harry Potter plot lines in detail.

For months now, Zoe had settled comfortably into Lena's life, at home in the Victorian near Capitol Hill. Tonight the two of them looked forward to welcoming the honeymooners, Josh and Skye, back from St. Kitts. Zoe couldn't wait to hear all about the trip from the source.

Lena already knew her charge had a major case of hero worship when it came to Skye. The girl had even written a composition for English class about who she most admired. The subject, Skye Cree. Zoe hadn't even considered calling her Ander yet. When Zoe had mentioned that very topic to Skye, the woman had assured Zoe that she had no intentions of changing her name. That was all right by Zoe.

Zoe had already decided she wanted to be exactly like Skye, Native American to boot. That's why she'd dyed her hair to match Skye's. She'd even taken to using feathered earrings as accessories and wearing faux black leather.

But lately Lena had been concerned more about Zoe preparing for college than how she accessorized her wardrobe. Getting the girl to keep her grades up had become a priority.

"It's never too early to start thinking about getting into a good school."

"But Skye didn't," Zoe tossed back. "She's done fine."

"That's not the point," Lena argued.

"Yeah, well, the newspapers write stories about how she catches the bad guys. I want to do that."

"If you want to catch the bad guys like Skye, then go to college, get an education, to do it."

The teen's response was a big harrumph.

"If you want your opinion to be taken seriously, lose the attitude," Lena said.

"Okay, okay."

When the doorbell chimed, Zoe took off to answer it.

"Look through the peephole, Zoe," Lena warned, her voice rising to the teenager's back. "Just in case it might not be Skye."

Zoe skidded on the hardwood floor all the way across the entryway. At the last minute she decided to heed Lena's advice. "It's them," Zoe shouted staring through the security slit.

"Lena and I baked double fudge brownies for dessert," Zoe announced, stepping back to let Skye and Josh inside.

"Good, I haven't had my chocolate fix today," Josh replied, noticing Zoe was all but bouncing on her toes. "As if you needed any more sugar in your system," he teased.

"Oh that, I'm just excited to see you guys."

"Did you find a house?" Lena asked from the doorway, wiping her hands on a dish towel.

"Not yet. But we did take the tour on a couple of open houses. We even went all the way over to Bainbridge Island for one." Skye went to wrap her arms around her friend and sensed tension in Lena. Eyeing the two, she finally turned to Lena. "This one giving you much trouble?"

"Just the usual stubborn streak a fourteen-year-old tends to have, a lot like someone else I know. Maybe you two could emphasize the importance of a college education to Zoe while you're here."

"Never got one of those myself, but I hear they come in handy for things like, oh I don't know, getting a terrific job."

Zoe rolled her eyes at the two women and flashed her eyes on the only man in the room. "Josh didn't get one of those and he runs his own company."

"Yeah, but a lot of days I wish I'd bothered, especially in negotiations."

"You guys are ganging up on me. Not fair," Zoe whined. "I'm still young. I've got four years yet to decide about stupid college."

"And getting ready to turn fifteen in two months," Skye pointed out as she tousled the girl's hair. She eyed Zoe's recent dye job. "What's with the all-black look?"

"That's easy," Lena said. "She's emulating her hero. You. Ask her about the composition she wrote for English class. It was five pages of Skye Cree this, Skye Cree that, the person she admires the most."

"Me? Really? I don't believe anyone's ever done that before."

"Sure they have," Zoe said. "They write about you on the Internet all the time. They say you make a difference. I should know. You got me off the streets."

Skye let out a heavy breath. "But what I do is dangerous, Zoe. Very. I wouldn't recommend doing it for a living."

"You're just saying that because you're siding with Lena in this thing. College isn't for everyone," Zoe argued, her face sporting the pout of a typical teen.

"I'm not defending Lena. You are right about one thing though. You're fourteen with plenty of time to settle on what you want to do in life before making a decision right now."

"You having a hard time at school, Zoe?" Josh wanted to know. "Because I've been told that college is nothing like middle school."

"Nah, things are okay. I told everyone that I'm getting a job at Ander All Games this summer."

Skye grinned at Josh and put her arm around Zoe. "By the way, any chance I could get a look at that essay? I'd like to see for myself what you really think about me."

Zoe elbowed her playfully in the ribs. "Sure. I was gonna write about Pink but the teacher said I had to actually know the person."

Lena shook her head. "You two go on. Josh and I will set the table."

Skye followed Zoe into the hallway and upstairs to her room. Once inside Skye asked, "What about Lena? She would've been my first choice."

"I thought about it," Zoe muttered. "But I needed action in my story. I couldn't write about Lena because she stays home most of the time." Zoe opened a drawer and took out a sheet of paper. "This is the one I started on Lena. But I ran out of things to say."

Skye read the words on the page. It warmed her heart to know the girl had waxed poetic about her foster mother. "You should have turned this one in, Zoe. Why don't you show it to her? I'm sure it would mean a lot, especially since you two are at odds over this college thing."

"She'll think it's silly."

"Not at all. I know Lena. She needs to know how you feel. This'll do it." Skye held up the paper, looped her arm through Zoe's. "Come on. Let's show her this one. Lena will be off-the-map ecstatic."

It was after dinner when Skye's cell phone dinged. Harry Drummond's number popped up on the digital readout.

"Hey, what's up?"

"I thought you and Josh might want to know. Shawna Langley woke up about three hours ago. She started talking."

"And?"

"She confirmed her stepfather followed her to school that morning, parked across the street from the bus. She remembered he honked his horn to get her attention as she stepped off. When Shawna went over to the car to see what he wanted, he convinced her to cut her first period math class and go with him to a diner nearby to get breakfast, which she'd apparently skipped. Once he got her into the car, he drove to a nearby park where he raped her."

"Then where was she for a week? Let me guess. The bastard panicked after the rape—"

"Not sure if he panicked or not but Shawna said he went crazy after the sexual assault, screaming at her that she'd better not tell anyone. But then while she was getting dressed, he started trying to strangle her from behind. I guess he decided he couldn't chance her keeping her mouth shut. She remembered them fighting, rolling around on the ground. She doesn't recall what happened after that. At some point she must have hit her head."

"Or maybe the stepfather thought he'd killed her and left her for dead. Somehow she managed to regain consciousness and walked off. Tell me Bob Houston's in custody."

"He is. Got an arrest warrant as soon as I heard Shawna's story, went out to the house and put the cuffs on him myself. I'll be doing paperwork for the rest of the night but it's worth it. I wanted you to know the outcome. You did it again, Skye. You got us the bad guy."

"Not me. All I did was locate the girl. Shawna Langley did the rest."

Chapter Seven

He sat on the ground among tall evergreens bounded by mountain violet that hadn't yet bloomed, looking up at a slender thread of stars in the night sky. With his hands resting on his knees, he breathed in the crisp, cool air and the peacefulness he found here.

That was because this stretch of clearing overlooking the soggy marshland below was his special place. For almost a quarter of a century he'd been coming here to find solace—a peace from the pressure and grind at work.

He dropped his head so he could look over at the recently turned earth, mopped his brow. He surveyed his boneyard. He liked to take this time alone to relive what he'd done, to picture in his head those buried here. If only he'd been allowed to keep his collection in one place. But he hadn't always had the foresight to do so. What was it the Roman philosopher Cicero said? *Ah yes, rashness belongs to youth; prudence to old age.* He could attest to that. He was careful these days, maybe too over-cautious for his own good. But all that would change soon. He'd already put the wheels in motion.

What stayed the same inside him was his difficulty in letting go. Putting them in the ground seemed almost too final. But it had to be done. The bodies, dismembered in chunks and pieces, wouldn't keep forever. No way around that, he thought now. Yes, a shame he couldn't keep them all here, he decided. But he hadn't always owned this piece of land. Because of that he didn't have access to all his early treasures. That's the way he thought of those he'd taken in his youth—his very own personal collection of treasures. At least, he was able to go visit them. It's one reason he'd never considered moving out of his home state.

He knew he wasn't as young as he used to be, nor as spry, not as agile or as quick. His looks were fading, too. It took him longer to coax his quarry into the car. He'd have to come up with a much more original ruse than relying on his charm. Unless of course, opportunity knocked, then he would take the opening and make the most of it.

Lately, he'd resorted to other methods, because in order to subdue them, he needed to get as close as possible. That he would need to work on, to perfect his methods. After all, when he'd first started out, there had been no such thing as text messages or instant messaging.

And like tonight, he found it took him longer to dig up the earth—not like it did in his youth when there was joy in each spade of dirt. Now, when he finally did let go, it took him twice as long to put them in the ground.

Not a good sign at all.

All that considered, it added up. He was slower to recover from each kill. He had to take the time to get his second wind, so to speak. If he intended to play Skye Cree's game, he had to be in tip-top shape. After all, look what she'd done to De Palo. The poor bastard had been laid up in the hospital for a week before ending up in county.

He didn't intend to end up like De Palo.

That's one reason he'd dropped fifteen pounds since Thanksgiving. He'd lowered his cholesterol. His last lab test showed it was down to one-ninety-two. He'd cut back on his meat consumption, avoided eggs, and stuck to eating oatmeal in the mornings.

The same week he'd begun his new diet, he'd started hitting the gym twice a week. That's when he'd gotten his inspiration, his most brilliant idea ever. While lifting weights he'd been watching the local news station do a story about some female who'd beat the crap out of a serial killer, some small-time punk who considered himself God's gift to women.

He'd sat there dumbfounded in stunned realization that this De Palo guy had been small potatoes in body count compared to him. He'd been at this far longer, and been far more successful than the rat bastard Skye Cree had beaten to a bloody pulp.

Then why had the son of a bitch gotten the spotlight? It wasn't fair. Back in December, he'd been sick and tired of listening to the reporters go on and on about the brilliant serial killer who had defied authorities for years. He was fed up with not getting noticed, tired of other people like Frank De Palo getting all the press. Didn't he work just as hard as De Palo? Didn't he deserve a little of that limelight coming his way for a change?

He was in a rut and he needed to get out of it. If not now, then when? If he planned to string Skye Cree along and lead her down the path he wanted her to go, then he needed to follow up in a big way. It was time to get her attention and keep it.

⋖⋗ ⋖⋗ ⋖⋗ ⋖⋗

Red-haired Maggie Bennett's life had taken an upswing in recent months. Her third year at UDub was turning out to be better than she'd hoped, certainly better than sophomore year.

And she'd recently met a cute guy at the part-time job she'd found. Earning a few extra bucks toward her rent every month would surely keep her parents off her back about grades, especially her dad. The hours were flexible, which meant she could devote more time to her courses. Besides, the new guy seemed to be more than happy to help her out with advanced chemistry and calculus.

They'd slept together half a dozen times even though they'd only known each other since Christmas. Earlier that day the two had spent an awesome Saturday together—all day long beginning at ten that morning. He'd taken her to breakfast for omelets. From there, they'd caught an early matinee and then got a burger afterward. But then he'd ruined it all by getting testy because she'd suggested they make it an early evening. Saturday nights were meant for dates, he'd said—and sex. But she still had a pile of laundry to do and a paper to write for her environmental class that was due on Monday.

Since they worked together and saw each other five times a week, she hoped it didn't start getting awkward between them. She wasn't ready for a serious relationship. How was she supposed to tell him that he was crowding her? Wasn't spending her Saturday with him enough?

As Maggie collected the laundry to take downstairs she remembered she'd run out of detergent ten days ago. She'd been meaning to pick some up but kept forgetting. If she didn't do it now, she'd just keep putting it off.

The convenience store was a block over. It would take her less than ten minutes to walk there. She wouldn't even need to move her car and risk losing her parking space. In her neighborhood everyone knew street parking was at a minimum.

Digging in her purse, she took out a ten dollar bill and stuffed it into her jeans pocket. No reason to lug her bag with her either, she thought.

With that, Maggie dashed out the door, planning to be gone no longer than twenty minutes. She was in such a hurry she didn't even remember to grab her phone.

※ ※ ※ ※

Two nights later, pretty waitress Willa Dover wound her way through the restaurant bussing tables as she went. The twenty-two-year-old server with long flaxen hair was about to end her shift at Country Kitchen, a job she'd had for less than three months. It was just shy of midnight and she'd been on her feet for eight hours straight taking care of the dinner crowd. Tuesday nights were usually slow—tonight had been anything but.

She didn't mind hard work. Having quit school when she was sixteen, she knew life would never be easy. If she could go back, she'd change a few of her stupid decisions.

Willa looked up from wiping down a particularly messy table—where a cranky two-year-old had just spent a couple hours crumbling up every cracker she'd given her into mush—to spot Velma Gentry, strolling through the door. Her replacement looked perky as ever.

"Been busy?" Velma asked.

Willa didn't know how the woman did it. Velma always seemed to be cheerful no matter what time of day or night it was. Not only that, but Velma had an outlook on life she envied. It's probably what made Velma such a good waitress. "We got slammed about four hours ago, been downright crazy ever since."

"Travis been in? I need to talk to him."

"He was here around six. Haven't seen him since. Why?"

"Bill and me, we got us a reservation in two weeks at one of those fancy bed and breakfasts outside of town. Four days. I'm gonna sleep till noon all four, read me one of those hot and steamy romance novels and never leave my room. I want to ask Travis for some time off."

Willa looked skeptical. "You got Bill to agree to take you to a B&B? That don't sound like Bill to me."

"I know. But it's our anniversary and I told that man, I'll he damned if I spend another year celebrating our wedded bliss without doing something special."

Willa guffawed. "Is there such a thing as wedded bliss?"

"Damned if I know. But it got me a reservation and I'm making the most of it and making him stick to the plan come hell or high water."

When Willa started to reach for the salt to start filling them up, Velma stopped her. "Honey, why don't you go ahead and clock out. I've got cleanup here." She looked around the almost empty dining room. "I don't see a rush hitting anytime soon unless the tokers come out for a little snack."

"You sure? I wouldn't mind getting off my feet and home to Charlie, although he's more than likely dead to the world this time of the night." Charlie Tucker was her sometime on-and-off-again boyfriend. Lately the two of them had been on.

"Make sure Charlie does something nice for you, you hear?"

"Believe it or not, we've been doin' lots better than we ever did before."

"Good. Good. 'Cause you're a sweet girl, Willa."

The blonde smiled. "I like you, too, Velma."

"Now go on, get outta here. Tell that boyfriend of yours to treat you right. Tell him I said so or else."

Willa didn't have to be told again to hit the road. Her feet were killing her. This time, she circled around the counter, went to the back of the diner to clock out.

The time on her card read twelve-nineteen.

Grabbing her purse and jacket she slipped out the door and headed for her fifteen-year-old Honda Accord.

She hadn't gone twenty yards when an older model Jeep Cherokee pulled into the lot and stopped next to her. He got so close that he almost ran over her foot with the left front tire. She watched as the man behind the wheel rolled down the driver's side window.

"I'm lost. I'm trying to find 90 but I think I have to get back to the I-5 first? By any chance could you give me directions?"

"Sure. But you don't have to get on the 5 to hit the Express." Willa stepped closer to the car. "Two blocks over is First Avenue. Take a right, then a left on Cherry. When you see Second Ave, take another right. Head south until you get to Seattle Boulevard. It'll dump you into I-90."

She made the mistake of leaning her hand on the car window so she could turn to point to the end of the street.

All of a sudden the car door burst open, thrusting her off her feet. Before she could struggle she had to right herself. But the man was quick. When she opened her mouth to scream, she felt the cold steel of a nightstick punch her in the head.

A handcuff snapped around her wrist. She tried to pull back but he yanked her with such force she hit her head on the edge of the door. He dragged her into the front seat and then shoved her face down hard into the floorboard. On the way down, her head connected with the console about the same time she heard tires squeal out of the parking lot.

By this time she lifted her head to scream. But his fist smacked her in the bridge of the nose. Despite seeing stars she began to grope for the handle on the passenger side door, trying to get out. But it wouldn't budge. It had been tied with rope.

"Why are you doing this? Where are you taking me?" Willa sobbed.

Entwining his fingers in her golden hair, he jerked it from the root. "My idea of heaven, sweetheart, but don't worry, honey. I promise it'll be yours soon, too."

Chapter Eight

Skye's phone rang a little after six. Rolling over in bed, she felt around on the top of the nightstand until her fingers landed on her iPhone. Lifting one eyelid, she slid the bar across to answer the call and mumbled a barely coherent greeting. "What?"

"Skye, you know that new waitress we got?"

She recognized Velma's voice on the other end of the line. Usually chipper this time of morning, Velma didn't sound sunny but worried.

Skye's brain did its best to line up the tumblers in the right order. "You mean Willa? Sure. What about her?"

"She ended her shift last night a little after midnight. Around four this morning I took a load of trash out to the Dumpster and noticed her car still parked on the side street. I tried to wait until a decent hour to call. But I'm worried about her, Skye."

"Maybe the car wouldn't start." Skye tried to sit up, tried to focus to get her bearings. Blinking in the direction of the clock at the early hour, she wondered what passed for a decent time where Velma was concerned. But then she remembered the woman pretty much lived at Country Kitchen.

"I thought of that already but if that were the case, Willa would've headed back inside to call her boyfriend so he could give her a lift. She didn't do that. She would've let me know, Skye. Willa's good that way. She hasn't worked here that long but she's gold when it comes to calling in, especially when she runs late. When she left here last night that girl was headed straight for home. She'd worked a busy eight-hour shift and she looked all done in, wanted to get home and go to bed. This isn't like Willa to leave her car on the street overnight."

Without voicing an opinion as to just how well you could get to know a person in three months' time, Skye did her best to reassure her friend. "Okay. Let's not panic. Let's think this through before we leap to any conclusions."

"Don't give me that wait twenty-four hours crap, Skye. Something's wrong. I called Charlie, that's her boyfriend, and he said she didn't make it home. I believe him, Skye. He had no reason to lie to me."

But Skye was skeptical. "Why? Why would you believe him? Maybe they had a fight and he doesn't want to admit it. Maybe Willa simply left on her own. Was the relationship a good one?"

Skye heard the intake of breath, the hesitation in Velma's slow reply.

"It wasn't ideal but he didn't hit her, if that's what you mean. They'd been back together for six months this time and she said he was good to her this go-round. He went to one of those therapists to get his anger under control."

Great, thought Skye, not exactly a glowing point in favor of the boyfriend.

As Josh stirred beside her, the cynic in Skye ramped up. "Relationships often go south without warning, Velma. You know that. But hey, I understand you're concerned about your friend. You're right to be anxious if her car never moved. Give me Willa's address. I'll talk to this Charlie, size him up for myself."

While Skye keyed in the number and street info into her phone, she realized she was anything but calm. A jumble of nerves began to crawl up her spine. Googling the address, she determined it was on the way to work.

"That's real good, Skye, talk to Charlie," Velma echoed. "He's a mechanic at Dalton's Garage around the corner from Country Kitchen. When you're done, stop in and I'll see to it you get breakfast."

Skye ended the call, saw Josh was all the way awake.

"Trouble?"

"Let's hope not. Waitress didn't make it home from the night shift. Remember Willa Dover?"

"At Country Kitchen? Sure, the cute little blonde, right?"

"That's the one. Her car is still parked near the restaurant. She's gone missing. But I suspect the boyfriend."

"That doesn't sound good. The boyfriend's definitely a cliché but the first go-to guy for a reason. Maybe she took off somewhere on foot, reluctant to go home."

"Not according to Velma. After waitressing eight hours on your feet, trust me, you're not exactly ready to go out and party. But I'll know more after I get through grilling the boyfriend. Wanna come?"

"You know I do."

"Good because Velma dangled breakfast as an incentive."

᠅ ᠅ ᠅ ᠅

By the time Josh and Skye reached Dalton's Garage, Willa had been off the grid since midnight, almost eight hours.

They found the repair shop a busy place where people were dropping off cars for simple stuff like a regular oil change and a variety of major work. They had to wait for the owner to hail Charlie Tucker, who was in the middle of overhauling an engine in an older model Suzuki.

When Charlie did crawl out from underneath the bay area, Skye watched from the window of the lobby as the tall, slender man with a long brown ponytail approached the waiting room. He was about her age, she decided, as he did his best to wipe the grease from his hands.

The guy didn't wait for introductions before he wanted to know, "You here about Willa? Any word yet?"

Skye noted Charlie's unease. At his next question she figured out why.

"Are you two cops?"

"No. And you're under no obligation to talk to us. But if you are so inclined, we'd like to know about your relationship with Willa. Maybe start with this. Did you file a missing person report yet?"

"I called the cops two hours ago around six o'clock, got the runaround about how I had to wait twenty-four hours to report her gone. They said, 'She's an adult. She has a right to disappear.' That's bullshit, if you ask me."

With a fair amount of prompting, Skye got him to focus. Once he did, Charlie settled down and went over the same story Skye had heard from Velma. To her, the more he talked, the more his apprehension faded away.

"Did you two have a fight?" Josh asked. "Even the happiest couples do fight from time to time."

"I won't lie. God knows Willa and I have had our share of them in the past. I've known her since she was seventeen. But we didn't have a fight last night because I'm telling you, Willa never made it home. We were doing real good lately, you know? I didn't even know she hadn't shown up at home till Velma called at five-thirty and said her car was still at the restaurant. I knew right away something was wrong then."

"Why is that?" Skye wanted to know. "Why is it you didn't miss her crawling into bed with you in the middle of the night?"

"I'm a sound sleeper. Besides, I took cold medicine before I went to bed around ten. You can ask anybody here and they'll tell you I felt like crap yesterday, thought I was going to hack up a lung. So when I got home I ate some leftover spaghetti Willa had made, drank a couple of beers, and went to bed before I dropped. I wouldn't hurt Willa like that. I love her."

Skye's heart clutched at the heartfelt declaration. "Did you ever tell her that?"

When Charlie hung his head, she had the answer. "Okay, here's what we're going to do. You give me a list of her friends and family, share a few phone numbers out of your cell phone I can check out."

"I called everybody I know after I talked to Velma."

"Doesn't matter. I'll give them a call, too."

"You might as well know, on my way to work this morning I stopped by Country Kitchen and checked out Willa's car. There's not a damn thing wrong with it. I replaced the spark plugs at Christmas and the head gasket two weeks after that. It might be old but it runs like a top. You ask me, somebody did something to her."

"Okay. But *you* should know I plan to call a detective I know to make sure Willa's put on the front burner and it sails past a uniform. Hopefully it won't get stuck in a pile on someone's desk. Any chance you have a photo of Willa?"

Charlie hitched a hip and dug into his back pocket, pulled out a billfold. With his grimy fingers, he inched out a photograph. "Here's one we took at the lake last October, a Sunday. We'd only been back together two weeks when I took this with my old Canon."

"I'll see you get it back."

"Thanks," Charlie said. "Will you let me know as soon as you hear something? Anything at all."

"I will. And Charlie?"

"Yeah?"

"If I find out you're lying, I'm coming back here to get in your face. Even though I'm not a cop, you'll likely need a lawyer if that happens. Or a doctor."

"Okay. Fine. But I'm not lying. Find her. Will you?"

"You got it."

"Do you believe him?" Josh asked once Charlie headed back to the Suzuki.

"I do. How about you?"

"I think he's telling the truth. Which means—"
"We need to find Willa."

They walked around the corner to Country Kitchen where Velma greeted them with a troubled look instead of her usual wide smile.

"So? Did you talk to Charlie Tucker?"

Skye went through the byplay back at the garage with the boyfriend. "I called Harry on the way here. He'll expedite it, put out a BOLO for Willa until the obligatory twenty-four hours is up. If they get nothing from the BOLO, he'll get Seattle PD to investigate it as a missing person case."

"But you both plan to still look for her, right? You have to do something, Skye. You can't just let Willa fall through the cracks like others have."

Skye grinned. "You bet. Now how about that breakfast you promised?"

"Sure. What'll you two have?"

"I'm craving blueberry pancakes," Josh admitted.

"Sounds good to me, make it two," Skye agreed. "Take a seat, Velma. Let's go over exactly what happened last night with Willa."

"Again?"

"Yep. Give it to me one more time."

In the middle of the rehash, Travis walked up. Skye looked him in the eye, pointed a finger and said, "You know what, Travis? As owner of Country Kitchen with waitresses working here 'round the clock, you really need to think about installing security cameras, both in front and in the back. And make sure they have a high-quality resolution, not that grainy stuff."

"Duly noted. I have a guy coming by this afternoon."

"A little late for that," Velma moaned as she got to her feet. "We need to get the word out."

"And we will. I'm having flyers printed up to put in the window. We'll circulate Willa's picture, maybe get the news media involved," Travis said.

"An excellent idea," Josh said, nodding toward Skye. "And this is just the woman to do it, the perfect one to hold a press conference right here in front of the restaurant."

"If I have to appear on camera, then I want my stack of pancakes first," Skye groaned. "I get nervous enough without my stomach rumbling in front of all Seattle's reporters."

Soon after that, Velma complied by slapping down two plates filled with steaming flapjacks onto the Formica table.

After he'd scooped up the last of the stack, Josh slid out of the booth, took out his cell phone. "Finish up while I set up the press conference."

"Where are you going?"

"I need to take a look around outside first."

"Why?" But she already knew. She stood up, tossed some bills on the table from her pocket. "I'm going with you."

"Velma said Willa left out the back door. Let's head that way," Josh prompted.

The negative energy blasted him the minute he reached the parking lot. He sensed an evil so dark it had him doubling his focus. He surveyed the area across to the alley and back again. Because he could still see Willa's Honda angled at the curb on the street, he headed that way. But when the images lessened, he stopped in mid-stride. Sensing that Willa had never made it this far, he turned on his heels to backtrack. As soon as he reached the middle of the lot again, the series of flashes became stronger. This is where he decided to concentrate his efforts.

"She didn't get into the car on her own. He dragged her. He tried to do it without getting out, but of course, that didn't work. He had to get out so that he could make room for her to get in. He's not quite six feet tall, has brown hair. Not sure what color eyes, but he hasn't shaved in several days." Josh frowned, considered the rest. "And he smelled. He was sweaty from some type of physical labor. His olive green shirt had major stains under the armpits and around the neck."

"Why would she let someone like that get so close to her?" Skye marveled.

"He asked for directions, got her talking, then pulled her into his smallish SUV. No, that's not quite right. The SUV was a Jeep. I don't know the model but I'd recognize the front grille. He peeled out of the parking lot right about there." Josh pointed to what would've been the darkest part of the area where the light from the alleyway didn't reach the entire scope.

"Going which direction?"

"South. He headed south on the I-5. I'm sure of it."

They exchanged looks. Skye picked up on the where, mainly because she had complete faith in his ability to read the situation. She didn't have a problem following his lead. Both knew the info was sketchy but more than they had had since six a.m.

"There are a lot of miles between here and Joint Base Lewis-McChord, Josh. Think about it. The fact the guy headed south means nothing."

"I know that," Josh fired back.

She might not possess the same skills Josh did, but she could pick up on his body language. Hands on hips, the stubborn set to his chin, told her he'd already made up his mind. "But you want to follow this through until it dead-ends, right?"

"I do. I know it's a longshot but I think it's worth a trip south anyway."

"Okay, then what are we waiting for?"

They were fine until they reached the outer edges of the military base. An outcrop of dated offices looked like products of a bygone era. They zeroed in on the derelict buildings, some with broken windows. They drove past an old service station, an abandoned hangar, a PX no longer in use.

"This part looks like a ghost town. You can feel the old souls here," Skye commented as she stared out the passenger side window.

"Troubled souls wrestling with an evil so dark most people can't comprehend it."

"Evil that lives and breathes here—somewhere—we just have to find where." Unnerved is the way it made her feel, like the victims might be long gone but they had left a part of themselves behind so someone would know they'd been here.

Josh turned down a back road and then another and another. But none of the streets led them to Willa.

Three and a half hours later after circling the base several times without actually going through the gate, Josh turned the car around and headed back to Seattle.

Frustrated and disillusioned with their efforts, by the time they reached Country Kitchen, Skye had to prepare to face the bank of media that had gathered in front of the restaurant. Skye recognized most of Seattle's field reporters who waited with cameras, microphones, and note pads at the ready, waiting to ask their tough questions.

News vans with satellite dishes lined the block, some from as far away as Vancouver and Idaho.

Of all the things she did for the Foundation, this is the one she hated the most. But appealing to the community had to be done. Willa wasn't here to speak for herself.

And that was the problem. After the eerie trip to the base Skye felt she'd somehow let Willa down already. The least she could do was get her photo circulated, make a public plea for help and beg for Willa's safe return.

About the same time Skye was addressing the media, Willa Dover woke to complete darkness. Battered and bruised, her body felt sore from head to toe. The man who'd taken her had already raped her four times. Her chest ached. Her head throbbed. Even the roots of her hair hurt.

There was no doubt in her mind that at some point he'd drugged her. With what, she didn't know. But she still felt groggy enough to have trouble lifting her head.

He hadn't blindfolded her or put anything over her mouth to keep her quiet. She realized it was probably because he had no fear of anyone hearing her scream. Willa had already kicked up a fuss. She'd yelled and hollered. But no one had come. She was pretty sure no one was going to.

Her arms were stretched over her head at an uncomfortable angle. When she tried to move she found she couldn't because her wrists were manacled to a bolt in the wall. Her feet were bound with heavy cuffs slapped around both ankles. Each time she attempted to roll or turn, she heard the clanging of metal on metal. It was her chains rattling with each little movement.

Outside in the distance, she heard nothing but the occasional bird chirping. Except for a few noisy sparrows it seemed quiet. Sometimes a jet flew overhead. Maybe she was near an airport. She tried to remember if she'd heard any other voices other than the man who'd abducted her and couldn't. Her brain was still having a hard time processing. Wherever she was life no doubt seemed to be speeding along without her.

All she knew for sure was she had to find a way out of this dark, dank place. She tried not to think about how bad it smelled. She needed to concentrate, to figure out how to escape from this horrible hellhole before her captor came back, which she knew could happen any minute. But how? She couldn't even get off the filthy cot.

That thought had her trying to sit up again. With all her might, she yanked on her chains. Was it her imagination or did they give a little? She tried again and again and again until her arms grew tired.

She thought about Charlie in their little apartment. Had he gone to work this morning without hearing from her? She thought about her mother and her sister. Had they missed her yet? She thought about Velma and wondered if her new friend would be angry when she didn't show up for work this afternoon. Was anyone worried about her yet? Would she ever see them again?

About that time she heard footsteps advance down a set of steps and knew he was back from wherever he'd gone. The door opened to the little room where she was. Her heartbeat quickened. Fear felt like a fist in her throat.

For a brief moment she caught the sliver of sunlight before he slammed the door shut. For one second she thought maybe he couldn't see her in the blackness. Willa licked her swollen lips and waited. She closed her eyes, not to block out light but to try and put herself in another place. It didn't work. How much more could she take inside this evil place?

When she felt him standing next to her, there was reason to be afraid. She might not be able to see him clearly but she could feel the large knife blade he held up to her cheek. He let it rest there, cold and sharp.

There was heat emanating from his body. She could feel the rage bubbling to the surface within him. As he knelt beside her on the bed, Willa drew in a tight breath. He crawled into her space, so he could run his fingertips down her throat. On one side, he began massaging the carotid artery. He licked the skin there and whispered to her, "It's time to play again, Willa my love."

When he unchained her, the gesture gave her hope. But then she heard the zipper go down on his pants. And knew her fate was sealed when his knife moved to the space between her legs.

Chapter Nine

Within a matter of weeks Josh had settled comfortably into married life. He admitted he loved having Skye fuss over him, fuss over the house. She routinely picked up flowers at the market, used them around the house to decorate the table at mealtime, or placed them in some conspicuous spot so that they were the first thing he saw when he got off the elevator.

She set candles around the loft for ambiance. The place always smelled like cinnamon or vanilla or jasmine. He loved walking in the door after a long day and breathing in the aroma of some tasty dish she'd put together from scratch or out of one of her cookbooks.

Even though they had established an easy domestic routine, it didn't mean they spent their evenings the same way other couples did. He didn't know another pair who routinely sat for hours at a time looking up missing children online. Who else kept track of reported runaways from as far away as San Francisco? And now, who else actively sought reports on missing women across the state of Washington? Who else concentrated on official police investigations from as far back as 1990?

Josh glanced up from his iPad, leveled his gaze across the table at Skye, who sat in front of her own laptop mesmerized with whatever appeared on her screen. "Look at us. What other couples do you know who are glued to their computers over dinner?"

"Oh. Sorry. But to find Willa we need to…do all we can, as soon as we can. You know as well as I do that time is a factor."

"No need to explain. I get it."

"I emailed that forensic anthropologist, Dawson Hennings, to see if he had anything for us yet. I know it's early but I'm anxious to hear what he has to say. I thought maybe we could set up a meeting with him. Push him along to get us a facial reconstruction on the skull."

Josh chuckled. "I asked him the same thing about fifteen minutes ago."

Skye grinned. "You know what they say? Great minds think alike."

While they polished off the leftover pork roast from two nights earlier, they went over recent abductions in the area, touching on specifics, drawing on similarities. Even attempted abductions, including carjackings, were included in their discussion. They checked off timelines, mapped grids, and rehashed other related crimes within the last several years trying to find a link.

Josh picked up his glass of wine, gestured at all the data. "It occurs to me we're looking for someone who doesn't stand out in a crowd, maybe even fits in to the point that people see him every single day without him raising any suspicions or warnings."

She lifted her glass as well, sipped. "He could even hold a position of authority, one where he has power over people. He'd get off on something like that. How much good do you think holding that press conference really did?"

"Harry said he got a few leads. He'll let us know in forty-eight hours if anything panned out."

"I'm worried about Willa, Josh. I have an uneasy feeling her disappearance is tied to our guy."

"You know that it's way too early to make an assumption like that. And yes, I know we already did, but let's try to keep an open mind about Willa."

"No, it's too much a coincidence not to be."

"You think he targeted her then?"

"Yeah, I do."

"To make a point right in your face?"

"There you go. I'm wondering how long he'll keep Willa around before he decides to... I can't let myself think like that yet."

"Let's hope we can get to her before that happens."

She forked up more meat and looked across their spread of computer devices. "Imagine trying to solve crimes without modern technology. What would we do without databases to use to cross-reference all manner of the stuff we collect?"

"No doubt we have valuable tools at our disposal. We could try using keywords, like say, dismemberment, to look up any cold cases involving body parts."

"That would work if he dismembered in the early years. You said once that maybe we could try syncing our thoughts together, working through a series of thought patterns. We already know that both of us have uneasy feelings about the military base, especially the older parts of it. I'd say trying to find Willa, there's no time like now."

"You're kidding?"

"What? Now you've decided trying to utilize that mind-meld thing you're so fond of is a waste of time?" Skye teased. After flicking through the last of the websites on her list, she added, "Come on, give it a whirl."

Although he wasn't sure how combing through her brain would help matters, he decided to humor her. "Maybe we use it on unsuspecting strangers to zero in on all kinds of secrets." He slid in to the chair next to hers. "So you want me to take a trip through your head and see what I come up with? Okay, let's try it now. Put your hand in mine."

She pretty much knew by the glint in his eye she was being had, but she decided to play along anyway. Because of the day's events, what harm would it do? They needed a diversion.

All the while he went through the phony steps, she continued to check her inbox to see if Hennings had replied to her email.

That is, until Josh finally cleared his throat. "If I could have your undivided attention it would make things a whole lot easier. I could be much more effective without having you distracted."

She complied but not for long. It didn't take but a couple of minutes for Skye to grow impatient with the game. "Getting anything yet?"

"Wait. Oh yeah. Lots of images. I'm seeing how much you want head-banging sex right about now, right this minute, right here on the dining room floor."

She frogged him in the arm right before elbowing him in the ribs. "Like you needed special powers to figure that one out."

"Power of suggestion," he said, nibbling her throat before moving to her ear where he gnawed on a delectable lobe. "Whaddya say we move to the couch."

She let herself be led over to the sofa until they both dropped down into the leather. "It amazes me you can do this on a full stomach."

He ran a finger down her cheek. Those violet eyes pulled him into their depths. "Do you have any idea how beautiful you are?"

"I don't think so. Why don't you show me?" Almost a year of being with him had made her more adept at flirting, at handling the sexy banter. After years of putting off intimacy, she gave Josh high marks for easing her into normalcy in that arena. "I want to rip your clothes off."

"Now we're talking. Don't let me stop you," Josh said evenly, a good dose of come-and-take-me in his tone. He wanted her under him, stripped down and eager. Or maybe on top, he thought now as he pulled her sweater over her head with one yank. He tussled with the zipper on her skinny jeans, watched as she wriggled out of them.

Heat thrummed between them hot as golden light.

"Now you." She tugged up his shirt, unbuttoned his pants. They finished ripping off whatever clothing remained till they got down to flesh, lean and hard, soft and supple.

Pressing her body to his, she threw long limbs around his waist. She needed to climb and conquer.

He locked his mouth to hers, feasted. Using lips and tongue, he moved to her breasts. Slow, lazy tugging drew out the longing.

Fast and fluid, fingers found little gems dancing in the glistening folds. Teeth bit down, gnawed and chewed, languished and savored.

Ripples rushed to the core and back again. A flood of sensations had her tumbling, quivering, shuddering into his palm.

She pushed him back into the cushions to ride, to triumph, to take.

He gripped her hips to fly higher, to drive deeper.

Her hair draped down over him as they rocketed up together, soaring, lifting higher and higher until they winged to the peak. The world tilted. It spiraled and fluttered, built to crashing crests. When the surf careened against the rocks with a roar, she called out his name.

"Is it possible we're getting better at this?" Skye fanned out, trying to catch her breath.

Laughter escaped in the way of the very smug at a job well done. "I'm pretty sure we just set a record for something."

With a grin, she rolled off, snatched up her top. "Good thing records are made to be broken."

"We'll just keep at it till we're legends at our own game," Josh muttered as his eyes fluttered shut.

"I need to shower. Want to join me?"

But when he didn't answer, she turned to stare at a still naked Josh. It always amazed her to see him like this.

Knowing she hadn't always been so at ease with the intimacy that came so naturally to him, she continued to stand there taking in the sight of him. His head lay askew on the cushion. His chin had already dropped to his chest. His eyes were closed. He'd fallen asleep right in front of her.

As she blew down the hallway to the bedroom, she decided she liked the progress she'd made. Feeling as though she'd come a very long way in a short amount of time, she rushed into the shower confident she'd conquered one more fear.

As the water sluiced over her like luxuriant rainfall, she lathered her body with the smells of lavender and vanilla. Appreciating this quiet time had her wondering if she really wanted to live anywhere but right here. It was nice to kick around the idea of moving into a new place. But really, when it came to pulling the cord, she wasn't sure she could leave the loft, leave Seattle.

She turned the water off, stepped out, and grabbed a thick towel to soak up her dripping hair. Rubbing a generous handful of body lotion from head to toe, she stood in front of the full-length mirror studying her reflection. *Was* she beautiful? She didn't see it. But somehow Josh never failed to make her feel that way.

After slipping on a robe, she headed to the kitchen. One glance at Josh told her he was still conked out. She tossed a throw over him and spied the mess they'd left on the table. The supper dishes waited. The temptation to leave them until morning was there but Skye resisted the urge and decided to clean up anyway.

When she realized she'd left her laptop open, she reached to shut it down. That's when her eyes landed on the notes Josh had jotted down on a legal pad. One section was about a young college student who'd gone missing two weeks earlier.

Before she remembered Josh was still napping, she blurted out, "Why didn't you mention Vanessa Farrington?"

Josh abruptly sat up, rubbed the sleep out of his eyes. "I came across it earlier when we were surfing the net."

"Sorry. I didn't mean to wake you up. I just read about the girl from Olympia who didn't make it back to her dorm room after attending a party on campus. It says here, she's a state senator's daughter. Maybe that's why the name sounds so familiar."

"Olympia College is sixty miles from Seattle. But it's only fifteen miles from Fort Lewis." He pulled his pants back on, crossed over to give her a kiss on the top of her hair.

Skye took a seat at the table, entered Vanessa's name and the circumstances surrounding her disappearance into the database they had created.

"Hmm, another jurisdiction that isn't King County, therefore another set of county cops to deal with. This website says the Farrington family's putting up flyers. Here's what she looks like…" She turned her laptop around so Josh could see the screen. That's when it hit her. "Wait a minute, I know this girl."

"What? How?" Josh sat down beside her to get a better look.

"She came to see me at the Foundation last fall. Had to be around mid-October, early November maybe."

"What on earth for?"

"She wanted to know if she could get college credit if she volunteered her time at the Foundation three times a week."

"What did you tell her?"

"I told her sure, if I had anything for her to do. That's when we were just getting up and going. By the way, at some point we need to talk about that. I mean, so far it's pretty much a one-woman outfit. But there's a chance in the near future this gets bigger than I can handle by myself."

"Skye, if Vanessa came to see you, that's one more connection to you. Like Willa. You can bet it isn't a coincidence."

"I agree. You did mention that he's probably been staking the building out for some time. He sees a pretty girl go inside, waits until she comes out, follows her back down to Olympia, grabs her there when the opportunity presents itself."

"You sure Vanessa came in last fall? You sure about the timeframe?"

"Positive. That means he's planned this out for quite a while."

"Planning to involve you all along."

"Exactly."

"That's disturbing. Have you thought about letting people man the office while you spend more time in the field, so to speak."

"Sure. The problem is I don't want a bunch of people sitting around with nothing to do, waiting for the phone to ring while I'm out circling Seattle. The point is I…I mean we," she corrected. "Need to be more organized. I had three people call the office while we were in St. Kitts wanting to volunteer their time after seeing a news story about the Foundation. But what would they do, Josh? I don't even have available flyers printed up yet with all the missing. The list is rather long. Plus, I'd need people I could trust."

"Don't be so hard on yourself, Skye. The Foundation is still in its infancy. It seems you already know exactly what to do. Have someone come in and organize your files, get flyers printed, get them in the mail, circulate as many as you can around Washington, starting with the immediate five counties."

She arched a brow, considering. "Jumpstart the searches, put new life in all the cold cases. That's a plan. I like it."

About that time her email dinged signaling a message from Dawson Hennings. She scanned the brief five-line missive. "He's agreed to see us tomorrow morning."

Josh shook his head. "He's agreed to see *you*. I'm afraid I have a meeting with my programmers. I can't miss it, Skye."

"Let me guess. Working on that new game featuring the red-headed female fighter? When is it set for release?"

"This coming Christmas, which means we have less than a year to bust our asses from now till then to get this product on the market without major bugs."

"So when it comes to this case…"

"I'm in this with you a hundred percent. Just not tomorrow. How about if I text you with any questions I come up with, though? We can always keep in touch to make sure we're on the same page as a team."

※ ※ ※ ※

The next morning, half the Ander-Cree team stood inside the office belonging to Dawson Hennings.

To Skye, the man, dressed in a white lab coat, came across as the perfect stereotype—a snapshot of the medical scientific nerd mesmerized by whatever ended up under his microscope.

His lab might have been meticulous but his office was cluttered with files and textbooks scattered around. Despite all the obvious work piled up, the bespectacled guy seemed rather organized in his chaos.

Reluctantly she followed Dawson into his lab and watched as the man busied himself with drying an upper arm bone that had been soaking in some type of clear solution. Much like at Bayliss's lab, she felt like an intruder. But unlike the coroner, Dawson seemed to relish having a visitor. He'd already given her a brief dissertation on the two types of DNA used most often in solving crimes: mitochondrial and nuclear.

"Mitochondrial DNA is found in the subunit of active cells known as the mitochondrion and deals with energy production. Bones, teeth, and hair are ideal for obtaining that type to use in missing persons cases. While nuclear DNA is found in the cell nucleus and pertains to growth and maintenance where blood, semen, and sweat are left behind."

"Mitochondrial DNA is inherited from the mother, right?"

"It can be used to determine maternal heritage, yes. A father's mitochondrial DNA is usually destroyed at fertilization. Although a few scientific case studies have shown people can inherit mitochondrial DNA from both father and mother."

"Really?"

"Those results showed subjects had parents who had used in vitro fertilization to help with their pregnancies."

"Ah. So nuclear DNA is the stuff found from evidence on things like blankets, clothing, weapons, stuff found at crime scenes?"

"That's right. Sorry. I know I sound like I'm lecturing you but the point is mutations and disorders routinely occur in science, in diseases, in molecular structure. And understanding the types of DNA might give you a better handle on what your expectations are in obtaining usable DNA for ID purposes in this case."

"Hey, any time I get to see things firsthand and learn more than I get from the Internet, I'm a willing subject." When the doctor turned his full attention from his work to her, she wanted to know, "Is that one of the bones you got from Bayliss?"

Dawson grinned and showed off his immaculate teeth. "No. This is another case I'm working on, another unidentified set of remains. This one had flesh and tissue still attached, which I've already removed."

Skye made a face. "On second thought, I'm not sure I'm ready for this."

"Think of it this way. Going through this process hopefully IDs this poor victim and gives a family somewhere some much-needed answers."

"Good point. I think I'm going to like you, Dr. Hennings. You didn't use that word 'closure' that so many tend to use which has a tendency to piss me off."

"I like you, too. Call me Dawson. Want to see how it's done?"

"Sure. Although I doubt it ever comes up again."

"You never know," he said, moving on to his task. "I soak the bone in a ten percent solution of bleach, rinse it in sterile water before making sure it's thoroughly dried. Like this." Dawson took her through the steps before picking up a grinder. "Now, I remove the outer coating with either sandpaper or in this case, I'm using my Dremel to drill down as much as I can to collect the bone powder. As I've already stated, the best chance of getting usable DNA is in the middle of the bone, the nucleus."

"Looks like you're avoiding the ends for a reason. Is it because they're more dried out than the rest?"

Dawson looked back up from his specimen, stared at his guest over his glasses. "You are observant. I don't use that part of the bone because it's usually too contaminated. Exposure to the elements takes its toll. Since this sample has pretty much degraded to what you see here, I've elected to avoid the marrow, for now at least. I might get desperate down the road though."

"Why's that? Wait. What you're really saying or trying not to say is that you don't have the skull of this victim to extract any DNA from the teeth? It's down to that bone you have curing in the solution."

Dawson cleared his throat. "It's unfortunate, but that's true."

"So, why not use the marrow?"

"In this case it's just too degraded. When that happens it produces a much lower molecular weight substance.

Using a descending concentration of ethyl alcohol, I hope to extract what I need for the size sample I want. The goal is to get fifteen grams. That's ideal. In this instance, it's soaked overnight in the extraction solution. But the process itself may take several tries." He picked up a conical tube, filled it with the liquid, set it in the centrifuge to spin while they talked.

"What does that do?"

"It dissolves the bone and collagen and releases the DNA into the mixture. We spin fifteen minutes and the spinning produces PCR to amplify that single piece of DNA we want."

"PCR stands for polymerase chain reaction. I read up this morning in preparation for coming here."

"That makes up the first attempt."

"The first?"

"We repeat this process up to five times. And it may take as many as that to get anything at all. When we're done we hope to have a pellet-sized concentrate we use to extract the DNA."

"I'm pretty sure you just simplified that for me. You're a smart guy, Dr. Hennings. I appreciate what you do here."

Dawson adjusted his glasses, shifted his feet. He went on as if he didn't know how to handle the praise. "When this bone gives up what I need, I'll move on to the silica extraction where the DNA molecules bind to the silica. I run it through a microchannel where I can remove the DNA."

Now Skye was positive her assessment embarrassed him so she diverted to her own pending case. "But when do you get to the bones Bayliss gave you? Right now, those are the ones I need analyzed. Seattle has a killer out there who likes to dismember."

As they stood there, Dawson fidgeted with his test tube, as if more ill at ease than before. "There's something I want you to know. Before we get to your case, you should know I've read about you. Extensively. You're an amazing woman, Miss Cree." He stared at her. "I can see by that statement I've made you self-conscious. I don't mean to. I just felt like I needed to tell you. We'll be working together."

"The thing is I don't feel amazing or extraordinary."

"I know. But that's what makes you all the more exceptional. You have terrific instincts. You really should be in law enforcement."

"Thank you. I think what we have here is mutual respect for one another. But I'm afraid I'm not cut out for the restrictions placed on cops."

"Ah. Well. A pity. I suppose I put my foot in my mouth. But then, I often say too much."

"Not at all. I think we can be friends though, don't you?"

"I'd like that."

"Your email did indicate you ran an initial test you wanted me to know about. Why don't you just tell me what you found?"

"Sure. The test I ran on the mummified hand indicates your second victim has been dead less than five years."

"Really? Okay. So we have one that's been in the ground for a long time versus another more recent."

"In addition to that, I found bruising under the soft tissue which makes me think this victim was tortured."

Skye pondered that development for about five seconds. "Hmm, he's all about getting off on the physical violence, the suffering of the victim rather than about the sex. You know, Bundy started out bashing their heads in once he got them into his vehicle. Then he'd take them to an undisclosed location where he had plenty of time to do despicable things to the body so that he could have sex with the corpse again and again. I wonder if that's what's going on with this guy."

Dawson swallowed hard. "You think he somehow gets them into his car, whisks them away from the area, and then goes to a place where he brutalizes them without detection."

"That's exactly what I think. Right now I have a missing waitress named Willa Dover. She worked at the same restaurant where I worked as a kid. I'm thinking this guy has done his research."

"Willa Dover," Dawson repeated. "I heard that name on the news this morning driving to work. You think he abducted her to make a point with you?"

"Yes. And it might be a giant leap on my part, but I'm thinking he took her so I'd know he could. Wherever Willa is, she's still alive, probably in bad shape but alive. If we move on this fast enough maybe we could find her before it ends up too late."

"What can I do to help?"

"Make those bones the killer sent me a priority." Skye looked around Dawson's lab. "Start with anything you think might give me a leg up on this guy. You mentioned taking samples of the dirt. Anything would help. Is that even possible?"

"Possible and doable. But not me. That's for a forensic geologist to examine the soil to see if it contains anything unique that makes it identifiable to a certain, specific location."

"You wouldn't happen to know one by any chance?"

Dawson grinned again. "As a matter of fact, I do. Kevin Holt. He works upstairs in his own state-run lab. Around here, he's the go-to guy. He can usually break down the mineral particles, determine the soil content, color, and come up with a source. He's actually testified in murder trials. He's very good at pinpointing where soil samples come from. It's his specialty."

"Sounds like just the man we need. You'll share the dirt found on the skull and bones with him, right?"

"I will."

"Then let's hope he's able to reveal something distinctive, something from the general area where this guy buries his victims. Otherwise, we're just flapping in the wind."

Chapter Ten

Skye wasn't sure why but she just couldn't let go of her studio apartment. When she'd left Dawson Hennings huddled in his lab surrounded by his specimens whirling around in that little machine, she'd made a point to stop by her former home.

Even having taken down the serial killer, Frank De Palo, in this exact spot where she stood now, the place could still tug at her heartstrings. Maybe it was because it had been her very first real home. Maybe it was because here in this place she had first come to the realization that she could make a life for herself doing what she wanted to do.

It was here—for the first time since the accident had taken her parents when she was just thirteen—that she'd felt she had a purpose. Whatever the reason, she couldn't let a stranger move inside these four walls and take up residence in the place she still considered her personal space. She didn't want just anyone living here, cooking here, or sleeping here. She couldn't handle subletting it.

She knew Josh wondered about why. But these past few months, he'd come to accept her decision to keep this part separate from everything else.

Because of that, she still had plants and herbs here, growing, thriving, though it was still winter. Despite the gradual change in temperature from February to March, her small balcony garden flourished. The lavender had survived the winter. The little blooming buds proved that. Of course, she'd moved a few of the smaller containers over to Josh's place—the rosemary and basil, the sage and oregano had found a new home at the loft. Josh had offered to cart more over but so far, she'd dragged her feet on doing it.

Today, she was there to water, spritz, and deadhead. Maybe replant those that needed it into bigger pots. The spider plants were okay the way they were, but the rootbound monstera had to graduate to a much larger container. When she'd finished with that chore, she pruned and snipped brown leaves off the dianthus and coreopsis. While she was at it, she cut a mix of both to use as a table centerpiece. She harvested the mint, did the same with the chives.

Sitting back on her haunches to survey her work, she realized the little terrace was crowded. She really did need more space. In the not so distant past, she'd dreamed about having an actual garden one day with rows and rows of veggies or flowers growing directly out of the ground.

She decided they should get more serious about making the decision to get a house. Maybe settle on the Tudor Revival in Ballard with a view of Shilshole Bay or the farmhouse on ten acres in the rolling hills of Bainbridge Island.

The 1935 Tudor had plenty of room—three bedrooms, two baths—with a brand-new deck. Plus, it had been remodeled with all the latest upgrades.

But something about its counterpart—the rambling country house on Bainbridge—pulled at her. Its age was a factor. The fact it had been built in 1909 just meant it had withstood the test of time. Its size was a definite deterrent for two people. With four bedrooms and three bathrooms, what on earth would they do with all that space?

The gabled windows and wraparound porch were huge draws for her though. The cherry orchard was a bonus. There were rows and rows of trees already budding with aromatic blossoms. It was like a picture postcard, a precursor to spring. The land offered plenty of space for planting and growing a vegetable garden or whatever else she decided to put in the ground.

She suddenly realized how much she wanted that old house. She took out her phone to text Josh. *What do you think about becoming farmers?*

Across town when his cell phone dinged, Josh had just finished up with the programmers. Sitting in his office with time to spare before his next meeting, he grinned at the readout and keyed in a response. *Didn't you know? I'm a regular Old MacDonald.*

A couple minutes later Skye texted back. *Good. B/c I think I want that farmhouse.*

When will you know for sure?

Smartass. Let's go for it. Now.

⊹ ⊹ ⊹ ⊹

Harry Drummond showed signs of fatigue as he knocked on the door of Skye's apartment. Not only had he trudged up four flights of stairs, he hadn't slept much the night before.

As soon as she flung the door back, he didn't wait for preamble. "Joggers found the body of a young woman this morning dumped in the park."

"Come on in."

"I need to know if you recognize her." He handed Skye a crime scene photo.

It was hard to look at what once had been a young, attractive female with such a youthful, pretty face. But she forced herself to study the picture of the nude woman and the details it gave up. Skye noted she'd had gorgeous red hair and deep brown eyes with a spattering of freckles across the bridge of her nose. But in death, her hair had been left in disarray, matted with blood and bunched in knots. Deep slashes across both breasts and the open wound to her throat told Skye the woman had suffered greatly.

"Jesus, this guy really likes to use a knife. How long do you suppose she'd been there, do you think? In the park?"

"At least twenty-four hours, maybe longer. Right now, I'm waiting on Bayliss to give me anything more concrete."

She handed the photo back to him. "I don't recognize her, Harry. I mean, she looks somewhat familiar but I can't place her. What about a missing person report?"

"Well, it doesn't match the twenty-four-year-old hooker I have who disappeared from Tacoma. That much I'm certain."

"Another person who went missing besides Willa? What's her name?"

"Andrea Harkness disappeared last Friday night, last seen climbing into a Jeep."

"A Jeep? I'll make coffee while you bring me up to speed and I'll do the same."

"That psychic thing you and Josh have going for you?"

"Right now, sad to say, it's all we have. Any word yet on Willa?"

"Not a thing. It's like she vanished into thin air. Pour that coffee and I'll tell you what I have so far."

That night at the loft, Skye deliberated over her decision. Buying a house was a big step. Since she'd never done it before, she was standing at the fringes about to get cold feet. As they relaxed after dinner, both were stretched out on the sofa, her legs propped up in Josh's lap. While second thoughts nagged at her, she finally said, "It's a really old house, maybe too old."

"Don't try to talk yourself out of it."

"Why?"

"Because it shows we're on the same page. Don't think about its age but about how happy we'll be there together. The present owners added a few nice upgrades. They put in all new appliances in the kitchen, a new hardwood floor in the dining room, and added a new roof last summer. Plus, it's located right on the water. The view alone is a nice benefit that you don't normally get with a farmhouse. I love the surrounding land, did from that first Saturday we looked at it. I was hoping you'd come around."

"You could've just said something. It's a big house, Josh, too big for the two of us."

"Nah, we'll fill it up with friends and…what about getting a dog? Maybe two?"

"I haven't had a dog since…well, a dozen years or more." Not since her parents had died.

"What kind? What was his name?"

"Her. Binky. A little apricot bundle of pug that followed me around everywhere."

"What happened to her?"

"She died of renal failure two months after I got out of the hospital."

"Jesus, Skye. You had a lot to deal with back then and you were so young." ˎ

She looked away and changed the subject. "I do like the hiking trails and bike trails in the area. You're right. You wouldn't normally get those kinds of amenities with a farmhouse."

"Then it's a go?"

"It's a go. If nothing else we can use it for a weekend getaway."

"What about going out every night?"

"Like you said, I can always take in volunteers at the Foundation. Maybe start making my rounds during daylight hours. Who knows, maybe settle into a normal existence?"

"You'd do that?" He lifted a hand to her hair, twirled his fingers through several strands.

"Yes, I would. What's bothering you? Something's wrong. I saw it tonight at supper."

"One of my employees didn't show up for work on Monday. She didn't bother to call in either. When she wasn't at her desk by four that afternoon to start her shift, her manager sent someone over to her apartment to check on her. Turns out, they couldn't get anyone to answer the door so they called the cops."

Her gut tightened, her instincts kicked into overdrive. She peppered Josh for more info. "Who? What did you do about it? What did they find? How come you didn't mention it until now?"

"Down girl. The who? A junior at UDub named Maggie Bennett, hired as a part-time tester. She worked twenty to twenty-five hours a week, depending on her schedule. I just learned about it this afternoon myself between meetings. And I'm briefing you mere hours after I was told about it. I suspect Maggie and Tate have been seeing each other, hot and heavy, for the last several months. He was pretty upset about her not showing up and not being able to locate her."

Since Tate Brock was the brother of his late wife, Annabelle, Skye knew Josh still considered the man family. "So tell me what happened."

"It was Tate who couldn't get Maggie to answer the door. He's the one who decided to place a call to the police. But when they got inside the girl's apartment, there was no sign of Maggie. None. Personal items were still there, her purse, her cell phone, but no sign of a break-in, nothing looked out of place."

Chills ran up Skye's spine. She tried to remember if she'd ever met Maggie. But she couldn't put a face to the name. "Hmm. Where was she last seen and with whom?"

"Tate said he dropped her off Saturday night around ten-thirty. Said she seemed to be upset about something. They'd spent the day together and agreed to meet for lunch the next day but when she didn't return his phone calls on Sunday, he thought she'd blown him off for some reason. He didn't think any more about it until she didn't show up for work on Monday. That's when he got worried, began calling their mutual friends to see if she'd been to class.

She was a no-show for Monday and Tuesday morning classes."

"Josh, what did Maggie look like? By any chance did she have red hair?"

Josh wrinkled his brow. "I think so. Why do you ask?"

"Harry dropped by the apartment this afternoon. I was there watering the plants. We compared notes. He has one missing woman from Tacoma that hasn't turned up yet. A hooker named Andrea Harkness, last seen by her friends hopping into one of her john's vehicles. Wanna guess what he was driving?"

Josh sat up straighter. "A Jeep Cherokee?"

"You got it. And get this. I knew Andrea Harkness through Dee Dee and Lucy Border. Remember Dee Dee and Lucy?"

Josh nodded. "They worked Sixth and Wheeler Streets here in Seattle as I recall."

"At one time so did Andrea. She was roommates with both girls during tough times. Had some disagreement with them and ended up turning tricks in Tacoma."

"So our guy resorts to hookers in a pinch?"

"Wouldn't be the first serial killer to do so, that's for sure."

"Okay, so what does Andrea have to do with my tester, Maggie Bennett?"

"As of this morning, Harry also has one new murder investigation. Joggers found a girl's body dumped in the park. She had ligature marks around her wrists. And Josh, she had red hair."

"Are you certain of that?"

"Positive, a natural redhead, I saw the crime scene photos myself. Harry wanted to know if I knew her, if I recognized her or had a connection to her in some way. If this is your Maggie, your tester, he dumped her there, nude and battered. To me, the girl looked to be no older than twenty-one."

"Damn it. You don't think…?" Josh took out his iPhone, punched in a series of numbers. "I need to find out one way or the other if it's Maggie. Her family's been frantic for news, tearing their hearts out with worry for two days. Harry needs to get on this."

"Then get him on it."

It took several minutes but Josh finally got Harry to pick up. Josh could tell a detailed explanation about Maggie's disappearance piqued Harry's interest right up front. "A missing person report was filed Monday. She missed her classes at UDub now for three days in a row, which Tate assures me is unusual for her."

"Okay, I'll contact my office and give them an update. Sometimes these missing person reports fall through the cracks and we don't make comparisons as quickly as we should. I'll make up for it though. After I get the desk sergeant to fax me a copy, I'll call you back."

At the click in his ear, Josh hung up. "It's amazing to me how many times information doesn't get to the right person, falls through the cracks. It's like two ships passing in the night and each one has no idea they were in the same general vicinity."

"Just one more reason so many people disappear and are never heard from again unless friends or family hit the ground running with a lot of fanfare and legwork."

"Harry's overworked. He sounded beat."

"This afternoon he looked it, too."

About that time Josh's cell phone rang. "Hi, Harry."

"Your tester's general physical description matches our victim. I'll get the coroner's office on board and notify the parents that the body might be that of their daughter. Thanks for the heads up, Josh."

Again Josh heard a click in his ear and the detective was gone.

Skye mulled over what they knew. "Maggie's been missing since last Monday, possibly longer, maybe even as long as Saturday night. That's when Tate dropped her off. In the photo I saw, her throat had been cut. She also had rope marks around her wrists and ankles, which means whoever kept that girl held her for days before the killer decided he was done with her and put the body in the park. He's keeping them for shorter periods of time, Josh. That's a similar method to the college coed we talked about who was found two weeks ago."

Josh got up to check his notes. "Vanessa Farrington was last seen around midnight when she left a frat party to walk back to her room. Alone. When they did find Vanessa's body she'd been dumped naked with signs of major trauma." Josh looked up from his iPad. "He's trying to impress you with a number count."

"I think you're right." Skye went to her own laptop, tapped the screen with her index finger where she'd brought up the map they'd created online with the data they knew. "Vanessa was found a week later in Bellingham. Here. But she disappeared in Olympia. That's over a hundred and fifty plus miles. On the other hand, Maggie was found in a Seattle park. Closer to home. Here. Roughly ninety miles separates each woman's case, but that short distance involves two different jurisdictions."

"As we've learned in the past, different jurisdictions often mean the cops don't share info about their cases, especially in homicide. Throw in the fact that in Vanessa's case, the tox screen showed no alcohol in her system."

"Even though the story on the Internet indicates she left that party so intoxicated witnesses said she had trouble walking, which means she had plenty of time to get it out of her system. He kept Vanessa a week, Maggie three days at minimum," Skye determined. "Depending on whether or not your tester went missing Saturday night after Tate said his goodnights."

"Yeah, Maggie could've been taken then or sometime on Sunday. Either way, he didn't hold her as long as he did Vanessa. And yet, Vanessa was dumped farther away from where she was last seen while Maggie is left practically around the corner."

"Which means he covers a lot of ground," Skye finished. "And there's no pattern to speak of."

"Both locations are well within the range of the military base though," Josh pointed out.

"We keep circling back to that."

"For a reason."

She stalked to the windows and back, rested her hands on her hips. "So where's Willa? She vanished well after Vanessa, and a couple of days after Maggie did. I don't want to think about Willa ending up like the others."

"We don't know a hundred percent that it's Maggie."

She tilted her head to give him a look that said he knew better. "You probably need to talk to Tate, prepare him for the worst."

Josh groaned. "Maybe it's another missing redhead." He paced in front of the bank of windows alongside Skye, looked out into Seattle's skyline and on past into Puget Sound. "So we have a string of recent abductions where the killer is now leaving the bodies in obvious locales knowing full well they'll be discovered instead of burying them as we suspect he's done in the past. We touched on this at the coroner's office. He's changed the way he does things—for you."

"We have more than that, Josh. Think about it. These women all had a connection to me or now, to you. Willa worked at Country Kitchen. I go in there at least four times a week to talk to Velma or Travis or to grab a meal. Vanessa had stopped by the Foundation months ago. Even if it happened some time back, it's still a connection to me. I knew Andrea Harkness through Dee Dee and Lucy. Now there's Maggie who worked for you. This is freaking me out."

"A 'six degrees of separation' kind of thing? You're onto something, Skye."

"But how does it help us, Josh? How do we catch this guy?"

"I'm not sure exactly. I do know we need to find the owners of every Jeep Cherokee in the state and run the numbers through the database. I'll call Leo. See if he can meet us here tomorrow night for an all-nighter."

Chapter Eleven

A pall fell over Ander All Games. Tate took the news about Maggie's death especially hard. Josh knew the younger man felt a chunk of guilt for not checking on her Sunday.

"You couldn't have known," Josh told his brother-in-law. He studied the man from across his desk. Tate didn't look like his usual self at all. There were circles under his eyes as if he hadn't slept all night. His clothes were the same as the day before and wrinkled.

"But I certainly know something about how you're feeling. After Annabelle died...well, you know what a hard time I had dealing with her death."

Tate nodded. "Maggie was such a sweet person. Like Annabelle, Maggie didn't deserve this. When I didn't hear from her, I should've gone over to her apartment Sunday to make sure she was okay. But I thought she was playing head games with me, you know? So I left her alone to stew and teach her a lesson. Imagine that. The whole time some sick bastard had her...raped her...while I...I...played video games."

"You couldn't have known what would happen, Tate," Josh repeated. "The day Michelle killed Annabelle, the day I walked into the house and found her dead on the floor, we'd had an argument that morning. Did I ever tell you that?"

"No."

"It was part of the guilt I carried around for so long. I don't want to see you doing the same."

"Her funeral's Saturday."

"I know. The entire company plans on going."

"Rumor has it you and Skye are looking for the guy who did this. What kind of sick person does this to another human being, Josh? Tell me that."

"You said it, Tate, a very sick bastard. Now get out of here and go home."

"I can't. I have to stay busy otherwise it'll just drive me nuts."

About that time, Leo Martin sauntered into the office. Long and lean at six-three, Leo sported dreadlocks down to his shoulders. Two gold earring studs pierced both of his earlobes. The look made him seem more musician than seasoned programmer slash hacker.

Leo's contractor gigs paid the bills. Companies like Ander All Games hired him to supplement their work force. In many instances, he made sure people such as himself couldn't hack their way into a secure system.

Added to that, Leo had a rep for helping out his buddies any time they needed it. Skye and Josh qualified when the situation warranted it. Working for them, it was almost like being part of a team with two of Seattle's own crime-fighters. The fact that he could hack into any website, retail or otherwise on behalf of The Artemis Foundation, made the work seem almost legit.

Leo had come to terms with how much time he spent in front of a computer screen at fifteen. Hacking came natural to him. He'd always been a risk taker.

After all, he never hacked to steal anyone's credit card info, unless of course they happened to wander across Skye's radar as a bad guy. He didn't make a habit of using the info for any other purpose than to narrow down a perp's particulars, to pinpoint a location, to zero in on whatever would aid in their capture. He didn't hack to obtain anyone's ID, or personal information, unless they were hunting and killing kids or women. In those cases,

Leo made it a point to come through for Skye and Josh. If they needed the deets and he could supply the tools necessary to capture one of the bad guys, Leo intended to do what he could to put the scum where they belonged—off the streets and behind bars.

That's why when Skye and Josh had asked him to help them narrow down the names of Jeep owners through the state's DOL, Leo hadn't hesitated.

"Hey, how's it going?" Leo finally said, shifting his feet when he spotted Tate. Not sure how much he should divulge about what was going on later, he traded glances with Josh. "Wanted to let you know, you can count me in for tonight."

"What's tonight?" Tate wanted to know.

Josh and Leo exchanged another long glance. "Poker game."

"That's bullshit. You don't play poker, Josh. If this is about Maggie, I want in, too." Tate dropped his head into his hands and muttered, "I have to do something. *You* have to do something, Josh."

"Tate, I will. But first you need to clear your head. Rage won't help you think, let alone help Maggie. Now go home. Get some sleep. Don't come back to work until you get at least eight hours. And if you need to talk, call me."

⁂

When Josh got off the elevator at the loft, he had Leo in tow.

"Something smells terrific," Leo said as he put his computer bag down in the living room.

About that time, Skye made her way into the dining room carrying a stack of plates to set the table. "I hope you guys are hungry. I made a meat lover's pizza."

"From scratch?" Leo asked.

Josh slapped the programmer on the back. "You haven't lived until you've tried Skye's pizza."

Over gooey slices of pie, they prodded Leo for what he'd learned on the Jeep owners. But he went them one better. He took out a printed list from his computer bag and handed it off to Josh. "I also have that data on my laptop. The problem is the DOL doesn't always distinguish between Jeep models in their records. You have Wranglers, Wagoneers, Libertys, which by the way, took the place of the one we're looking for, the older model, the sporty Cherokee XJ."

"There must be ten thousand names here," Josh groaned.

"But that isn't the issue. Not all DOL records reflect the vehicle model. They do provide year though. That's why I'm moving on to plow through surveillance tapes the night Willa Dover went missing." He'd already used his skills with protocols and firewalls to pull anything he could get on the surrounding buildings from the area around Country Kitchen to the ramp leading up to the interstate.

After dinner the three of them spent several hours at the keyboard until Leo finally announced, "I've got nothing but a grainy video from the bank opposite the I-5 onramp that shows a Jeep Cherokee crossing in front of the building at twelve-thirty-three. That doesn't help much because we already knew the make of the car."

"What about a license plate?"

Leo shook his head. "I got a side view. And as bad as the images are it wouldn't yield a number anyway."

"Well, that's just great," Skye muttered. "That leaves cracking the reports on all the missing women in the area."

"What age group, specifically?"

"Don't leave anyone out."

Leo whistled through his teeth.

"Okay, narrow it down to females under the age of thirty. How's that?"

"I'll try."

A couple of hours later, they hadn't counted on so many surprises.

"I'm astonished to find the list is so long. This tops the information I've been trying to maintain for the last five years," Skye uttered as she skimmed the names.

She looked over at Josh. "Maybe we can get Hennings in on this. I understand he and Harry have been going through boxes of cold case files. They even asked Bayliss if he'd revisit the remains of people he hasn't been able to identify yet. Some go back as far as 1985."

"That's farther back than we know our killer was active," Josh added. "But it might be a good idea to eliminate a timeframe and move on from there, although that would make our guy in his fifties."

"Age doesn't mean he stops killing. BTK was sixty when they caught him. And Dennis Rader began to want attention more than anything else, enough to reach out, make contact with several news outlets. That's what tripped him up. Technology. If we're lucky this guy will trip up as well."

Josh stared at his wife. "It amazes me how good you are at this, Skye Cree."

She sent him a glowing smile. "You mean Ander. Skye Cree Ander, that's me. Besides, you always say that."

"Because it's true."

"I hope you guys don't mind but I've asked Harry to join us tonight when he gets time."

Josh looked at Leo who had a deer-in-the-headlights look on his face. A hacker coming face to face with a cop might not be a smart move. "Is that wise? I realize you trust Harry, but after all, Leo's putting everything he is on the line for us."

Skye patted Leo's hand in reassuring fashion. "I wouldn't expose what you do unless I thought it was important. Harry's thinking of retiring after we nab this guy. He's been a little down now for several months. For a guy who used to follow the straight and narrow down the line, I think he just wants an end to these recent murders and cases he hasn't been able to crack. He's looking to get justice for the families."

"Less than a year ago this was the same guy preaching about how we shouldn't cross a line and now he wants to see how we do it?"

Skye smiled. "Something like that."

"If that's true then why don't we just ask the cop to share his official list of people who've gone missing like Willa Dover?" Leo wanted to know.

"His commander's been giving him a hard time about us. Cops don't generally trust consultants. That's what we are…unofficially."

"But we're supposed to trust him?" Josh said clearly troubled by this one tidbit he couldn't ignore.

"We need him in on this, Josh. He shares with us to find Willa. We share with him. He did help us give Maggie's family some answers once we pointed him in the right direction. By the way, how's Tate handling this? And what about the rest of your staff?"

"Tate's devastated. So is everyone she worked with. I need to be there for him and them."

She squeezed his hand. "Of course you do. We both will."

When the buzzer rang signaling someone was downstairs, Skye got up, drifted over to the panel. "That's Harry now."

"Make sure it's him before you let anyone in," Josh cautioned.

Skye rolled her eyes in response as she spoke into the speaker on the security plate. "Who's there?"

"It's me, Skye."

Recognizing the voice, Skye pushed the button, granting access. "Come on up."

Out of the corner of her eye Skye saw Leo fidget in his seat, clearly not comfortable with the new arrival. She felt she needed to reassure him one more time. "It'll be okay, Leo. Don't worry. I know Harry."

She'd been hounding the detective for two weeks to send over copies of any files he had that might fit their killer. When he stepped off the elevator, he was carrying a banker's box.

"These are from my own stash I brought from home," Harry explained. "Do me a favor, don't advertise it around."

"Sheesh, there's an awful lot of mistrust floating around here tonight," Skye said, shooting a knowing look in Josh's direction. "With so much suspicion on both sides, I guess we know now this is going to take a while."

"What's to eat?" Harry said, sniffing the air. "Smells like Italian."

"How's leftover pizza sound?" Josh offered. "Homemade."

"I'm starving. Skye always puts on a great spread. I wouldn't say no to a beer either. It's been a rough day."

Once Harry settled into his seat at the dining room table, several awkward moments hung in the air until Skye said, "Leo thinks we shouldn't trust you. Josh isn't so sure about it either."

Harry frowned into his slice of cheese and pepperoni. "I'm not here to judge anyone. I want resolution. I'm sick of these cases going unsolved." Harry looked first at Josh, then at Leo. "That's the same thing we all want, the reason we're pulling an all-nighter."

From there, everything began to click into place. The men began to trade good-natured barbs. The more they talked, the more they found they shared common ground. Despite their age difference, Leo and Harry discovered they had a lot in common. They both rooted for the Mariners in the spring, the Seahawks in the fall, and both believed with every fiber it would be a damned shame if the Sonics ever won another game in Oklahoma City.

"I'm glad you two don't still hold a grudge about the team's move," Josh mused.

"Nothing against the players, but it's the principle. Moving out of Seattle was just wrong," Leo asserted.

"Leo's right, the team's owner screwed the fans. Big time," Harry vowed.

"How about we table this discussion and do some real work?" Skye prompted as she brought in a tray with another round of bottled Redhooks.

"Spoilsport," Harry grumbled.

"She's such a taskmaster," Leo said in agreement.

"No fun at all when she's in Skye-mode," Josh added with a wink.

She ignored the teasing and decided to test Harry's intent so the guys would know he was a team player. Using Leo's surveillance video for the night Willa went missing would be perfect to make her point. "So even though Country Kitchen didn't have cameras installed, what about looking at other buildings in the area?"

"Nothing substantial has surfaced so far. We have a distorted view of a vehicle passing in front of the bank around twelve-thirty or so. But you can't make out much of the driver or the plate," Harry answered.

Skye met Josh's eyes as if proving a point. She cut a glance in Leo's direction, got a subtle nod of the head. Satisfied they were all on the same page, she picked up the list Leo had compiled, held it out to Harry. "Take a look at these names. Some of these match the ones I already know about, the ones that correlate to the map I keep. A lot of these are kids. But I'm thinking what we need now is to expand my list and include yours."

"Sure, make one master list."

"Exactly, and then narrow down the ones, if any, who fit our guy."

"You mean like his type? But we don't know his type yet," Harry questioned.

"We look for three key points. Timeframe. Location. Age. Anything at all that looks like a pattern," Josh clarified.

"This list is huge," Harry said, putting on his reading glasses. "Open that box, Skye. Let's go through what I've got, compare it to what Leo's come up with."

Inside the box were notes from the original missing person reports, info collected by investigators who hadn't spent a great deal of time digging and looking. That conclusion was evident by the lack of information in each individual file.

Skye handed off the photos. Most were females ranging in age from twelve to mid-thirties who'd gone missing under mysterious circumstances. They tried to eliminate runaways but it became clear that would be difficult because of the scarcity of details.

"Wait. Some of this pertains to murder victims," Skye realized. "There are crime scene photos at the bottom of the box."

"I brought those along because I thought we should take a look at homicides of women who fell into the time fit in 1993."

"Then we need to separate the data into two groups, one for the missing. The other for those we know were found but not yet identified."

"Why don't we enter the particulars of each case into the database? Easier to keep track that way," Josh suggested.

"That's a lot of keying," Leo pointed out.

"Not really," Skye returned, thumbing through the mess in the box. "Some of these files are incomplete. Your organizational skills leave something to be desired, Harry."

"How about we each take a stack of files, enter the names and notes and then merge the info into one database," Josh offered. "It'll go faster that way."

For almost two hours the three of them with the most computer skills—that left out Harry—sorted through reports and notes, keyed in information, and sorted it all into chronological sequence until they each had a workable spreadsheet.

For the missing, it included names, physical descriptions of those people last seen with them, witnesses, name of the person who had reported them missing: anything from the investigation, such as it had been, was added.

For the cases they knew were homicide, they added columns to include where the body had been found, its condition, and any details from the coroner's office. After finishing with that, they scanned victims' photos, and any pictures from the crime scenes that included additional pages relating to the autopsies.

Once that was done, they spent another hour making sure every crime scene photo matched to a name on the list. Next, they combed through each entry, line by line, checking for errors.

As Leo said, it took an incredible amount of keying, but when it came time for Leo to merge everything into a single database, they each felt confident in the work.

While they had been busy inputting names and dates, stats and descriptions, into the computer, Harry had scoured the remainder of the case files the old-fashioned way. One by one, he looked for any kidnappings of women that had gone awry, searching for any reports on anyone who might have escaped.

Hours later, Skye pushed back from the table, stretched her back and looked around at the group. "Who wants coffee?"

"I need the caffeine jolt if we intend to break down the spreadsheet in more depth," Leo admitted.

"I'm with Leo," Josh agreed.

"I need something to stay awake just so I can make the drive home…eventually," Harry said with a yawn.

"No need for that. It happens we have two guest rooms at the Ander Inn tonight. You're welcome to bunk here," Josh offered.

As Harry took out his cell phone to check in with his wife, Skye came back in from the kitchen. She glanced at the stack of reports Harry had already gone through. But one open file caught her eye. "Did you see this?"

"See what?"

"The Judy Howe case from 1999. Her assailant drove a Jeep Cherokee. The timeframe fits." She thumbed through the pages, read the first page, then the second, then the third. "Oh my God. We may have found a survivor, a girl who managed to escape his torture chamber and live to tell about it."

Chapter Twelve

Both Josh and Harry believed it best if Skye talked to Judy Howe without them being there. They made that decision based on what Harry had uncovered overnight about the woman and the aftermath of her ordeal. Judy hadn't done well.

So later that morning, Skye took a twenty-minute trip down to Kent. She found the woman's apartment building in a modest section of town known as East Hill. Ahead of the visit, Skye took out her cell phone and punched in the number Harry had given her as she'd been instructed to do. Good thing he had already set up the visit because Judy didn't like having people in her home.

Once she arrived at the little condo, it took several long minutes for Judy to open the door. Skye heard locks flipping on the other side.

When the woman did open the door, the first thing Skye noticed was how old she looked—far older than her thirty-five years indicated. Her face was pale, her dishwater blonde hair looked brittle and dry from lack of sunshine.

Fifteen years earlier Judy had been a twenty-year-old sophomore at Evergreen State with hopes of getting her degree in Marine Science. But a case of bad judgment one night had ended any hope of realizing her dreams.

Skye got comfortable on an old plaid sofa. Judy finally sat down beside her because there was no other place to sit in the tiny living room. "Judy, I know Harry told you why

I'm here. We have a series of murders and abductions and we think it's the same man who kidnapped you years ago."

Judy nodded. "I let you in because I've seen you on the news. I know your face, your story. I know you help victims. You find people who've been taken. I saw your press conference about Willa Dover."

Skye took Judy's hand. "Why don't you tell me what happened the night he abducted you? You were living in Olympia at the time."

Unsettled at having someone in her space, even someone whom she considered a local celebrity, Judy hesitated. She spent a good minute ringing her hands before she finally said in a low voice, "I was. Olympia is my hometown. I didn't go very far from where I was raised to attend college. My family didn't have much money."

"Evergreen State is a good school."

"I loved it. I was a good student, but even good students get tired of studying all the time. That was the way I felt that Saturday night. I wanted to let my hair down a little. I'd been invited to a party about a mile from my apartment. I thought what the heck? I'll go have some fun with friends, have a few drinks, get back around midnight, get a good night's sleep before spending all day Sunday finishing up my term paper for my hydrographic science class."

"Sounds like very technical stuff."

Judy's brown eyes grew moist at the memory of what she'd lost. "Oh, it was. I loved it. At one time I pictured myself a marine biologist traveling all over the world collecting and mining data from the ocean. Can you believe that?"

"Absolutely."

Judy glanced around her shabby little rental, threw up her hands. "Look at me now. I'm afraid to go out my front door, afraid to look my own friends in the eyes. I have difficulty interacting with my own family. My sister does my grocery shopping for me because I'm petrified I'll go out and see him. I spend my days and nights afraid he'll come back one day for me and finish the job. I sleep with the lights on. At one time, I wanted to move, to get out of the state, but in the end I didn't even have the courage to do that."

Skye couldn't help comparing how her life might've paralleled Judy's if she'd let terror take hold. If she'd been paralyzed with fear that day, she never would have gotten out of Whitfield's apartment, at least not under her own power.

"But he didn't come back for you, Judy. You're still here, strong as you were the night you got away. Did you get counseling after the attack?"

Judy nodded. "Every day for two years. Therapy didn't matter."

Skye took her hand. "It probably mattered more than you realize. We're both survivors. I hate to ask this but I need to know. How about going through your story one more time? Tell me what happened that night."

Judy let out a huge sigh that reverberated off her tiny four walls. "I'd met a few friends at the party. But I didn't know most of them. Around midnight someone brought out cocaine. I decided this is crazy, not my kind of crowd at all, so I slipped out the back door. I hadn't driven so I set out on foot. I was a little tipsy because I'd had five margaritas in those little plastic cups. I wasn't used to drinking that much. It's about forty degrees out and cold. All I had on was a sweater and jeans. Anyway, I got four blocks down the street when this guy pulls up driving a Jeep Cherokee."

"By any chance do you remember the color?"

Judy twisted up her mouth. "Hmm, I think it was red."

"What did he look like?"

"He looked normal, you know? Attractive, well-groomed with brown hair, pretty green eyes. He looked like a thousand other guys I'd seen hanging around my neighborhood since moving there. From behind the wheel, he told me I looked cold and wanted to know if I needed a ride. At the time I thought that was sweet. I told him I lived nearby."

"But it was freezing out and you got in the car because he looked like a safe bet."

Judy let out another loud sigh. "Exactly. And when he rolled the glass down on the window, I could feel the warmth inside from the heater. I remember that. I decided it was just a few blocks away. What could it hurt? So I ran around the side of the car and hopped in. Everything was fine for the first couple of minutes. But then he reached over to touch me and I backed away. *That* got him mad. He bashed the side of my head into the passenger window. As soon as my head hit the glass, it seemed like he floored the accelerator. I don't remember exactly. I was dazed. But at some point, he gunned it out of there and headed to the highway. We drove for a short time, maybe three miles or so till we got away from town."

"Do you remember where? Was it near the army base?"

Judy nodded. "I remember the general area even though it was dark. I was able to catch a glimpse of the sign for the base out of the corner of my eye. You know the one that hangs over the road. But he drove past the entrance, past that sign and turned onto a side road, off the freeway where it was even darker. There were no streetlights. It wasn't long after that he pulled to a stop on a bumpy stretch of road out in the middle of nowhere. My head was still pounding so much I thought I might pass out. In fact, I remember hoping I would. But then…he dragged me out of the car and into something that looked like an old shed. It only had three walls."

"How did you get away from him, Judy?"

"After he…after he… He hit me several times. And while he was raping me…he had his hands around my throat. He said he'd been watching me, liked what he'd seen and that he had to have me. But he kept hitting me. I was sure he was going to kill me right then. I think he would have but…after he finished the second time, his pager went off. Those were the days when most people had one. Anyway, I remember he looked down at his pager and mumbled a curse word. He said something about having to go back to work. After that, he seemed distracted, not the same man. And when he reached to put on his pants, he turned his back to me. I got up and stumbled out of the opening. Remember the place only had three walls.

"As soon as I felt the dirt under my feet, I took off running. I'd been a runner in high school, so I was pretty fast. I didn't know where I was going but I couldn't stop. I ran to get away from him thinking any minute he'd catch me. I was screaming for someone, anyone, to help me. I was really loud."

Skye grinned at her. "I bet you were. You didn't have your clothes on either, did you?"

"No, or my shoes. And it was freezing cold. I ran and ran until I fell into a ditch. I stayed there for a long time, didn't make a sound. I stayed like that until I guess he gave up looking for me. I finally heard the car start up and leave the area."

"Who found you?"

"As soon as it got light enough for me to see where I was going, I started walking toward what I thought was road noise, traffic. When I reached a paved road, a trucker saw me and stopped. He's the one who called the police."

"Wait a minute. Back up. Are you saying this guy didn't take you very far from where he first talked you into getting in the car that night?"

"That's right. It wasn't far at all from my apartment."

"And he didn't take you that far away to where he stopped the car to assault you in the shed?

"I'd say no more than five miles away total."

"Okay. Do you think you could find it again?"

"The cops asked me that at the time. They went where I showed them. But I must've been confused. They couldn't find a shed of any kind."

Skye frowned. "What do you mean?"

"I mean the cops checked out the area and the shed wasn't there."

Skye rubbed her forehead and got up to pace in front of the couch. How was that even possible? "Is it possible he could've moved the shed? If we went back to the general area now, do you think you could point me in the right direction?"

Judy shook her head. "I won't go back there. Not ever."

"How about drawing me a map from your apartment at the time to where you *thought* the shed was located? Do you think you could do that?"

"Sure, I'll try."

Judy took out a pencil and legal pad from an end table drawer. She went over to her little kitchen table and sat down. An hour later, Skye had a decent idea of where Judy had been during her ordeal. While the location wasn't on the base, it was in the general vicinity.

"You did great, Judy. Thank you. I want you to work with a sketch artist, help us get a composite of what this guy looks like. You okay with doing that?"

Her shoulders slumped. "I guess. Could you arrange for the artist to be a woman? And could she come to my house?"

"Not a problem." Skye put a hand on her shoulder, left it there. She could feel Judy tremble.

"I came so close to dying that night. Maybe I was meant to die. I don't know. Maybe I wasn't supposed to survive because I've had so much trouble coping ever since."

"I don't believe that. The same thing could've happened to me. I wasn't facing death but a life sentence in the sex trade. I got away. You got away. There's a reason we did."

"Is…is there any way I could help you at your Foundation? From home? From right here? I'd be willing to do just about anything. I could stuff envelopes from right here."

Skye chewed her bottom lip and made a decision. "I think that could be arranged. But how about this? At some point, if you ever want to get out of these four walls I could offer you a full-time job as my receptionist where you'd answer the phone and take messages."

"Really? But…" Judy looked around her apartment. With sad eyes, she added, "But I can't leave this place."

Skye took her hand. "I'll find this guy, Judy. And when I do, you won't have to be afraid anymore to leave. Promise me you'll continue with your therapy. Give it some thought, okay? Any time you're ready to take the job, you call me. If you say yes, I'll have to get you an honest to goodness desk because right now, all I have is a folding table." Skye could see Judy wanted to take the offer. But old habits, especially those reaped in fear, didn't go away overnight.

Skye couldn't think of a better candidate for the job than someone who had been through hell and escaped from it. "You let me know whenever you're ready to take that first step. The job isn't going anywhere. It's yours whenever you want it."

Chapter Thirteen

The same day Skye found out the owner of the farmhouse had accepted their bid, the mailman dropped off the third package from their psycho to the Artemis Foundation—an innocuous-looking carton decorated with little red hearts drawn on the front and back.

A little late for Valentine's Day, Skye surmised as she used a letter opener to cut through the tape. This time he'd sent the upper and lower arm bones, presumably from the first victim. Another job for Bayliss or Dawson to figure out, Skye decided.

She lifted the note on top with the same tongs she'd used before. Sad that she'd kept the utensil here at work rather than using it for its intended purpose in her kitchen at home. Holding the note out, she read the message, brief but to the point.

> *You're in over your head. Admit*
> *it.*

Maybe she was, Skye thought as she reached for the phone. But damn if she wouldn't give it her best shot to find this bastard. She dialed Harry's number first, then Josh's, then had to look up the contact information for Dawson Hennings.

Harry decided the best course of action this time was for Skye to bring the box directly to the medical examiner's office.

There, Skye watched as a technician dusted the box and its contents for fingerprints. They took Skye's so they could eliminate them from the carton.

Disgusted with frustration, she pointed out, "You do realize that the mailman's are probably all over the outer shell and the dozen or so other people who handled it at the post office, don't you?"

"Sure I do. But when you've got nothing, you have to reach for anything. Process of elimination," Harry barked.

Josh looked around the room at the faces of the same people who'd started this quest. "No fingerprints leave us with exactly what we had before. Nothing."

The grumbling had Dawson offering up a tidbit. "It isn't all bad news. I can tell you this much. I was able to extract DNA from the first set of bones to get a profile. It's female. I entered it into the FBI's National Crime Information Center and CODIS, category, unidentified human remains. I also got fingerprints off the mummified hand which I entered into IAFIS. We might get a hit there if the victim was ever picked up for anything. But to get a match to the profile in NCIC or CODIS…"

"A family member would have had to enter theirs."

"You already knew that," said Dawson with a wry smile. "I urge patience because the labs are backed up and sometimes it can take as long as four to eight months for results."

Josh looked around the lab at the glum faces. "Let's hope whoever this is has family out there somewhere who cared enough to submit a swab."

Skye spoke up. "It isn't that, Josh, sometimes the family members just don't know to do it. Unless they're a fan of *CSI* or *Criminal Minds*, they don't know they can obtain a kit free of charge specifically for that purpose."

"Maybe we could push that to the forefront through the Foundation," Josh suggested before turning to Dawson. "Any idea how old she was? The victim from the first set of bones?"

"Young. My guess is between seventeen and twenty," Dawson answered. "As for DNA from the hand, I'm still working on getting a strong enough sample to profile."

"Protocol has changed quite a bit in recent years on how we handle missing cases versus human remains," Harry revealed. "Now when a person goes missing we approach the family to ask for a DNA sample. In the Maggie Bennett case for instance, it's routine if she had remained missing for longer than thirty days. The lead detective would have simply gone to her loved ones at some point and requested a cheek swab or some personal item he could use down the road for DNA comparison, like a hairbrush. The sample is sent to the lab, analyzed and then uploaded to the database where it's kept there."

Bayliss assessed the troops. In his no-nonsense way, he added, "Drummond twisted my arm so that my office would revisit a few cold cases for him, to help out. You might want to listen up to what we've found. Back in 2000 they brought in a female, dismembered and unidentified. At the time the body was in an advanced stage of decomposition. But there were marks on the upper vertebrae indicating that whoever killed her tried to remove the skull."

"He tried to cut off her head?" Skye asked in astonishment.

"Exactly. There were saw marks. But he was unsuccessful."

"You have photos?"

"Of course."

Skye watched as Bayliss scooted around evidence boxes and took out several file folders until he handed one off to her.

Drawing in a solemn breath at the sight of the gruesome autopsy images, Skye shuffled through the pictures in rapid order. But then stopped, realizing she needed to suck it up. What was the point of asking to see them if she had no intentions of really looking at the details? This victim deserved better. She reshuffled the stack, scanned each one at a time in slower study.

"She obviously died a horrendous death, got dumped in a field until a hiker stumbled upon her body," Bayliss said in a somber tone.

"So we don't know who she was or what she did for a living," Josh said, taking the photos Skye had given him. "How old do you think this one was?"

"I'd say by the condition of her skin, the condition of her bones and teeth at the time of autopsy, a best guess, early thirties," Bayliss answered.

"However long she lived, it wasn't long enough, that's for sure," Skye grumbled. She stared at Bayliss, met intense eyes and asked, "By mentioning this one, you think we should include her on the list." It wasn't a question.

"That's up to you. I'm giving you the facts as to what the autopsy told me. Then there's this one." Again, Bayliss hunted through the files until he found the one he wanted. "The victim had bruises from her face to her shinbone like she'd been repeatedly whacked with a blunt instrument. What instrument exactly is indeterminate, but I did take impressions if we ever have anything to compare them to."

Skye took the pictures again after they'd made the trip around the room. She noticed the grotesque condition of the body almost at once. These photos were even worse than the other victim's had been. The images made her a little sick at her stomach. As the taco she'd eaten for lunch wanted to come back up, she tamped it down, considered another point. "But she wasn't dismembered."

"True. But here's the thing. The killer tried. See the back-and-forth knife marks at the throat, then again on the torso. They indicate a primitive sawing motion. Could be he was interrupted or changed his mind for some reason."

"Or, it was an impromptu killing where he wasn't at his usual location. He tried using whatever he had handy and it didn't work out as well and he gave up. Two for two in that regard."

Bayliss and Dawson both turned to stare at the woman in surprise. It was Dawson who told her, "You're quite good at this. It's as if you have some kind of second sense. It's your Nez Perce heritage, I think." He turned to Josh. "Yours is more...feral...and new to you while Skye's ability is...innate."

Josh eyed Dawson. For several long seconds the two men scowled at one another until Josh figured out why. It seemed the anthropologist had a little crush on Skye. Like any good pack leader worth his salt, Josh determined he needed to keep an eye on the doctor. He wasn't sure how he felt about Dawson so obviously enamored with his wife.

Sensing the tension between the two, Skye cleared her throat. "My father's people. The second sense, it comes from my father's people."

Dawson's gaze fell away from Josh to Skye. "Is it true what the Native American legends say about part of getting through life means staying true to your spirit guide? How does that work exactly?"

Skye tilted her head, assessed the man's demeanor. Noting the anthropologist seemed to be veering off the subject at hand for a reason, she decided to humor him. "Staying on your path, a path thought to be destined before birth, is customary in many types of folklore and culture, predominant in Native Americans."

Dawson nodded. "I believe you're meant to do this type of work. You both are," he finally admitted. "I've talked to a few people in law enforcement about you...both of you," the man corrected, glancing over at Harry. "Drummond is one who sings your praises the most." Now, Dawson acted embarrassed when he sent Skye a smile. "That Foundation you started is something to be proud of. What you do for victims is amazing. If you ever need a hand don't hesitate to ask. I'm happy to help out any way I can."

Bayliss nodded and threw in, "My office is committed to working round the clock on this, too. Anything you need expedited, you have only to let us know."

When they were done with the meeting and walking back to the car, Skye leaned into Josh. "I was worried about you back there. For a moment, I thought you and Dawson were…ready to tangle."

"He's a strange man."

"Not as strange as some. Why are there so many mean sick bastards out there walking among us? Who does this kind of nasty business and keeps their jobs, their families, their souls intact?"

"People screwed up early and often," Josh returned. "But we're going to stop this messed up son of a bitch. He'll make a mistake and when he does, we'll be ready."

※ ※ ※ ※

That night, before they left to walk the streets, Travis showed up at their door, unannounced.

"What are you doing here?" Skye asked surprised to see him holding a box clutched to his chest.

"This nut job has me worried about you," he looked over at Josh. "About both of you. I brought you what our people believe is protection of the strongest kind."

"What, you have a loaded .45 in that box?" Josh quipped.

"Maybe something more powerful than that," Travis told him. He took out a soft leather bag decorated with ornate beadwork. "It holds something from Daniel, the one you considered your father for so long a time, and something from me. Daniel's spirit guide was a hawk named Deata. Mine is a crow named Eotyuu."

"Dee-ah-tay and Ee-ot-tu," Skye repeated. "Yes, I know. What are you up to, Travis?"

"Feathers from both are thought to hold great power. Native custom dictates that long after the mortal body dies, the spirit still inhabits the earth taking whatever form they

143

used as a guide. Deata will watch over you. I can't be with you every single second of the day. No one can. So my spirit guide will help you along the way until you're able to defeat this man and bring him down."

"You're assigning your crow, Eotyuu, to me for the duration? But what about you?"

"I am. The shamans have told many stories, sung many songs about such things where guides are transferred to others to protect their loved ones in battles."

"I don't know what to say. Thank you, my father."

Travis smiled. "That's the first time you've called me that. I don't want to sound greedy but I'd settle for dad at some point."

Skye wrapped her arms around him. "Okay, *Dad*. You humble me." She held the soft leather pouch in her hand as if weighing its contents. "This is fairly heavy for just having feathers inside."

Travis grinned again. "It's a little more than that, precious stones, locks of hair from the people who love you, old tribal arrowheads, herbs used for medicine. The usual stuff, think of it as your shield."

It was Skye's turn to grin. She turned to Josh. "Did you know about this?"

Josh gave his wife a sheepish look. "Hey, these days I don't give up my hair easily without a fight or a good cause. Travis and I thought it was a good idea. Why don't you do the honors, Travis?"

Skye moved her hair aside so her father could place the thin, leather strap around her neck. The pouch was small, no more than two inches across by three inches in length, but as soon as the bundling hung in place, she could feel its power. It already made her feel capable and confident.

Her father began to chant in brief ceremony until finally taking her by both shoulders. "It isn't uncommon for the warrior to feel the power kick in. In times of great stress or danger, accept it, wield it. To take this man down you'll need strong medicine to combat him. Even though he's become reckless of late, the malicious aura that surrounds him is very strong. There is no greater strength than knowing here," Travis put his hand over his heart. "That those who love you will not let you down and will be there for you when you need it. Never fear. Together, through this, Daniel and I will always be with you in spirit wherever you find yourself."

Chapter Fourteen

Later, she and Josh faced a steady downpour as they headed out the front door of the building. But before they took two steps away from the entrance, something caught Skye's eye. Taped to the glass was an envelope with her name written in block letters. The paper had gotten wet, which made the ink run.

Standing under the covered portico as rain pounded the canopy above them, they traded looks until Skye snatched the note off.

"What the hell do you suppose this is?"

"Maybe you should wait to—" Josh advised too late as he watched her rip open the seal on the letter. He chuckled. "Or not. What does it say?"

She bounced on her toes while skimming the words. "Holy shit, there's another body in a Dumpster at Brawley and Edgewater near the harbor."

"That's a construction site close to the viaduct project. I hope this isn't about Willa."

"Me too. I'll call Harry, get him to meet us there."

They took the Subaru and drove the ten blocks well above the speed limit. Pulling into a dark alleyway, Skye turned the headlights to high beam and let the luminous streaks guide them along.

"The note said it was eight doors down on the right."

"Very specific instructions if you ask me."

But they counted down anyway till the Dumpster in question came into view. They found a light bluish steel box with ugly rusted places around the bottom. The steady rain had made the blood trail watery. But there were still faint traces of red stuff running down the front and sides.

"This is no joke," Skye stated. It looked as if the killer had had a good deal of trouble hefting the body to get it inside and left smears on the metal. The rain shower had streaked the rest.

"Are we ready for this?" She asked as they both opened the doors at the same time. Skye skirted the hood to get closer. "This is sloppy work, Josh. I'm thinking this isn't our guy."

"Maybe he was in a hurry."

Skye studied the entrance to the alley they'd driven down and then the other direction that dumped into Western at the end of the block. She took in the harbor to the left, noted the twinkling lights of the empty docks. Turning her attention to the row of abandoned manufacturing buildings to the right, she said, "Why? There's no one within four streets of right here. And we wouldn't even be standing at this spot unless he'd directed us here. Yet, it's messy and rushed."

"Makes you wonder how this guy kept from getting caught for so long."

That's what troubled her and she couldn't let it go. "Why would he lead us here when it's obviously such a fresh kill?"

"Point taken. Should we look inside or wait for Harry?"

"Unless you want me to lose my supper, I think I'll elect for you to dive in and explore what's in there." At the sound of a car, she looked up. She recognized Harry's gray Volvo. "Keep that in mind. We're about to see what a pro thinks about this whole thing."

Harry surveyed the scene dressed in a rain-slicked jacket, a pair of jeans drenched at the cuffs, and an equally soggy T-shirt. He wore comfy tennis shoes without socks on his feet. In the end it was decided the detective should do the Dumpster diving.

Standing inside the relatively empty container, Harry gave them the play-by-play. "We've got a young female still wearing her bra and panties. Light brown hair tells me it's not Willa. This one had pretty brown eyes that were left open after someone bashed her head in. See this gash here? Fractured her skull at the base."

"That's not our guy's MO," Skye said.

Josh peered in from above. "And the note was different than the others printed not typed. I'd say this one looks no older than twenty-five. Not a lot of blood at the scene. I don't think she was killed here."

"Somewhere else. Yeah," Harry agreed. "Good observation."

"Let me ask you this. Why is she still wearing her underwear? If our guy tortures before he kills, then why would she have on anything at all? The others were dumped naked."

Harry nodded. "This one wasn't tortured. Either he didn't have time or… You guys are getting better at this. Bayliss is on his way." When a patrol unit pulled up, he added, "And this uniform is here to secure the scene."

"Is that a polite way of telling us we're done here?" Skye prompted.

Harry gave her a sly look, his way of telling her, *you two lead, I'll follow and no one needs to know about it*. Instead of that, the detective merely asked, "What do your instincts tell you on this one?"

"You've changed, Harry," Skye said in response, stealing a glance at Josh. "I believe our mutual friend here is encouraging us to use our creative side for the most impact."

Josh grinned. "We're very good at following a trail, no argument there. And this is the freshest trail we've seen in quite some time."

"Exactly. Now get out of my crime scene," Harry directed, loud enough for the uniform to turn his head.

"Remember to text me with…whatever it is…you find to…report."

The two had plenty to say once they crawled back inside the car and out of the drizzle.

"What do you make of it?" Josh wanted to know.

"Harry's change of heart or the careless way this killer disposed of the body?"

"The killer."

"I don't know yet but let's leave the car here. I do my best sorting things out while I'm on foot. Even in the rain, walking helps me think."

Just as Skye suspected, with Kiya's assistance, they picked up the killer's trail near the entrance to the alley at Brawley and Western. While the activity back at the Dumpster buzzed with more cops and crime scene techs, the wolf had them heading in the opposite direction. They crossed the train tracks, kept to the water's edge, along the wooded greenbelt lining the harbor.

The pier came into view. A foghorn sounded somewhere over the Sound. When they reached the bike path, Josh told her, "It's for damned sure he didn't ride his bike all this way to dump the body."

"No, but you can bet he lives in the area. Not sure it's our guy though."

"The victim was the right age."

"There's that, but the bra and panties are the bonus round. I still don't think the serial we're looking for would take the time to put underwear back on. Think about it. Our guy didn't dress Maggie Bennett or Vanessa Farrington. So why would he do it now, tonight?"

"He had to be rushed, which again isn't like our guy. Not to change the subject but you know Dawson Hennings has a major crush on you, don't you?" Josh tossed out.

"I know. You handled that fact pretty well today. Since he's only the second man to feel that way about me, it's kind of sweet in an ordinary sort of way. The idea that this is a very ordinary thing that happens to people—I guess I'm flattered."

"Yeah? Well, I'm not. I guess I'm jealous."

She grinned before elbowing him in the ribs. "You have no reason to be. By the way, when I was surfing the Internet this morning, I picked up on a disturbing story, a trend. It's about what's known as 'rehoming' disruptive children who have been adopted out but are no longer wanted. The parents dump these kids with people who haven't even been vetted. They pass them around to anyone who's willing to take them, a horrific practice that has to open up all kinds of opportunities for abuse. I'm wondering if the Foundation needs to take a closer look at this practice in the Seattle area."

He picked up her hand, kissed the palm. "And that's one of the reasons I love you. You're always thinking how to help, how to fix a problem, especially when it concerns kids, those most vulnerable who usually can't help themselves."

"Come on, you make me sound…"

"Beautiful?"

"I was gonna say corny."

"You're a lot of things but never that."

They rounded a bend in the path and spotted the apartment complex, a high-rise overlooking the waterway. Skye noted the wolf turn her regal head to look upward. "Kiya's better than a police tracking dog at this job. That's Alpine Court. Twenty-five stories. Five-hundred units. Wanna take bets which floor the bastard lives on?"

Josh whistled as he lifted his head skyward to check out the tower. Some units had windows blazing with light. Others had already gone dark for the night. "That's a lot of condos. How do we get in? This late hour not too many people will be coming and going."

"What's the first thing you do after you've just murdered someone?"

He sent her a wide grin. "Get rid of the body. But we can fast-forward past that step. I see where you're going with this. When you get back from dumping the body, you're compelled to clean up the crime scene."

"Exactly. There's no need to lurk in the lobby. We head around back, wait for him to take out the trash or something or stake out the underground parking lot where he's sure to use his car to dump stuff somewhere else."

"You don't think he'd be that stupid, do you?"

"He killed someone in this very building and then left a note for us to find the body. I'd say he's beyond stupid."

"Okay, so he's dumber than a box of rocks. I'm not sure which I hate more, the fact that he's trying to use us, or that we're getting used by such a dumbass."

"I say we go around back to where the waste receptacles are kept. We stake them out. He's bound to toss stuff if he hasn't already."

They headed around the corner of the building just as someone threw back the lid on a tan, nondescript-looking Dumpster. The cover flew back and clanged into the wall with a thud. A man stood in front of it, tossing out a section of blood-soaked carpeting.

"Whatcha got there?" Josh asked from three feet away. In the dim light, he saw the man's face go white at getting caught. There was a brief moment when Josh thought the guy might take off in a run. But the culprit turned, bold as brass, to stare into his eyes.

Josh caught the hint of madness mingled with a good dose of desperation.

"Who the hell are you? Get out of here. This is private property and none of your damn business."

"Murder's everyone's business," Josh said evenly, eyeing the murderer, then the garbage bin. He got a whiff of blood first, right before he smelled bleach. The mixture, a sickening combo indicating the killer had tried to use the strongest chemical on hand to get the stain out of the carpet. When that hadn't done the job, the guy had simply removed a sizeable chunk of rug from the floor.

As Josh took in the scene he wondered. Could this be the serial killer who had escaped capture for two decades and wanted to get caught now?

"I don't know what you're talking about," the man insisted.

Josh stared at the guy's bloody shirt and the dark stains on his jeans. "Sure you do. You dumped the woman, left her there beaten and battered, left her with no ID in that alleyway."

"Then you decided to write a note sending us to Brawley and Edgewater to find the body. Which we did," Skye added.

The man's eyes darted back and forth between the two of them. Nervous, from the waistband of his dirty jeans, he pulled a revolver, waved it first at Skye then aimed it at Josh. "You get back now. Just stay back both of you. I told you this doesn't concern nosy neighbors."

Josh assessed the man, decided an unpredictable cornered rat could bite if the teeth were sharp enough. This guy's teeth were primed. It wasn't in their favor to try reasoning with him. Rattling him seemed the best way to go.

"Who was she?" Josh demanded. "Your wife? A girlfriend?"

Skye exchanged furtive glances with Josh. An unspoken dynamic ignited a plan of action. All it took was the nod of heads for Skye to take a step to the side. She faked to the left, distracting the killer long enough for his head to turn at the movement. Josh took the opening and barreled into him with a fist, knocking the man backward, dislodging the weapon. The gun skidded on the wet pavement.

Skye went over, picked it up while Josh kept the guy in a firm chokehold.

"I'm texting Harry. It's up to him to find out who this jerk is with a search warrant in hand." She took out her phone, keyed in: *Address is 8515 Alpine Court. We're in the back of the complex. Get here soon before Josh breaks him into little pieces and there's nothing left to lock up.*

Chapter Fifteen

Twenty-four-hours later Harry stopped by the Foundation. "I don't know how you two do it but you were spot on. I used the carpeting you found in the Dumpster to get a warrant for the owner of that unit."

"No doubt that took some fancy talking."

Harry grinned. "I told them the beat cop followed a blood trail, didn't bring you guys into it at all."

"Whatever it takes. Who is this guy?"

"His name's Benjamin Zaharia. With the warrant we went through the security tapes at the building for the night of the murder. It shows he wrapped the body up in a comforter, carried it out using the service elevator and put it in the trunk of his BMW."

"Was she his wife? Girlfriend?"

"Diana Weatherly, Zaharia's girlfriend for about two years. I had forensics go over the entire apartment from floor to ceiling. We found blood drops on the remaining carpet he didn't remove. We also found sizeable spatter in the bathroom that he hadn't had time to clean up. That was the murder scene. He lost his temper one time too often, got mad, bashed Diana's head in while she was getting ready for bed."

"He hit her from behind?" Josh asked."

Harry nodded. "Standing at the sink. He hit her with one of his golf clubs."

"Geez, why?"

"Because Diana defied him one time too often. His words, not mine. He's sitting in jail where he'll be staying because the judge denied him bail."

"Zaharia doesn't have anything to do with our serial, does he?" Skye said, wanting to make certain of what her gut already knew.

"You got it. This is a case of domestic violence gone bad in every way possible. Turns out, the asshole has a history of abuse a mile long. The cops on the beat were well aware of the girlfriend's list of complaints against Zaharia over the years. Why she didn't just pack up and get out of there—?"

"No one understands the syndrome."

"I guess not. Anyway, I spent six hours interviewing Zaharia where he confessed to killing Diana. When I grilled him I pushed quite a bit about the other murders. He told me how he got the idea to blame Diana's death on the serial killer in the news. He thought the plan was brilliant and decided he could fake us all out by sending the note to Skye Cree. He used the Internet to look you guys up, found your address, and the rest is…" Harry let his voice trail off, shrugged. "The bastard decided if you guys found the body the discovery would play into one more victim. We'd link Diana to the serial and Zaharia would get to play the grieving boyfriend and go on with his life. I guess that was his undoing."

"No, his undoing was not breaking up with his girlfriend like normal people do but grabbing that golf club to make his point."

Less than a week later the authorities found Willa Dover's body thanks to an anonymous tip. Her remains rested on a gentle slope in Discovery Park near the south meadow bordered by straw-colored nut grass and golden buttercups. The wildlife had gotten to the body. It was so decomposed the coroner's office couldn't immediately tell how she'd died. Putting a name to the deceased had to be done through dental records.

Because the killer had picked Skye as his contact initially, Harry had invited both her and Josh to sit in on a newly formed task force. Inside a conference room on the third floor of the Cherry Street police station, they listened to various reps from law enforcement—sheriff's deputies from King, Pierce, Snohomish, and Whatcom counties—go through case files and procedures.

"The vehicle description is a huge break. How did we obtain that?"

Harry shot Josh a look that clearly said, "Do not bring up any paranormal crap." The detective answered the question with his usual unruffled demeanor. "A witness reported Andrea Harkness jumped into a Jeep. And we have the surveillance video from the bank. It might be grainy but it's an obvious side view of an older model Cherokee, which we think means they're connected."

"You think he'd actually keep the same car for two decades?"

"Some people use older models if they intend to put a lot of miles on a car, using it like their own workhorse. My uncle has a Toyota 4Runner he's had since 1985."

The chatter continued like that as members of law enforcement debated the plausibility of such a thing until Harry directed the focus back on Willa Dover. "No doubt Willa's killer intended for the body to be found much sooner."

For the first time since she'd sat down, Skye waded into the discussion. "But it rained buckets for the past seven days which made for less foot traffic on the nearby hiking trail fifteen yards from where she was found."

"When no one came along, he took the initiative," Josh added. "He made the anonymous call so everyone would know he's in charge."

"I'm sure Skye will get another gruesome package with a taunting message pointing out how sloppy we all are," Harry advised.

"I read your initial report from the handout you gave us. You think there's a connection to Joint Base Lewis-McChord. Do you think it's significant that the killer dumped the Dover woman near historic Fort Lawton housing?"

"Good question. But the area hasn't been used for military in years. I think he was simply looking for the maximum effect."

"Or it might be symbolic," Josh tossed out.

Skye bobbed her head in agreement. "What I'd like to know is how he got her there." She stood up, went to the map Harry had attached to an easel. "Not only has it been muddy for the past week, but according to the crime scene techs, there were no obvious tire tracks or footprints left around anywhere."

"The rain washed everything of value away."

"I understand that. But the trail was too narrow there for a vehicle anyway. He had to carry her a good fifty yards before picking that spot."

"Unless he brought her there by boat," Josh assessed, letting that settle into their heads before he added, "The body was closer to the shore than to the road on the other side of the park near the Sound. Between the sewage treatment plant, hidden by the marsh and the lighthouse on the westernmost point, you're dealing with more than five hundred acres of land."

Skye nodded again. "That actually makes sense. He chose that spot for a reason. He wanted her on display where he could get the biggest charge out of someone finding her."

Because the others in the group thought so too, the assembly took it through various scenarios.

"Maybe he watched from a vantage point."

"There's a thought. Check out all the places where he could have staked out the area from higher ground."

"He knew the area…well."

"Well enough to have no fear of getting caught."

"What about the time of death? Does Bayliss have any idea how long Willa was out in the elements?"

Harry shook his head. "Not yet. We're hoping he can narrow it down."

After the meeting ended, a few detectives approached Skye and Josh in the hallway. A group from law enforcement that hadn't exactly welcomed them with open arms in the first place encircled them. It made them understandably leery of any attempt at camaraderie or small talk.

"I wasn't sure about letting civilians near the task force, let alone have access to crime scene photos," one of them admitted. "But I have to say I'm impressed. Coming up with that boat theory showed you could be an asset to the team."

The other deputy turned to Skye. "And you've saved countless abduction victims. *And* you caught Frank DePalo, beat the holy crap out of the sadistic bastard, as I recall. Your input should also be invaluable to us."

A third stuck out his hand and added, "Good to work with you. At least you two aren't claiming you're psychics. We tried that shit some years back with Ridgway, found out real quick they couldn't see their own asses through a hole in a doughnut."

"Yeah, name me one crime that's ever been solved by a psychic?" the fourth man demanded. "Now if those shysters could ever come up with the numbers for me to win the Mega Millions jackpot, then I might become a believer."

There were laughs all around as the cops continued to make fun of using psychics or mediums.

"We take any tips the public offers. That doesn't change no matter where the tip comes from. That includes anything called in by a bunch of kooks," one of them added. "We treat every lead the same way. We process the information and run it down until we hit a dead end."

"Old-fashioned police work is what solves crimes."

While Skye and Josh didn't disagree with that, they had no intentions of ignoring a second sense. If a supernatural element could be utilized to get scum off the street, they'd keep with what they did best.

As they headed back to the car, Skye turned to Josh. "Was that conjecture about the boat, or something else?"

"When you called me that they'd found her body, I went out to the park. I watched the cops and the crime scene techs mill around acting as if they didn't care. Sure they were doing their jobs, but I knew Willa, had seen her lift trays at the restaurant, carry food to my table. The woman took my order not four days before she disappeared."

"You were upset. It's understandable."

"Seeing them all stand around or wander about, seemingly without a care, got to me. That was my first reaction. My second was this. How the hell did he get Willa to that spot? The closest road is back the other way near the parking lot, a good half mile. If he wanted her found quick, then why didn't he simply dump her there near the main entrance? The only thing that made sense was he motored there with her in the boat."

Skye dipped her head in agreement, able to see it play out in her head. "So he comes in from the west. We had a storm churning then. The water had to be choppy as hell. In the pouring rain, he trudged up that hillside carrying Willa's body."

"Or dragged it out of the boat and up to that ridge. Any drag marks, footprints, or indications of either, were lost to the lousy weather conditions."

"Did you get anything studying the pictures of the crime scene?"

"Other than outrage, disgust and the fact I'm fed up with this guy? Sure."

"You held something back." It wasn't a question.

"Yeah. I think he had help getting Willa's body into the park."

That bombshell evaporated any hope of shifting from murder to downtime before they had to go back out again. Relaxation took a backseat. For four hours they batted around the two-killer angle till they reached the same conclusion. If the guy did have someone willing to help him dispose of a body, it had to be someone he trusted, someone in his closest circle, someone he could depend on who knew his darkest secrets—someone he trusted with his own life.

Chapter Sixteen

It wasn't until that night that Harry stopped by the loft to share more detailed information face-to-face.

"Bayliss found a drug called rocuronium during Willa's autopsy. He says there is absolutely no need for anyone to have rocuronium show up, let alone the amount that was there. The drug is used primarily for general anesthesia, used to induce muscle relaxation for endotracheal intubation, or mechanical ventilation. It paralyzes the lungs. You suffocate to death. You're able to see what's going on around you, but can't move or breathe on your own."

"Poor Willa."

"Yeah. She didn't go easy. There were marks around her wrists and ankles, rope burns around her throat indicating she'd been bound for some time and tortured. Willa went through a lot before she succumbed to a cut to her throat. Insect activity showed she'd been at that spot where we found her for about three days."

Harry turned to Josh, "Look, I need to give Skye a little bit of background info before continuing. You want to leave us alone for a few minutes?"

Skye brooded into her coffee mug, gave her longtime friend an anxious frown. "Whatever it is, Harry, I don't mind it if Josh stays."

Harry lifted a shoulder. "All right. You know that I've been going through cold cases to see if I could find any victims from around 1993 who might fit into the 'possible' category. I came across two cases in HITS. And one is a little bizarre. Try to hear me out first before you jump down my throat."

Puzzled, Skye said, "I feel like I should sit down or something."

Harry cast a bleak look at one, then the other, before letting out a heavy sigh. "Might not be a bad idea."

"Maybe we should both sit down," Josh proffered. "What exactly is HITS?"

"A database used by law enforcement that stores crime-related information. Various agencies put in characteristics of crimes so if anything similar pops up, we know about it statewide. It's been around since 1987, first used in Bundy's crimes and then utilized by the Green River Task Force."

Skye and Josh exchanged glances. "This sounds promising."

"The thing is I have a box of evidence from a cold case that goes back twenty years, a verified homicide. But I'll get to that in a minute. The other case is a bare-bones file folder on a young soldier's wife who went missing about the same time of the murder. Both have a connection to Fort Lewis, Washington, before it was known as Joint Base Lewis-McChord.

"When she was twenty years old, Trisha Danes went missing. Trisha was originally from Charlotte, North Carolina, a newlywed who had moved across the country to be with her husband, Milo. The night she disappeared, the two had had a fight. Milo locked her out of the apartment they shared on base and sent her packing with the clothes on her back. After that, she essentially vanished into the night and hasn't been seen since."

"Milo sounds like a prince of a guy. I'd bet the husband did something to her," Josh tossed out.

"You'd think. That was my initial gut reaction, too. But I called in a favor from the base and got hold of the old file yesterday. It seems two witnesses came forward at the time and told the CID investigating officer—"

"Military? Because it happened on the base?"

"That's right, they had jurisdiction. Anyway, the witnesses said they saw Trisha get into a car not far from the apartment building. That car was listed in the file as a Jeep Cherokee."

Skye's jaw dropped open as chill bumps ran along her arms. "Any chance Trisha's family has looked for her?"

"This morning I got off the phone with Trisha's stepmother, Brandy Sue Grainger. Brandy never liked Milo and always thought he had something to do with Trisha's disappearance. Brandy spent years doing what she could to help find her stepdaughter. She didn't have a lot of money but back then she pleaded with a friend to loan her enough cash to hire a private investigator. The private eye worked on it for about two months but gave up when he found nothing new on Trisha and decided the woman simply vanished into thin air leaving her family devastated."

"But a stepmother won't be much help with DNA," Josh declared.

"True. But even though Brandy and Trisha's father divorced years earlier, Brandy put me in touch with him. Local law enforcement in North Carolina has scheduled a trip to collect his DNA."

"You really are amazing, Harry," Skye proclaimed.

"I hope you still feel that way after I finish explaining about the homicide, the other case. The victim's name was Ellen Schreiber, a young, pretty army lieutenant who grew up in the Los Angeles area. "

"Okay. I suppose we have another victim," Skye determined. But the look on Harry's face told her it was much more than that. "What's so special about this particular victim?"

"I'm sorry to have to tell you this, Skye, but Ellen Schreiber had a connection to your father."

For a second time, Skye's jaw fell open in shock. "How so?"

"At the time of Ellen's murder, Daniel Cree's name appeared on the suspect list, both from CID and the jurisdiction where the body was eventually discovered. It took years, but when they started adding lanes along the I-90, specifically near State Road 519 and Fourth Avenue near downtown, they dug up a body. This was long before Safeco Field. The Kingdome was still home to all our major sports teams. I didn't get the Schreiber case, but it fell to Seattle PD to coordinate it with Army CID. Seattle PD took the lead but…"

"It remains unsolved," Skye finished.

"It does indeed. Along with the bizarre case I mentioned. According to what was in the evidence box, Ellen's makeshift grave still held her clothing, as well as the weapon, a fourteen-inch butcher knife with a rosewood handle."

"So she wasn't dismembered?"

"I didn't say that. The killer tried to slice off her hands at the wrists. Instead of cutting them entirely though, he left them dangling by a string of muscle tissue. Parts of the hands were still attached even though she'd likely been in that grave a couple of years."

"We might have DNA, Harry," Skye said, excitement dripping in her tone.

But Josh got the implication. "It doesn't seem Harry is as excited by that as we are, Skye. How did this Ellen Schreiber and Daniel Cree know each other?"

"Daniel worked at the base as a civilian contractor. Ellen was an officer. They worked in the same department. Witness statements back then said Ellen and Daniel used to see each other quite a bit—outside of work. They were essentially colleagues, Skye. There were rumors of an affair."

Skye bristled at the mental picture. "So?"

"When Ellen first went missing the investigator on the case was an MP by the name of Jason Berkenshaw. He's the one who interviewed your father. Berkenshaw wrote in the file that there were major inconsistences in Daniel's statement, his alibi."

"Which was?"

"Daniel told the cops he'd gone to visit his daughter in Seattle. The report in the file says your mother, Jodie, backed him up. He was eliminated as a suspect."

Skye blew out a relieved breath. "So that was the end of it?"

"It was, until I went through that evidence box. Ever since this guy decided to start sending you all these boxes with bones, I took the liberty of going through all our cold cases from that timeframe. I went through boxes and boxes of evidence from at least thirty homicides narrowing the focus down to the 1990s, all females. I pulled out whatever articles of clothing were inside. Anything in there that could be tested for DNA, I sent off to the lab. They've been working overtime testing everything. They got to Ellen Schreiber's stuff last week."

That feeling of impending doom landed in Skye's stomach. "You're getting to the point soon, I hope. And it doesn't sound like good news."

"No, it isn't good news. In Ellen's box there was a scarf. Touch DNA on her scarf is a match to Daniel Cree's."

"That's impossible."

"I thought you'd say that. I brought the report." He handed off a manila file folder.

She skimmed the piece of paper, read the results with her own eyes. "What the hell? I don't understand. Touch DNA, that's a transfer of skin cells, correct?"

"Sloughed-off skin cells or nucleated sweat. They call it CNA or fragmented, free-floating DNA."

"You're certain of the results? I mean, there's no mistake."

"The DNA doesn't lie."

"No chance of cross-contamination in the lab?"

"You know better than that."

"I'm grasping at straws here, Harry. How do you know it was a match? I mean what the hell is Daniel Cree's DNA doing in CODIS?"

"It's a long story."

She threw the file folder on the coffee table, spread her hands out wide. "Do I look like I'm going anywhere anytime soon? What gives?"

"When you went missing, for that span of time you were gone, we found the body of a young girl in Andrews Bay. Since you were the most recent missing child we had, we asked your father for a DNA sample to see if our dead girl was a match to you. Daniel complied."

Her temple throbbed at the thought. "I don't understand. But it wasn't a match. It couldn't have been a match to me anyway," she mumbled, almost to herself. "Why on earth would he provide DNA knowing that?" All at once she realized she'd spoken out loud and couldn't take it back.

Harry scowled beginning to get the gist. "Why wouldn't it match yours, Skye? Unless... You can't possibly mean that Daniel wasn't your biological father?" Harry sat back as lines formed along his forehead, the idea sinking in.

"That pretty much sums it up. Seems like when my parents wanted a child, they learned he had trouble with low sperm count or something. They turned to a third party," Skye explained, doing her best not to feel totally immature about the disclosure.

"Okay. Then who is your father?"

What the hell, she thought. She got up from the sofa, crossed her arms over her chest and paced to the window and back again, decided she might as well go all in. "Travis. He and my mother hooked up and then decided down the road to make it a whole lot more, if you get my drift."

"They had an affair? Jodie Cree and Travis Nakota?"

"You got it. It lasted for some time, too. And now you're telling me during that same time when my parents were separated, Daniel's main squeeze turned up dead. That's uncanny. And yes, bizarre."

"But if Daniel wasn't your real father then why would he provide us with DNA? He knew it wouldn't be a match." Harry scratched his head. "Why would he do that?"

"That's what I said."

"Maybe Daniel wanted to keep up appearances. Maybe he didn't want to let that info out of the bag and have you deal with that along with everything else, so when I asked for a sample, he complied to make it look good."

Skye drew in a sigh, smiled at her friend. "You do have a habit of saying the right thing. There's just one problem with that theory. He didn't know for sure that wasn't me pulled out of Andrews Bay. It could just as easily have been me."

"That's a horrible thought," Josh stated. "But accurate."

"I was there, Skye. Your father, er, Daniel, and your mother were absolutely terror-stricken that they'd never see you again. Now that I look back, Travis was right there with them every step of the way just as petrified."

"I know. But let's get back to the subject at hand, for now anyway. I don't understand why you kept his DNA all this time. It's been years since I was abducted. The case closed. I got away from the bastard, alive. Why didn't you just toss it in the trash?"

"It doesn't work that way. Once Daniel's DNA was put into the system, or anyone else's for that matter, it stays there, whether it goes into CODIS or NCIC, it doesn't matter. Even though it wasn't a match to our young victim at the time, there was still hope that you'd be found alive. Once you showed up, we obviously didn't think any more about the sample, the DNA that is, because a couple of days later, you were found wandering around an apartment complex parking lot."

She closed her eyes remembering that day she'd escaped the clutches of a monster. It still haunted her enough to cause nightmares every so often. "I wonder... Is there anyway Daniel and Travis could have switched cheek swabs?"

"I don't see how that's possible. When did you find out about all this, Skye?"

"About my father not being my father? Several months back. I had to pull the info out of Travis though."

"I never would've guessed. But now we have to figure out how Daniel's DNA got on Ellen Schreiber's scarf. That's the issue."

"Hey, I intend to dig into that with a shovel the size of Mercer Island. I want to see the evidence box, Harry."

"I thought you'd say that. That's why I made a few copies of info I thought was pertinent."

"Thanks for that."

After Harry left them, the two went back over the entire conversation. She had to face facts. Her father had worked at Fort Lewis two decades earlier. His connection to Ellen Schreiber was unmistakable.

"I refuse to accept that Daniel Cree killed Ellen Schreiber," Skye finally said. "That isn't even on the table for negotiation. The father I knew, the man who raised me, was a good and decent man."

"I didn't know Daniel. But yeah, I'd say that's a bogus theory. I don't buy it either."

"So how did the killer manage to get Daniel's DNA on the victim's clothing?"

"Whoa, back up. Touch DNA just means that at some point, Daniel had hold of that scarf. A scarf is a simple accessory that could've been draped around something other than her neck at any given time while he knew her."

"Like a chair or on a hook in her closet, even in a public place?"

"That's it. Daniel could've handed it off to her when they had dinner out and got ready to leave a restaurant, or picked it out of a drawer for her to wear with an outfit, or touched it when he removed it from a peg in the closet. See? There are a number of scenarios that work other than it's a definitive piece of evidence against him."

"Okay. So what does it prove anyway? That Daniel and the victim were spending time with each other and he had access to her clothing. He never denied he knew Ellen. The two obviously had an affair, which means Daniel touched a great deal more than Ellen's scarf. So what conclusion does that leave us?"

"Exactly. All it says is he touched the scarf at some point. Big deal."

"Who are we kidding here, Josh? There are people in prison serving time with less evidence than this. As I said before, DNA is pretty strong. I have to face facts. Daniel Cree had some kind of tie-in with our killer. We just have to find out what it is." All at once, Skye shoved out of the chair, grabbed her satchel. "There's something I have to do."

Irritation flashed through Josh. He recognized that withdrawn attitude on her face, a demeanor he thought she'd rid herself of—until right this moment. "I'll go with you."

"No. We aren't joined at the hip. The sooner you realize that the better off this marriage will be."

"Don't shut me out like this, Skye. There's no need for it. You're hurting. I get that. But—"

"Right now, I need for you to back off." With that, she stalked to the elevator, hit the Down button hard with the palm of her hand, and disappeared inside the car.

⚜ ⚜ ⚜ ⚜

Skye drove around for a while to clear her head. When that didn't work, she made her way to the cemetery to visit the graves of her parents.

She hadn't thought to bring flowers. But as she stood among the headstones dealing with another painful memory of a different kind, she took out the medicine bag from under her pullover.

With her hand clutching the power of the talisman, she stood over the ground where Daniel and Jodie Cree had been buried side by side. She went through the only chant she could remember in her native tongue, a simple recitation that spurred memories from childhood.

"Oh Great Spirit, protect our family. Mother Earth, shine your sun on us for many years to come. Father Sky, let peace and honor be with us always. I believe in you, my father, my mother. I know you believe in me. Oh Great Spirit, bring joy and light as we all travel down life's road."

Glancing up at the heavens and the low-hanging clouds, she spotted a hawk, circling overhead. The magnificent bird wasn't alone. Not far away in the drifting layer of mist, a crow flapped its wings as it came into view. She breathed in the cool air and let a sense of peace wash over her. And decided there were pluses to having so many protectors looking out for her.

One in particular was very real and could be a pain in the ass when the mood struck him. It was one of the reasons why Skye fretted over her visit with Travis.

The two of them hadn't had much of a chance to revisit the subject of his affair with her mother since last fall. There were still a few crinkles that needed to be ironed out. She had to admit now as she drove through the gate, past the sign that read The Painted Crow, she'd acted a bit like a child when she'd first found out. She'd been feeling somewhat betrayed at the thought of what her mother had done to Daniel Cree and what Travis had done to the man he considered a brother.

Now that she knew Daniel had moved on with Ellen Schreiber, was that enough to temper her outrage at all of them?

She wasn't sure. It hadn't been Daniel's fault that Jodie and Travis had continued to sleep together well after their initial agreement to make a baby. But at some point, Daniel *had* begun an affair with a coworker. Perhaps out of loneliness, perhaps to seek out someone who gave him a measure of happiness, no matter how brief it had been.

Didn't Daniel deserve happiness as much as anyone else?

For that reason, she was done judging the actions of her parents and those of Travis. It wasn't her place. What happened was unfortunate for all concerned but it was ancient family history. It was time to let it go and move on. And she would have, if it hadn't been for the Ellen Schreiber murder. If not for that, she would gladly have put it right where it belonged—two decades ago in the past.

But not having all the details of the story bugged the hell out of her.

Knowing how much Travis valued his privacy, she figured he would never have come clean in the first place if she hadn't pushed him to do it. That day she'd seen too many emotions on his face to describe the turmoil running through him. She didn't take that angst lightly.

And now, here she was again with an inquiring mind and a head full of questions. She doubted Travis would be happy about it.

To escape Seattle's hectic lifestyle, Travis raised and bred American Paint Horses on forty acres of ranchland outside Everett. She knew the place to be a picturesque spot he'd bought during one of the darkest times of his life.

Crawling out of the Subaru, with the earthy smells of manure and hay hanging in the damp air, she understood why he found solace here among the rolling hills and evergreens. Maybe she needed a great big dose of it herself. Maybe she needed a retreat where she could get away from all the hassles her life had become.

When she spotted her father making his way from the stable, she sent him a wave.

"What a wonderful surprise," Travis said as he pulled her into his chest for a hug. After kissing her cheek, he put her at arm's length to study her face. "Something's wrong."

The sky started to mist rain so they looped their way up the pebbled walkway past the corral and inside the stable.

"How about I help you groom the horses?"

"Sure. But you didn't drive all the way up here in traffic to become the stable hand for the afternoon. What gives?"

"I used to hate being Native," Skye blurted out as she took off her jacket so she could move around better. "Don't worry," she assured him as she picked up a curry comb. Eyeing the disappointed look on his face, she quickly added, "It was a phase. I've been out of that mode for several years now. I was young and stupid and didn't appreciate my heritage back then."

"Okay. Glad to hear it. You want to tell me why you're here? Not that I don't appreciate the visit. Did something happen between you and Josh?"

A layer of guilt moved in at the question. She wasn't proud of the way she'd stormed out of the loft. She'd have to deal with her temper later. First things first though, she decided. "I'll fix things with Josh. I promise. Right now, I need to know more about the time Daniel spent working at Fort Lewis."

Travis narrowed his eyes to slits. "Why's that?"

She told him about the meeting with Harry, about Ellen Schreiber, about the DNA on the scarf linking back to Daniel.

"What? That's impossible. They made a mistake, that's all," Travis insisted after hearing it pour out of her.

"No, it seems they took DNA when I went missing. They found a young girl about my age and needed to make sure it wasn't me. They entered Daniel's DNA into CODIS, where it's been sitting all this time. I'm not even sure why he'd bother with providing a sample knowing it wouldn't match to me."

"That's just it, Skye. I'm telling you they made a mistake."

She focused on his dark brown eyes, beginning to pick up the implication. "Why are you so certain of that?"

"Because the DNA belongs to me. The day they collected the swab, Daniel and I did a switcheroo."

She stared at him with her mouth gaped open. Letting the words sink in, she finally got her brain to work. "That's impossible. How?"

"They weren't as particular about it then as they are now, standing over you with a long Q-tip every single second, watching your every move the entire time. When the tech handed Daniel the stick, he distracted her long enough that I was able to snatch it out of his hand then swab my own mouth, handed it back to Daniel. It took maybe an extra four seconds."

Skye shook her head. "You're kidding? While the tech did what exactly? Harry was so sure you two couldn't have pulled it off."

"So you put it on the table, huh? Thanks for thinking the worst of us, kiddo," Travis teased.

"Turns out, I wasn't that far off the mark. So if the DNA belongs to you instead of Daniel, who actually knew Ellen intimately, if you get my drift, then what the hell is going on with the evidence?"

"It could mean her killer had access."

"That's crazy. I don't even believe that."

He paced away from her and then turned to head back, covering the same band of space. "I knew Ellen."

"What?" Skye's shoulders slumped. "How?"

"Not well, of course, but Ellen came into your mother's ceramics shop a couple of times when I was there. I watched the place while she and Jodie went to lunch at a little cafe two doors down."

Skye huffed out a breath. "I don't understand how it is that the four of you could be so civilized during what had to be a very awkward encounter. If Josh cheated on me I'd want to scratch out the other woman's eyes. You're saying my mother and Ellen sat down, broke bread together, and then had a conversation. Unbelievable."

"Civilized? I guess we were. Jodie had a tremendous chunk of guilt over our affair. She struggled with it for some time. The three of us had to maintain a certain amount of civility because of you. Try to remember, in the end, Jodie chose Daniel over me. Besides that, I'm pretty sure Ellen wasn't that serious about Daniel in the first place. She had a boyfriend or rather an ex-boyfriend she couldn't seem to shake. At least that's what Daniel told me. She continued to see the guy the whole time she was with Daniel."

"I need to find out his name. It's odd but Harry never mentioned anything about Ellen having an ex-lover. Do you happen to know who it was?"

"No idea. Probably some guy on base. But it has to be somewhere in her file if they did a thorough enough investigation. Harry couldn't possibly believe Daniel had anything to do with Ellen's death."

"No, Harry didn't give me that impression. But there are people sitting in prison who were convicted on a lot less. DNA of any kind is a powerful piece of evidence to overcome in court."

"But it's my DNA found on the scarf, not Daniel's. And you can't take a dead man to trial," Travis argued. Scratching his chin, he leaned up against one of the stalls. "What if you're dealing with a cop who had access to the evidence room?"

"Wow, where did that come from? That might explain a few things though."

"Like access?"

"More like, the ability to evade arrest for all this time. But before we start down that path, let's back up a minute. How exactly did this DNA switch work?"

"That day we were both very nervous and anxious about you still being—out there somewhere. When the tech showed up, we were in the garage changing the oil in Daniel's car just for something to do and to keep our minds from thinking the worst."

"After everything, the two of you still managed to remain friends. It's still hard to digest."

"Why? We were friends, brothers really, neither one of us was a monster."

"No, you weren't monsters, just two guys who got caught up in something that got out of control. I'm sorry. I didn't mean to take a detour into that again. Go on with what happened."

"When the tech asked for the swab, Daniel and I traded looks. We both knew full well what we had to do. Daniel picked up a quart of oil and there were several others lined up on the fender of the car. Luckily, the cans had been opened. Anyway, he knocked one of them over and it ended up all over the tech's pants leg. She was pretty pissed about it. While she was busy doing an 'ick, look at this, black-stuff-all-over-me-type dance,' Daniel handed me the swab. I ran it around my mouth, handed it back to Daniel. Once she stopped dancing around the mess and stopped worrying about her shoes, the tech was none the wiser."

It was too simple, thought Skye. But this time she kept her opinion to herself. "What if you'd gotten caught?"

"In that case, we were prepared to disclose everything to the cops, anything to get you back, to get answers. Keep in mind, Drummond had a dead thirteen-year-old across town. We found out her age much later when she was identified as Brenda Bradbury. And then days later you found a way out of that rathole of an apartment and came back to us.

"They took you to the hospital and the next thing I knew the phone rang. It was Daniel calling to tell me you were alive. I'd never dropped to my knees before, but I did that day. I've never been so relieved in my life. That day when I walked into your room and saw you were headed into surgery, I…I wanted to go to you, to tell you...right then that I was your father. Everyone had to give blood that day. Not sure they used it on you, but all our mutual friends showed up for a donation to the blood bank. I kept thinking the doctor would come out any minute and set everyone in the room straight."

Stepping to him, she laid her head on his shoulder and then a hand to his cheek. "I understand you couldn't disclose anything. You were there for me later when they died. I needed you then, too. I just wish I could have grown up here."

"I do, too. But it wasn't our path, Skye. That's changed now. Nothing can keep us apart."

After finishing up grooming one of the horses, regret had already taken its toll. She felt petty for shutting Josh out like she had. And she wanted him here with her. There were times a person had to admit they'd been a horse's ass and deal with it.

For that reason, she took out her cell phone, punched in his number and was relieved when he picked up. "I'm sorry," she said quickly. "I can be such an idiot at times."

"Where are you? Are you okay?"

"I'm better. I'm at Travis's place. Come out for dinner. There's a lot you need to know."

Darkness fell, as she waited at the gate for him to drive up. At the first sign of his little car coming up the lane, her heart lurched.

As soon as he crawled out of the car, Skye rushed to him, locking her arms around his waist.

"I thought you'd never get here."

"That's what I like to hear." He snatched her up off her feet, held her up off the ground. "Traffic was awful. Are we staying the night?"

"I missed you."

"I missed you, too. Does your bad mood qualify for having makeup sex?"

She chortled with laughter as they headed up to the house. "We definitely should explore that once Travis heads to bed. You do qualify for grilled steak fajitas. I know you like those."

After dinner she caught Josh up on the conversation with Travis as they took a walk in the rain down to the narrow cove of rocky coastline below the house. They passed through rolling pastureland, ambled under magnificent nobles and western hemlock. The tops of the giant trees looked as if the branches could reach the heavens.

On their way to the little strip of rock-strewn beach, Skye breathed in the moist breeze. "The air always smells fresher up here even with the horse dung hanging on the fringes."

Josh laughed. "Get used to it. Once we close on the farmhouse, we'll have access to this smell every day."

They stood there taking in the waves crashing up against the rocks. As squawky seagulls dive-bombed the water looking for a meal, Josh asked, "What's troubling you the most?"

"I'm still a little raw each time I'm reminded that my parents were so flawed. I suppose we all want to believe our moms and dads are perfect role models."

"Sure we do, but the bottom line is that isn't realistic. Our parents make mistakes."

"Yours seem perfect."

"They're far from that. My father was a workaholic. My mother had an addiction to pain pills during my high school years."

"Really?" That was news to her. "But they seem so…normal now."

Josh stuck his hands in his pockets. "Looks are deceiving. You should know that."

"I guess I do. I'm prepared to put their past behind me, stop my immature reaction to it every time it comes up. But it's easier said than done."

"All you can do is work on the way you feel and keep trying. What else is bothering you?"

"At the time Ellen Schreiber dated Daniel, she had an on-again-off-again relationship with another guy. We need to find out who it was and where he was the night Ellen went missing."

"The thing I don't understand is how Travis's DNA got on the woman's scarf."

"Travis said he met Ellen a couple of times when she had lunch with my mother. Maybe...somehow…"

"Okay. So what did Travis do, grab her by the scarf before she headed out the door to eat?"

"I know. It's bizarre. Travis mentioned we might be looking at a member of law enforcement. Think about it, Josh. Who else would have had access to the evidence? Do you think he could've somehow managed to *put* Travis's DNA there on that scarf?"

Josh considered that, shook his head. "How? It was Seattle's jurisdiction. They're the ones who kept what was found at the crime scene. The scarf was at the grave site, buried with the body. It was Harry who sent it for testing. No one knew the DNA wasn't Daniel's, except Travis."

"A link to Seattle PD then? I can't help but think there has to be a flaw in the handling of this whole thing, in the course of the investigation, somewhere they missed a step."

"There's no way it could've played out that way, Skye. It's a coincidence, nothing more. Travis must've touched the woman's scarf at some point."

"I suppose you're right."

"What about Daniel's fingerprints? Were they found on anything else with the remains? That might indicate more than the DNA on the scarf. Since he went through a detailed background check in order to get the civilian contractor's job, his fingerprints have to be a matter of old military records."

Her brow creased into fine lines. "But that would mean Daniel might've had something to do with her death. Harry didn't say a word about anything else in the evidence box pointing to Daniel as her killer. It was the DNA on the scarf he assumed matched Daniel's."

"Like you said earlier, I'm grasping at straws. Nothing makes any sense."

"Unless it's as you said, a coincidence. One thing I'm sure of is that Daniel did not kill Ellen. He was a kind man, Josh, a truly lovely soul who thought of other people before he ever did himself. I can't imagine the man I knew and loved taking anyone's life." Her shoulders dropped. "I'm suddenly tired of talking about all this. I'm exhausted and ready for bed."

"Not going out tonight?"

"Are you kidding? I doubt I'd do anyone much good. My brain refuses to engage. My body refuses to cooperate. Besides, I'm ready for that makeup sex now along with a good night's sleep thrown in."

"Good thing I can take care of both," he vowed, as he pulled her along back to the house.

Chapter Seventeen

The next morning as Travis cracked eggs into a bowl for scrambling he was still trying to figure out how his DNA got on that damn scarf. He'd spent the better part of the night brooding about it but all his theories had giant holes in them. Nothing made any sense.

Skye wandered into the room, looking for coffee. He watched his daughter fill up a generous mug and then lean back on the counter to enjoy that first taste.

"Good morning," she finally uttered.

"Feel better than you did yesterday?"

"I do. Good night's sleep, fresh air, what could be better?" She looked at him over the rim of her coffee. "Something's on your mind."

"I've been thinking," Travis began. "About one of the times Ellen came to the shop."

"Okay."

"One of those times, she and Jodie came back from lunch and Ellen's car wouldn't start. Jodie and I had to give her a ride home. That means Ellen was in my car for almost an hour. There was traffic on the 5 that day. It took some time to get her back to the base. I could have… I don't know, touched her scarf or handed it off to her maybe. There has to be a logical explanation how my DNA got on part of her clothing."

"But you can't think of even one. Was she wearing a scarf on one of the days she came into the shop?" She noted the disbelieving look on his face. "Okay, it's been far too long for that kind of memory to stick," Skye answered for him.

Travis sent her a grateful look. "Hell if I remember what the woman was wearing. I barely remember what she looked like. But I can tell you this. She was driving a sporty little Honda Prelude that shouldn't have had mechanical problems that day. It couldn't have had more than a year's worth of wear and tear on it, if that."

"What was wrong with her car?"

"Someone had tampered with her distributor cap. As I recall, she later had to have it towed back to the dealership."

"Interesting. Maybe someone was stalking her. I keep coming back to the ex."

"Isn't it always the husband or boyfriend, ex or otherwise?"

"Generally speaking," Josh said from the doorway. "We've kicked this around quite a bit." Josh nodded at Travis. "How long after you saw her that day, did she go missing?"

"Good question," Travis said in response, rubbing the back of his neck. "Maybe a week. But that's a guess on my part."

"Could be the boyfriend, who wasn't Daniel, followed Ellen to Jodie's shop that day thinking she was seeing you, too. Wanted to get a good look at you," Josh suggested.

"Daniel and Travis did look alike. But these questions just tell me I need to find Ellen's sister, approach her about this ex, or not so ex, and see if she remembers his name, what he looks like."

"Even if you could find her, Harry says her family still lives in the Los Angeles area. With things the way they are around here, we can't go down there to talk to her in person," Josh pointed out. "It isn't practical right now for either one of us to leave."

"I agree we have way too much going on to take a road trip. And Leo's too busy for a thorough search on the

Internet. That's why I'll take care of finding Ellen's sister myself."

"I can spare Leo, Skye. It isn't that. You have access to any of my staff you think will help. But I still believe our best lead is the Judy Howe composite."

"I haven't forgotten. I'm not without computer skills when it comes to doing searches, locating what I need, especially finding out last known addresses and phone numbers on someone. That's fairly simple stuff."

Having said that, though, it turned out Harry had an old address for the Schreiber family. It took her most of the morning to locate the right relative, one who fit the age for Ellen's sister. She got comfortable in Travis's study, dialed the six-two-six area code for Pasadena and waited.

She introduced herself when someone picked up. "Hi, my name's Skye Cree. Are you Tracy Schreiber?"

"I go by my married name now, Tracy Sands, even though I've been divorced for five years. Why?"

"I tracked you down through an alumni association from your high school. I was wondering by any chance if you might be the sister or a relative of a murder victim we had some time back here in the Seattle area by the name of Ellen Schreiber."

Skye heard an intake of breath on the other end of the phone and the woman began to sob. "I'm sorry. I take it you knew Ellen?"

"She was my sister. One of the sweetest girls you'd ever want to be around. No one in the family could believe it when Ellen wanted to join the army. She was the least likely person to follow rules and regulations back then. But she changed after basic training, got into the rhythm of the service. We supported her decision, of course. We had no way of knowing she'd end up murdered. She was only twenty-five. They've never even found who did it. Is this about her cold case?"

"It is, yes. What can you tell me about the men she dated? Do you remember any names? Anything at all about them might help."

"Oh my God, you think it might've been someone she knew? That's horrible."

"It's a possibility."

"Well, let's see. Once Ellen got to Tacoma, she had quite a social life. I mean, she always loved music and used to go out to clubs and concerts all the time. She did have one steady guy who seemed to always pop up or hang around whenever I talked to her. They'd break up and then get back together."

"On-again, off-again?"

"Oh, definitely. They spent quite a bit of time apart. His name was odd-sounding, something that always made me think of those Birkenstock shoes. Then there was another guy who was really nice to her. His first name was Daniel. I don't remember his last name though. That doesn't help you much, does it?"

It was never her intent to discourage a victim's family, so she replied with an upbeat tone in her voice without being specific. "You know, it's always the little things that help a case turn the corner. We're hoping anything you remember might make it pop."

"For the last ten years or so I believed Ellen might have been killed by that Ridgway guy. You know? But when they arrested him and the story made the news, I called the Seattle PD for details. The detective couldn't give me much hope on that score, though. So we've waited for the last two decades for any word, anything at all. My mother died four years ago without knowing what happened to her youngest girl. My father died last year. They were both brokenhearted at losing Ellen."

When Skye ended the call she was more determined than ever. Maybe back in the nineties they didn't have a clue who had killed Ellen, but now she would do her damnedest to find the woman's killer. She would do it to clear any suspicion from Daniel and to give Ellen and her family some long overdue answers.

Chapter Eighteen

At an upscale bar near Pike Place Market, he nursed his glass of Johnny Walker Red sitting at a table in the back. The pub was dim and noisy but it made for an almost perfect perch to watch Selma Tolliver meet up with her friends from work.

Her little outing gave him opportunity. He couldn't very well approach her as long as she was with her friends. That would leave an impression, an imprint. Someone could remember the man she'd talked to at the bar. No, this way, there would be nothing to tie him to Selma.

Instead of dwelling on the 'how to' of intercepting her, he'd have to play it by ear, play out the entire scene with aplomb and patience until he got what he wanted. He didn't doubt for a second that by the end of the night Selma would be his.

He wasn't worried. The only thing he needed to get around was the pesky security cameras in the bar, in the parking lot and the one across the street. It reminded him how good he was at what he did. In twenty years he hadn't been caught because he'd kept up with technology. He'd been willing to change his methods and he'd learned on the job and continued to evolve over time.

When he heard Selma laugh he turned to stare. He doubted the prudish woman would go easy. Selma might be a little older than he was used to but age didn't matter when abducting her would make another in-your-face statement.

He wanted Skye Cree to remember without a doubt that he was around. He wanted her to know he was nipping at her heels.

Selma relished these nights out on the town with her friends. As an accountant with one of Seattle's best firms she sometimes put in a seventy-hour workweek, especially during tax season. With her head jammed with things like capital gains and deductions, it was one reason why she and her associates tried to plan one of these happy hour gatherings at least once a month. Plus, since her ugly divorce three years earlier, Selma made a point to get out more to socialize. She had to. At forty-three, she wasn't getting any younger.

She made her way off the elevator and into the garage parking to where she'd left her silver Lexus. Her heels clacked all the way on the pavement making an echo sound. The dark lot had her considering the late hour. She reminded herself that Seattle was one of the safest cities in the country.

Maybe she should have taken Tyler Elliott up on his offer to walk her to the car. The good-looking CPA had flirted with her all evening. But when he'd asked, she'd had to pee really bad. By the time she'd gone to the restroom and returned to the table, all her friends had left the bar, including the hunky Tyler.

When her vehicle came into view, she let out a sigh of relief. Her car was one of several still sitting among a throng of late-night partiers. She got a kick out of being one of them. Even that small thing made her feel a bit more at ease.

Pressing the remote on her key ring, she slid neatly into the driver's seat. She made sure her doors were locked and started the engine.

She headed toward the exit and her loft, a short eight blocks away. With her mind on Tyler Elliott, she drummed her fingers on the steering wheel to Blondie's *Heart of Glass*. When she had to stop for the red light at the intersection of Valiant and Premier, she turned up the volume on the CD player. All at once, she heard the sound of a police siren, three short bursts coming from behind her. It made her look up into the rearview mirror but all she saw was a set of bright lights. Checking her side mirror, she saw the officer jump from his vehicle. It didn't look like Seattle PD, but he tapped on her window anyway.

Her first impulse was to keep it rolled up.

"Have you been drinking?"

That question and the badge he flashed ended any reservations. Selma hit the button to lower the glass—and saw the barrel of a gun leveled at her face.

Chapter Nineteen

By one-thirty, Skye was exhausted. She'd stuck Judy's composite drawing under at least fifty noses without getting any reasonable results. Oh, there had been plenty of people who had insisted the sketch looked familiar. The boozehound trying to catch a nap on Howell was convinced it was the guy down the block panhandling, encroaching on his territory. The bartender at Magistrate's believed it looked like the man behind the counter at the convenience store on Freemont. The streetwalker on Darrow felt like it resembled the cop who walked the beat between Fourth and Bell. But no lead panned out, nothing came of any of it.

Her boots were beginning to pinch her heel. Her feet were starting to cramp. Her head ached from defeat. It wasn't the first time in eight years that Skye had grown weary of the hunt. But it *was* the first time she felt like giving up.

She turned to Josh. "Look, it's the weekend. Let's take some time and do something for us. We have the move coming up. I say we're entitled to take a day or two off from this crazy pace we're keeping."

Josh eyeballed the woman he loved. She'd been hinting at it for weeks. Dropping little nuggets that she'd grown fed up with the slow progress of the case. But this was the first indication she'd actually broken and given in, the first time she'd suggested they shirk patrols two nights in a row.

"You mean not go out tonight either?"

"If we do go out, we go somewhere other than the streets. Let's do something for ourselves for a change."

"Take the whole weekend off?"

In the dim light from the street, she stopped walking to meet his eyes. "Why is that so difficult to understand? I'm saying as clearly as I can that I need some time off from this case, if for no other reason than to have time to think because it's driving me nuts. We're no closer to nabbing him than the day the box showed up."

"We *are* making progress, Skye. You have a piece of paper in your hand with a decent likeness of what he looks like."

"Fifteen years ago," she pointed out. "From a woman who has been too afraid to leave her apartment all that time. For all we know he could have been in a car accident and had plastic surgery to change his appearance by now."

Josh rolled his eyes. "You're reaching because you're tired. I suggest we swing through the harbor area and call it a night. How does that sound? Then tomorrow we reassess taking two nights off."

He picked up her hand, placed a kiss on the palm. "Let me take you to dinner Saturday night. Someplace that has tablecloths and candlelight, somewhere we have to dress up to get in the door."

"It'll be our date night."

They settled on that as they made their last pass of the night through the neighborhood. Finding nothing out of the ordinary, the two headed down the quiet streets to make their way back home.

⟡ ⟡ ⟡ ⟡

Their much-needed day off began by sleeping till almost noon. Wrapped in a sheath of soft blankets, they lay bundled basking in the late-morning hour.

"It feels downright indulgent to wake up this late, rested and refreshed. Nine hours of uninterrupted sleep is what I call bliss."

"We haven't done this since St. Kitts. I'm starving." When she started to move out of bed, he snagged her hand. "But first, we should stay right where we are and make the most of the situation." To prove it, he rolled on top of her.

"So there's a situation?" she asked with a lazy stretch of legs and arms while he made the point with his mouth.

In between velvet kisses, she nibbled an earlobe, ran her lips along his throat. "Then you should definitely take advantage of me, maybe a couple of times, as long as you're thorough. Are you thorough, Josh? Do you take care of the little details?"

"I like to think so. But talk is cheap. How about I show you?" He cruised to a delectable part of her neck before running his tongue down to the fleshy curve of a breast. Pulling, tugging, savoring the textures, he made his way down her long, lean torso.

"I like being married. Who knew there would be so many perks?"

That sentiment had him looking up into her shimmering eyes and grinning. "Yep, the benefits package is great."

Her laugh, rich and smooth, was playful in return. Because she could, she held onto his hips, bucked up, took him into her. "Yeah, I like the way the benefits package fits. It's a real bonus."

That got him laughing as he shifted deeper, found a fluid tempo. Clinging to each other, that tempo quickened. The ultimate fall came in shattering feathers of glowing light around the fringes.

Breathless, they lay bound, still linked as one. He trailed fingers through her loose hair. "I'm a lucky man."

She guffawed with laughter. "Damn straight you are, especially this morning. And I'm not about to let you forget it."

Later, Skye discovered they didn't even have a box of cold cereal in the house. In fact, they were fortunate to have enough coffee beans for a full pot of brew.

"Who runs out of Cheerios?" Josh wanted to know, his head stuck in the cupboards as he dug past four different kinds of cracker boxes, each containing no more than four crackers.

"People hunting for a killer, people too busy to stop at the grocery store to pick up a carton of milk." Studying the contents of the fridge, she ran through the inventory. "We have exactly four eggs and some frozen hash browns in the freezer. It's either peanut butter on crackers or I throw together a scrambled mixture with potatoes. Your choice?"

"At this point I'd settle for a stale piece of bread. We don't even have an apple or a bottle of orange juice."

"I know. The pantry is down to the stash of stale crackers, a box of macaroni and a jar of olives. You could eat the olives with the eggs," she suggested.

After making do with what they had on hand for breakfast, they headed to Pike Place Market to remedy the bare cabinets. They bagged fresh fruits and vegetables, hunted down the best fish possible, and picked out the prettiest batch of gerbera daisies. They even sampled tamales from a man who promised them a genuine "south of the border" flavor.

But like other trips she'd taken here, as they made their way through the vast array of merchants, Skye had a hard time stopping at picking up produce. There were too many pots of herbs to pass up, too many shiny things that caught her eye.

They ended up hitting the jewelry booth, picked out a sterling silver charm bracelet for Zoe's upcoming birthday and decided on a plum tourmaline necklace for Lena as a little reward for being Lena.

They stopped to eye the pottery display and ended up buying several pieces of bright red stoneware that would look good in their new white and blue kitchen. While Josh browsed through the comic book shop, she snuck in several hardbacks on gardening and growing organic veggies under the bottom of his stack.

When that was done they took everything back to the loft to put away and then went furniture shopping. It didn't take long to discover they had different tastes in style and fabric. It took them several hours of back and forth before they were able to settle on a plump-cushioned, contemporary design in a durable, honey-color fabric.

By the time they got back home, Skye looked at Josh and grinned. "After all that I'm too tired to get dressed up in a fancy dress to go out anywhere. How about I grill the fresh salmon we picked up for dinner instead?"

Put on a suit and tie or stay home? No man he knew in his right mind would push for wearing formal attire unless he had to. When the opportunity to lounge around in a comfy T-shirt and jeans was thrown into the mix, he went with the prudent thing. "Whatever you want to do is fine with me."

They stayed in, ate the fresh fish they'd grilled and watched a movie, a romantic comedy that got their minds off murder. The light and silly film made them laugh and feel as though they were like any other couple spending a Saturday night under normal circumstances instead of tracking a serial killer in their spare time.

Sunday was spent packing for the move to the new house. As they jammed to hard-hitting classic rock, they stuffed whatever went to the farmhouse into boxes or bags.

Neither one was allowed to go near their laptops. But as afternoon approached they decided to wander out and ended up eating lunch at Country Kitchen. It was the first time back for them since Willa's body had been discovered. It was painful to walk inside and know Willa wasn't coming back.

Their upbeat weekend pretty much ended there. The same way as all the other days had since the box of bones had shown up: the realization the killer was still out there, doing whatever he wanted, whenever he wanted to whomever he felt like targeting. And no one seemed to be able to find a way to stop him.

Chapter Twenty

By Monday evening, Josh was ready to sit down and have a beer, maybe watch a replay of the Mariners preseason game from Arizona. He pulled his Fusion into his parking space about the same time Edna Grossman did hers.

Edna wasn't yet ready to give up the job she'd had for a quarter of a century. At sixty-seven her brown hair might be almost completely gray but she still got up to go to work five days a week at the marketing company she'd founded twenty-five years earlier.

Her husband had died the previous year of cancer, leaving her with a sizeable estate as well. But Edna wasn't one to trot out her bank account. Other than the ten-year-old Mercedes she drove and the prestigious loft address, she much preferred downplaying her lifestyle. A testament to her thrifty nature was the fact she still wore the same coat she'd bought in 1998.

Glad to be home after a long day, Josh grabbed his briefcase from the passenger seat and started for the elevator. When Edna joined him in the wait for the car, he nodded at her in polite fashion and asked, "How's it going?"

"Did you hear about Selma Tolliver?"

Josh's radar went off. The hair stood up on the back of his neck. "What about Selma?"

"She went out Friday night with friends, never made it back home. No one's seen Selma since she left that bar over on Pike where they were partying."

"Maybe she met up with someone, went back to his place." But even as he tossed the theory out there, he didn't believe it.

"And not call anybody the entire weekend, especially her sister, Suzanne?" Edna leaned in toward him. "You don't know those two women. Suzanne spends almost as much time here with Selma as she does back in Sammamish." Edna shook her head. "No, you don't know Selma at all if you think she'd get lucky at a bar on Friday night and not tell Suzanne first chance she got on Saturday."

Josh had to admit he'd lived in the building for years and hadn't done much to get to know any of his neighbors, let alone the perky brunette he'd only met a few weeks ago. "What do the police say?"

When the elevator doors dinged open, Edna let out a harrumph. "Don't know their asses from a doughnut hole if you ask me. With all these murders and abductions of young women in the news, you'd think the cops would do a whole lot more than blow smoke up the family's ass."

"Is that what they're doing?"

"Oh, the police eventually found Selma's Lexus parked on Valiant this morning—two days later. That's seven blocks from here, but right around the corner from the bar. They told Suzanne that maybe Selma had car trouble and someone gave her a lift." Edna made another noise in her throat. "Selma's Lexus was less than a year old, not a thing wrong with it."

"When did the sister call the cops?"

"Suzanne came in from Sammamish Saturday afternoon, went through Selma's apartment herself to see what was what. That's when she got scared, when she knew Selma hadn't made it back to the apartment."

By the time Edna stepped off on the fifth floor, Josh was doing a checklist in his head of all the coincidences since that box of bones had showed up. Vanessa Farrington, Maggie Bennett, Willa Dover, and now Selma—all people connected to them in one way or another.

As soon as he got to his penthouse, he dropped his briefcase and went in search of Skye. He found her in the kitchen layering noodles in a pan to make deep-dish lasagna.

"Were you aware that Selma Tolliver vanished Friday night and hasn't been seen or heard from in two days?"

Skye stopped what she was doing long enough to look over at Josh. "Your neighbor? The one from the lobby? No, I hadn't heard."

"Our neighbor," Josh corrected. "And yeah, the woman who was heading out the door that night and found the second package. This guy's hitting us close to home, Skye. Too damn close to home."

"And doing a damn good job of it," she groused.

"Neither of us has bothered touching base with Dawson Hennings the last few days. I think it's time we rattled his cage."

Inside the Artemis Foundation, for the first time, Skye had volunteers. Zoe, Lena, and Velma were joined by Karen Houston and her daughter, Shawna Langley. Today, they were all hard at work stuffing flyers into envelopes. To accommodate them she'd had to borrow chairs from Ander All Games to make sure everyone had a place to sit.

When the door opened Skye looked up and was surprised to see Dawson Hennings standing in the doorframe with another man she didn't recognize. Dawson was his usual awkward self, but Skye got the sense that the man he'd brought with him was anything but.

"After getting your message last night, I thought about returning your call this morning to let you know what we found over the phone." Dawson looked around the room. "But I wanted to see this place for myself. As it turns out, so did Kevin Holt, the forensic geologist I mentioned. So here we are. Kevin, meet Skye Cree."

Skye stood up, shook the sandy-haired man's hand, made the introductions all around to the others. "As you can see, we're mailing flyers complete with pictures of the missing along with information packets about the Foundation. Businesses from Vancouver to San Francisco will receive them in an attempt to get them more active within their own neighborhoods. We hope to get owners to agree to put up flyers in their front windows or near the cash register on a regular basis, get them more involved. That way, we keep a higher profile across the western states, maybe increase visibility and awareness."

She spread her arms out wide. "So what do you think?"

"That it's an incredibly good idea," Kevin concluded. "But you know there's bound to be some who get the letter and just toss it out with the trash."

"I'm sure they will," Skye agreed. "But if we get even fifty percent participation, it's more than we had before."

"I didn't expect so many people here," Dawson confessed.

As the phone jingled on the desk, Skye looked on proudly as Lena stopped what she was doing to pick it up. "We're growing," Skye proclaimed. "Lately it seems like all at once. We're still taking baby steps though. I'm sure we'll stumble along the way somewhere."

Dawson adjusted his glasses. "Is there someplace we could talk? We have some news. And I think you'll be interested in what we have to say."

"Sure, let's go in the kitchen." The small coffee bar area was a little crowded with three people but Skye felt determined to make them feel at home. "How about coffee?"

"I never say no to caffeine," Kevin proclaimed.

After she'd filled up three mismatched cups she'd brought from her apartment and passed them around, she motioned for the two men to sit down at the little round ice cream table she'd used on her balcony.

"Kevin here identified the dirt particles on the bones you were sent."

"And?"

Kevin took a taste of the hot liquid before putting down his mug. "The soil contained microscopic traces of Camassia quamash, a perennial herb that predominantly grows in marshy areas. Quamash is actually a Nez Perce term for the bulb at the end of the stem that's edible. It tastes similar to a sweet potato. But I guess you probably knew that."

Skye sent him a grin before she sipped from her own mug. "I did but it's good to know you've done your homework. If you're about to disappoint me, Kevin, I need a disclaimer. I'm not sure I can handle any bad news today."

"Understandable. But there's much more to what I have to say than about the quamash. Most people don't realize you can log a lot of interesting stuff, minerals and chemicals and particles, out of the smallest dirt sample. Dirt can tell us a helluva lot more than just the organic nitrogen and carbon makeup."

"Okay." Maybe she'd misjudged Kevin. He seemed as nerdy as Dawson. But what he said next proved her wrong.

"The government has even started making the most of the data. Geologists launched the U.S. Geological Survey Project in 2001. Ever since then, there's a lab in Denver that maintains a database with a collection of soil samples taken from one end of the country to the other. Like your Foundation, the database is small, but growing."

"You're a fascinating guy, Kevin."

"I try to be. Forensic science is just now beginning to recognize the importance of dirt. Like the bones you were sent, if a victim has dirt under the nails, it can tell us a lot. Was the person killed there or were they dumped?"

"You've got my attention."

"Good, because I'm not trying to confuse you. No, I'm trying to lead up to what I think is very good news. As for the Camassia quamash, or camas as they are commonly known, the only problem with the plant is that it's found growing from British Columbia down the coast of Washington, in abundance. On that alone, it would be almost impossible to pinpoint a precise location of where exactly those bones rested for all this time."

"But you found something else?" Skye asked with hope rising in her chest.

Kevin grinned. "Oh yeah, something significantly identifiable. The soil tested positive for traces of BTEX, an acronym we use for benzene, toluene, ethylbenzene, and xylene—all four make the components in aviation fuel. Wherever those bones were buried, the ground was contaminated with the stuff. If you take into account the traces of quamash, I'd look for an airport or military installation near marshland. BTEX will take the path of least resistance until it finds a water table. A marsh or wetland area has a very low water table. That's why I sent what I found off to Denver. I'm encouraged that my results may help you solve this case or at the very least, lead you to a location."

Hope went from resting on the bottom of the floor to a blast of optimism. She felt like hugging Kevin. Instead, she said, "Encouragement is putting it mildly. For the first time in weeks, we have something solid to follow up on."

"Then I hope it helps. I realize you might consider it like looking for a needle in a haystack at first, but if you stick to the parameters I've outlined, I think you'll be surprised. Besides, I'll send you more data as it comes in to help you narrow the area down more."

As soon as the men said their goodbyes, Skye snatched up her case binder and took the elevator upstairs to Ander All Games.

As usual, when she strolled inside the busy office, she saw programmers with their heads down. Each seemed chained to their laptops until they polished up the beta application of the new game. She spotted Leo hanging out with Winston and Reggie, their heads buried together comparing lines of code.

With that dedicated attitude, Skye had no doubt they'd stay on schedule for a Christmas release.

Once inside Josh's office, she slapped down the binder on his desk. Everything Kevin Holt told her came tumbling out. "You know what this means, right?"

"Joint Base Lewis-McChord has an airstrip."

"You bet it does. But we shouldn't rule out the area around Sea-Tac Airport either."

Josh scowled into his coffee mug. "That's a lot of ground to cover, Skye."

"I know. So we narrow it down. I wonder…"

"Might as well lay it all on the table."

"In the not so distant past, I read that sections of the base had an overabundance of abandoned buildings. They've demolished a lot of them but not all. Maybe this nutcase has specific knowledge of the region and has found one he utilizes for his sick torture chamber."

"On base? I don't think so. But he is familiar with the lay of the land. Maybe he snapped up a tract of it when the government sold off part of the base to individuals."

"We have to figure out a way to check out the area without raising suspicions. How do we get near a military base without anyone charging us with trespassing?"

"We don't necessarily have to get on the base." Josh went to his laptop, brought up a map of the area. "And neither does our killer. He could take advantage of almost a hundred thousand acres of vast space including the lowlands near the hiking trails that wind back all the way into the canyons here."

He pointed to the topography. "This is what I was talking about earlier. There's a creek that runs through all kinds of wetlands, a perfect growing place for quamash. It drains into Puget Sound. A trading post used to be here, as well as several missions. There was even an old fish farm located here once."

"Are you up for a little exploration?"

"Why not? The only question is when is the best time, day or night? We go out there at night, it's a fact one of us has trouble seeing."

"I might not be able to see as well as you do but I'm game. Although I'm not even sure Lewis and Clark would brave the area at night, so I guess the sooner the better. We still have five hours of daylight left."

"Then let's make the most of it."

Chapter Twenty-One

It took them an hour to grab what they needed. They stuffed a backpack with essentials—a map of the area, water bottles, power bars, flashlights, matches—anything they might need on the trail.

After crossing over into Pierce County, they picked an isolated spot where they could leave the car. Sunshine broke through the gray floating clouds overhead as they started up the narrow trail.

Sniffing the air, Kiya went first through the dense brush.

For now, they stuck to the lush creek corridor where mossy red alder and big leaf maple mingled with tall Sitka spruce. Bog birch and red-stemmed dogwood hugged the ground, home to families of squirrels and cottontails. Pacific wax myrtle crowded the creeping spikerush.

Josh pointed to a jungle of maidenhair fern. Nestled among its fan-tailed branches was the flowering quamash. Its blue buds reminded them spring wasn't that far off.

"We must be in the right area. Should we take soil samples for Kevin?"

He chuckled. "Don't tell me you actually packed baggies?"

"Of course, why wouldn't I? Kevin said he'd continue inputting the data to narrow down the area as much as possible."

"The dirt may very well be contaminated, even though corporations have done their best to clean up the land as far back as the 1970s."

"Progress. It ran off the Native American population." She glanced around at the lush greenbelt, home to a variety of deer and rabbit. "It's still a beautiful spot though. How far are we from the base?"

He took out a pocket GPS. "By my calculation the nearest gate is south southeast about two miles from where we're standing."

"The good news is we're here in broad daylight. We blend in with all the other hikers and runners."

"The bad news is in order to find a lair of a serial killer we need remote and secluded, away from the public eye, somewhere he could do his business, undetected."

With that in mind they hiked down another ravine, climbed up an embankment full of bitter cherry. When the trailhead ended they veered off into a creek bed covered in what looked like poison oak.

She tugged on Josh's sleeve. "Don't go near that stuff or you'll be itching all night."

"There's the tunnel and the railroad tracks. The rails are supposed to lead to a dock."

In different time she would have liked to explore the tunnel with its colorful graffiti and rusted railway from a forgotten era. "Out here? Don't we need water and a shore for that?"

"Due west."

"Too bad we're headed east."

A salamander chose that moment to run across her boot. To her credit, she didn't shriek out an expletive. Instead, she charged ahead through the yellowcress that dotted the slope surrounding them. Even though they'd left the paved path some time back, they surveyed the jagged landscape looking for anything out of the ordinary.

"Kiya hasn't picked up anything since we got here. What about you?"

"Only that the land has seen its fair share of bloodshed."

"Historic or more recent?"

"Both."

"Are we in the wrong area?"

Josh shook his head. "Just because we haven't found anything yet, doesn't mean it isn't here."

When they came upon one of the empty buildings Josh had mentioned earlier, they went on alert, standing outside the copse of sturdy western larch and Douglas fir that guarded what used to be a train station.

"We have to check this place out," Skye whispered.

"We'll circle around back."

The wood frame still had a faint trace of paint on it that had to go back decades. Since no one had bothered to board up windows or doors, they were able to get a look inside. Nothing remained, except a lopsided floor, rotting and unsteady. The last owner, whoever it had been, had left the place to the elements and the wildlife. Once they deemed it was only a shell and that it hadn't been used for anything other than a marker for hikers, they moved on.

A mile later they decided to rest near a shallow basin. Skye sat down on a rock and dug into her backpack for a bottle of water. She chugged down half before handing it off to Josh who drained what was left.

"Kevin Holt was right. This is like looking for a needle in a haystack. Why do you let me do these crazy things?"

"Because hunting is what you do. It's in your blood."

"God, I love you. Who else would put up with this insane life we lead, or more to the point, put up with me?"

"Right back at ya."

"So what do we do now?"

"We head back home and go through the case binders, again. Look for a better place where this guy could set up shop," Josh decided, drawing in a tight breath. "What else can we do?"

"Then I guess we'd better start back. We're losing the light."

He took her hand, brought her closer. "The realtor called today to tell me we close on the house tomorrow. Are you ready for this?"

"I'm more than ready. I want this new start, mainly because my brain feels like mush. If we don't solve this thing soon, I think I'm looking at burnout, Josh, full-scale burnout. For the first time in eight years, I feel exhausted, both mentally and physically."

"Me too. Maybe it's because we aren't getting enough sleep."

"We might need to cut back on the nights of the week we hit the streets, consider taking a break from all this. Maybe it's just too much. Sometimes I think what we need is an army instead of just two people."

"We have troops," Josh declared. He thought of the stellar team he had back at work and Skye's eager new recruits. "We just need to utilize them better."

Through binoculars, he watched the pair's movements. He wasn't afraid or worried. He'd never been that. The fact that Skye Cree and her bumbling partner had gotten so close might have rattled a lesser person. But it didn't bother him. After all, getting close wasn't the same as *finding*. He had to remind himself that the inept couple hadn't been successful on much of anything. Let alone their jaunt from their swanky penthouse in the city to where the common man lived and worked.

He wasn't ashamed of who he was, even though he'd slid out of a meth addict. He'd never known the bastard who'd fathered him. His mother had become a painted whore who sold herself for pittance. She'd overdosed a week before his fourteenth birthday. If he'd followed in mommy's drug-addled footsteps, he'd more than likely be dead by now, too. So he'd carved out a better life for himself by recognizing opportunity and seizing his chances.

That's why he didn't intend to spend two minutes of his time worrying about the Cree woman and her sidekick or how they had ended up so near his turf.

He told himself he wasn't getting sloppy. He knew where sloppy got you.

Letting his hands drape from his sitting position, he took in the view of the pretty valley below. Remembering another time, another place, a bad place, he'd sworn to never go back there again or anyplace like it. Nothing they could do to him could make him go back there again. Ever. If he had to, he'd fight to the death if that's what it took to stay out of jail. Recalling his time spent in that depressing, closed-in space was his salvation. A person had to want to crawl up through shit to get out of the sewer.

He'd climbed kicking and screaming through the waste of his life.

He'd been young and foolish the first time. He wasn't either of those things now. Youth and foolishness rarely garnered accolades unless there was a special talent involved. He had a special talent. It was that reassurance that had him getting his priorities straight.

Glancing to his right, he brought the dark-haired woman into the curve of his arm. Ignoring the fact that Selma was naked, cold and battered, he stroked the top of her head, patting her like a dog.

Without preliminary, he unzipped his pants, picked up her stiff hand and stuffed it down into his crotch and began working her fingers around his shaft.

And remembered back to the time he'd been seventeen.

He'd been horny as hell then, too. He also remembered being head over heels in love with Margo Jamison. At the memory of how his youthful heart used to race each time he saw Margo in the hallway between classes, he smiled.

He recalled how he'd stood like the weak dumbass he'd been at the time, waiting for Margo to show up at her locker.

If he was honest with himself it was that time with Margo that had made him what he was today. If the bitch had just given into him sooner, given him what he'd wanted then, he'd never have had to travel down this road in the first place.

Probably.

He smiled at himself and his soppy mood. What was it about getting older that made a man reminisce about his misspent youth? After all, he couldn't keep his mind wandering so much in the past, revisiting his every flaw or the times he'd messed up. That was for fools.

"I can't keep you, baby," he proclaimed, placing a kiss on Selma's cold, blue lips. "For some reason, I can never keep the ones I truly care about. But I promise to put you some place real nice. You deserve real nice."

Chapter Twenty-Two

Thirty minutes west of Seattle across Puget Sound, Skye was sure she'd found her own personal sanctuary. Bainbridge Island, with its bucolic countryside and gentle slopes, sand dunes, and a forest of trees, had an old world feel to it. A mix of Native American history combined with a European heritage, she decided she could feel right at home here.

From the back door of the farmhouse Skye could see the jutting coastline and rocky outcrops that made the land so diverse.

The furniture truck had already come and gone. The delivery men had already carted heavy bedroom furniture, mattresses, and a new flat-screen TV upstairs. They'd arranged the living room for her with the new sofa and love seat—several times, in fact.

She wandered outside to walk the grounds. Their ten acres included rolling hills, wooded patches that stretched to the rear of the property, and a small shallow pond the previous owners had let grow in knots of creeping ivy and ragwort. Skye intended to fix that.

When she heard a vehicle turn into the long drive, she dashed around the corner of the house in time to see Josh and Tate crawl out of a rented truck.

"What took so long?" Skye wanted to know.

"Had to wait forty-five minutes for the truck and then another thirty to get aboard the ferry. Did the furniture show up yet?"

"All set up, just waiting for you and Tate to bring in our treasures."

Josh swaggered over and planted a kiss on her mouth. He scooped her up off the driveway and into his arms, started heading toward the front of the house.

"What are you doing?"

"You've been married so long you forgot a man always carries his bride over the threshold. That's a good sign."

"But you did that when we checked into the hotel in St. Kitts and again when we got home to the loft."

Toting her through the front door and into the entryway, Josh covered her mouth again before setting her on her feet. "Then I guess the third time is the one that counts."

Tate followed them inside and looked around. "Wow, this is some hacienda. Next thing we'll hear is that you've decided to start a family! Imagine, having little Anders running around this place."

Skye met Josh's eyes. "We're getting us a dog, maybe two."

"Even better," Tate returned. "Have you decided what kind?"

As all three lifted and hauled in their share of boxes, they stacked them in every room of the house. Many trips back and forth gave them time to kick around the best dog breeds.

"I'm fond of border collies myself. They're supposed to be smarter than all the rest," Tate threw out. "There's a no-kill shelter in Snohomish that's so overcrowded right now they're begging for people to adopt. I know because Maggie was planning to go down there and pick out a dog for herself before she was…" Tate's voiced trailed off. He couldn't bring himself to utter the word, murdered. "Maybe she should have. Maybe a dog would've saved her somehow."

Skye took his hand in hers. "We don't know that, not even the circumstances of what really happened. I'm so sorry about Maggie. I still feel Josh and I have some degree of responsibility."

"Why? You shouldn't feel that way because the sick son of a bitch who did those despicable things to her picked her out of all the other employees. It could've just as easily been Terry in accounting or Jeanie in marketing. I'm the one who blew her off that Sunday. I'm the one who didn't go by her place to check on her until Monday. I was trying to teach her a lesson. What kind of boyfriend thinks that way?"

"Oh, Tate," Skye said, wrapping her arms around him. "It's not your fault."

Josh slapped Tate on the back. "I already told you to let go of that guilt. None of us has a crystal ball."

"I want to help you guys catch this bastard. I'll do anything you want me to do."

"You really want to help, volunteer at the Foundation," Josh suggested. "Skye could use all the help she can get going through case binders we've put together. Another pair of eyes couldn't hurt."

When they had finished unloading the van, they dropped into the comfy living room chairs, exhausted.

"How about I call in pizza?" Skye offered. "I found a pizza flyer mixed in with all the junk in our mailbox. How about we order takeout?"

"That'll work. Hard to believe they deliver pizza to the boonies." Tate joked. "Do they deliver beer, too, if not I'll take the biggest bottle of Coke they have."

"We aren't that far from downtown Bainbridge," Josh explained. "Less than four miles from downtown, that means we fall into their delivery guidelines."

Skye laughed. "We checked before we signed the paperwork on the house. Do you believe that? But you guys go ahead and argue the point while I go dig the ad out of the trash."

After she took off for the kitchen, Tate looked over at his former brother-in-law. "Should we tell her she could just look up the phone number on the cell?"

"And miss the five-dollars-off coupon that probably came with the advertisement? No way."

Tate grinned. "She is a sweetheart the way she always watches out for your money. That Foundation is bare-bones, Josh. She refused to spend excessively to outfit the place. I mean, it does the job but… That sure isn't like any woman I've ever known. And that's including my sister. We both know Annabelle loved to spend your money. "

Josh nodded his head in agreement reminding himself it was wise not to get into a rant about Annabelle's spending habits, which boarded on extravagant. All he said was, "Don't I know it."

The pizza guy showed up about the same time a cloudburst decided to break open in a downpour, which earned an additional tip for him.

They stuffed themselves on pepperoni and Italian sausage and told funny stories about dogs they'd owned, steering clear of any more mention of Maggie.

A couple of hours later after Tate said goodnight, Josh braved the rain to go out to the back and bring in firewood. He built up a blaze in the fireplace as they listened to the steady rain coming down on their new roof. When the fire caught, Josh settled back, propped his feet up in Skye's lap to the sound of Bach coming from their iPod docking station.

But just as they got cozy, the landline rang. Skye got up to answer it with all the enthusiasm of a teenager waiting for that special person to finally call.

"Our first phone call in our new house," she said, excitement dripping from her voice as she snatched up the receiver from its cradle. "Hello?"

"Skye, I've got news."

Because Harry was the first person who'd called on the brand-new landline, Skye told him as much. But even on a

Saturday night the detective was in no mood for small talk. Harry's demeanor was all business.

"Dawson got a match to the bones you were sent. They've been identified through DNA and came back a match to Trisha Danes."

"The young soldier's wife? But the note said they belonged to a Janie or a Julie, he couldn't remember which?"

"He was obviously way off. He either planted a false lead early on or maybe he just couldn't recall her name after so much time had passed. Either way, now we know. Look, I've got to get back to the living room. My wife popped in a movie already and she's waiting for me to come back from the bathroom. I wanted to tell you as soon as Dawson gave me the word."

"You're in the bathroom? What movie?" Skye wanted to know.

"My wife says if I don't sit still for two hours to watch some chick flick with her called *The Big Wedding,* she's cuffing me to the chair or filing for divorce. I forget which. By the way, when did Robert De Niro start doing fluff stuff?"

"About two decades ago," Skye told him.

"Well, the wife tricked me with that one, didn't she? Promised me De Niro. I'm thinking gangster, or cop, definitely drama. And what I get is silly and stupid."

She got a kick out of Harry's take on the movie. "Such a critic. Go have fun with the wife. But hey, if you play your cards right that handcuffing thing could be a lot less expensive for you than a divorce."

Josh was laughing when she hung up. "I don't even want to picture detective Drummond and the missus like that."

"Me either."

"So Dawson identified the bones?"

"Yeah, but the guy's note said they belonged to a Janie or a Julie. Trisha doesn't sound like either one."

"But the DNA doesn't lie," Josh replied. "Maybe he didn't know Trisha's name."

"That's what Harry said. But it bugs me, is all. I've been searching for missing Janies and Julies all up and down the Pacific Northwest. I can't believe I fell for a false lead."

"It happens." He didn't like the troubled look he saw on her face. They'd been having a nice evening and now she seemed preoccupied. Harry's fault, he thought now. "Okay, do you plan to tell me what's bothering you for real?"

"Yesterday, after we got the keys to the house, I made contact with a former FBI profiler named Emmett Cannavale."

"The obvious question isn't why but why another one? You know the task force already talked to one."

"Yeah, but that one shut us out. I want to know how this guy thinks, Josh. The only way to do that is get our own guy on board. Cannavale has spent time with serial killers on death row. He might bring a different perspective to the case than what you and I do. I want to pick Cannavale's brain, get a bead on who we're dealing with."

"When?"

"I set up a meeting with him for next month. He'll be in town then for a seminar."

"A month is a long way off. I hope we nab him long before then. But let me know when and I'll be sure to clear my schedule to make it to the appointment." He picked up his beer and chugged it down, stared into the fire. "At least tonight we can go to bed knowing Trisha is no longer missing."

"Yeah. After such a long time, she'll finally get to go home to Charlotte."

The first night in their new house Skye spent tossing and turning. She listened as the old house creaked and cracked, settling in with disturbing pops and groans. Twice since going to bed she'd gotten up to recheck the locks on all the windows and doors, which was unlike her. It was now five-thirty and she hadn't closed her eyes for longer than sixty minutes straight.

She did her best to attribute her restlessness to the new house, a new environment. But try as she might, she knew that wasn't it. She'd hoped their new refuge would give them something else to think about other than the string of murders and autopsy photos she'd seen lately. She couldn't deny the circumstances were getting to her.

She made her way to the kitchen, a large rectangular space with white cabinets, slate-blue walls and contrasting wide-plank cypress floors.

While they hadn't unpacked every dish yet, they had taken care of getting the kitchen squared away for breakfast by bringing a few necessities from the loft. She went through a reusable grocery tote until she found the bag of coffee. Tearing into the beans, she breathed in their deep aroma. Even the smell woke her up a little. Once she'd located the grinder, she started the brew.

After the machine kicked in, she stepped to the window over the sink, watched the sun peek its way over the Cascades. Skye stared out past the porch to the yard, a generous stretch of lawn that even now was brilliant green. The fragrant glacier lily growing there drew her outside. She threw on a sweater and stepped onto the back porch.

She noticed the patch of wild lettuce had almost overtaken the chamomile. In the corner of the yard a bunny munched on pineapple weed. She decided she'd have to do something about the rabbits if she intended to plant a garden. Until this moment, she hadn't realized how much she wanted to live here surrounded by nature and gleaming water.

When she felt strong arms wrap around her waist, she leaned back into Josh's frame.

"What are you doing out here? It's so early. Couldn't you sleep?"

"Not with the excitement of being here."

He wasn't buying her excuse but for now, he chose not to pursue it. Instead, he kissed the back of her neck and could feel the tension emanating off her. Determined to do something about that, he slid her top off to the side, exposing a bare shoulder. His tongue moved along silky skin so smooth it reminded him of the softest rose petals.

He guided his hands over her breasts till he found a ripe nipple. When she began to relax, he coaxed her with deep kisses. "Come back to bed. We didn't get a chance to christen the brand-new mattress last night."

"We'll have to fix that." Turning her body further into his, she ran her fingers under the robe he wore, pressed hard into his space. Molten pleasure spread like the sun bursting out of the clouds.

"Oh yeah. We'll test the newness with hot and sweaty sex." He captured her hand, bundled her up in his arms. With the sea breeze at his back, as blue herons soared across the bay, he carried his wife into the bedroom.

Sunlight began to glimmer through the wispy drapes as he laid her on the bed, followed her down. Stringing kisses from neck to belly, they tangled and rolled. Flames speared into rocket flares, bright as red stars. They flew up, winging their way to the crimson heat together. Mated, their bodies kept the beat through a wild pace until that rhythm brought them into a glorious freefall.

Sated, after hours spent cocooned between the sheets, lack of food finally forced them to crawl out of their nest.

For their first breakfast in their new home, Skye dug out the fixings for chocolate brownie waffles and blackberry sauce. She'd squirrelled away the ingredients hoping to surprise Josh. It hadn't been easy. Lately, it was difficult to catch the man off-guard.

"How did you put this together in twenty minutes?"

"It's a miracle," she cracked. "It's simple really. I used stuff I bought at the store."

"Imagine what you could do with your own restaurant. Like Travis. I wonder if it runs in the family."

"Hmm, I never considered where I get my knack for cooking. My mom was a whiz in the kitchen so I just assumed... I guess it's in the genes."

Before putting another bite of tasty waffle in his mouth, he decided it was time to drop the bombshell he'd been keeping to himself. "I have a little surprise. I hope you like the idea. I bought that old rundown motel."

Her mouth fell open. "What? I fix waffles for you— that's my surprise—and you go and buy... You mean the one we saw the night we found Shawna Langley? That old motel?"

"The same. The first thing I get rid of is that tacky rooftop billboard."

"I can't believe you're really planning on turning that building into little apartments for the homeless."

"It'll take some work but I'll hire local, anyone who can swing a hammer I'll consider an asset."

"That's not a bad idea. Like Habitat for Humanity. They'll let anyone volunteer no matter their skill level." She looked at him then with a big smile. "What do you say about bringing in a new addition to the family? Let's go check out that shelter. It's time to get us a dog."

Debbie Rodriguez had worked for the Adopt-A-Best-Friend Shelter for almost five years. Being a kennel keeper wasn't a job that came with glamour or benefits. But since Debbie loved animals, dogs particularly, she got to spend her time doing what she loved. There was a lot of cleaning up poop, feeding and grooming, and taking her charges outside for a walk.

That was her favorite time of the workday when she could get outside, rain or shine, let the dogs out of their enclosures to run and play. The four acres of donated land where the shelter sat had plenty of space for just that purpose. The dogs got to stretch their legs and run around. It's one of the reasons Debbie stayed.

She had her favorites. All the workers did. For the last week, she'd had her eye on one particular little female, about four months old, that had come to them as a sick stray. A jogger had found the canine at the side of the road near starvation. That had been several weeks earlier. Since then, she'd kept track of the girl's progress.

The on-site vet hadn't spayed the silver-colored malamute mix yet because of her young age, but the doctor had brought the pup up to speed on all her shots.

That's why Debbie was confident the puppy was healthy enough for adoption. She couldn't wait to see the cute little thing find a forever home. If she didn't have three dogs already she'd snap this one up in a heartbeat.

As Debbie put her charges through their paces outside under the threat of rain, she watched the sweet expression on the pooch. The fluffy ball of fur made her laugh. For some reason, the little pup had gone off to one corner of the lawn all by herself. There, she seemed to delight in playing with what looked like an imaginary playmate.

The dog pranced and jumped, put her front paw in the air as if to touch her new bestie. The only problem with all of it was that there was no other dog within ten feet of her. The pooch was literally romping in a meadow with no one else around.

When Skye and Josh pulled into the lot they saw what looked like a private residence, stately and grand. They'd already learned from the Internet that the house and surrounding land had once belonged to Frederic and Eleanor Brandenhall. After the couple perished in a 1952

plane crash near Seattle, the city found out Frederic and Eleanor had arranged to leave their sizeable estate in a trust to help with the care and feeding of the island's animal population.

For more than fifty years Adopt-A-Best-Friend had stood as one of the best in the state. The place had a good reputation as a well-run facility that provided quality care on a full-time basis with a competent veterinarian and medical staff on call twenty-four-seven.

As soon as they crawled out of the Subaru, every dog in residence set up a din of barking. Whether it was a showy welcome or to get attention, the gesture worked. Skye went through the gate first and spotted Kiya.

She nudged Josh in the ribs to take a look. In a corner of the huge yard the wolf played with a baby, a silver-gray Alaskan malamute mix with big blue eyes and the largest feet she'd ever seen on a puppy.

Skye wasn't surprised when Kiya scrambled over and the pup followed. Though her wolf sat like a dignified lady at her feet, the cute little bundle of fluff did not—the idea of manners seemed foreign to the fuzzball. She jumped and danced around Skye's legs before bounding into her arms with a lick to the face.

"Aren't you a pretty girl? You're just a puppy, aren't you?"

"The vet says she's between four and five months old." From a few feet away Debbie went through the pup's story and how she'd been found.

Once the dog nuzzled Skye enough to win her over, the puppy moved on to Josh, making sure all her bases were covered.

Josh crouched down, ran his fingers through the girl's fur. "You're a roly-poly wad of energy is what you are. Does she have a name?"

"Not yet. That's up to her new owners. I think you've found a new best friend."

Skye met the woman's amused eyes. "Your sign says this is the place for it."

"It's true. We've hooked up quite a few serious relationships since I've been here. This one is a sweetheart. Got a name picked out yet?"

Skye looked at Josh.

"Your dog, your call."

"Our dog. But I think I'll call her Atka," Skye asserted as she rubbed the pup's ears. "She's Alaskan so it seems fitting."

"That's a beautiful name," Debbie decided. "Does it have special meaning for you? I've never heard of it before."

"It's Inuit. The name means guardian spirit." Skye scooped the dog up into her arms and said, "Come on, Atka, let's go fill out some paperwork so we can get you home."

They worked the rest of the day unpacking boxes while Atka settled in around them, most of the time underfoot. The curious pup sniffed and explored her new home, but didn't stay very far away from her owners for long.

That was okay by Skye. Standing in the kitchen perched on a stepladder, she stacked plates in the cabinet as Josh handed them up to her.

"Don't worry, we've almost got this room knocked out then we'll move to the living room, get that squared away."

Like a general with a plan of attack, she'd been working like a fiend to put the house right. Josh shouldn't have been surprised in her resolve—she put Mr. Clean to shame. "Do we get to break for lunch?"

She grinned. "I'll ignore that while you make sandwiches. If you're bored, I can finish up. Why not take the dog out?"

"Come on, Atka. Let's get some fresh air." He took the leash down off the peg as the dog made a mad dash for the door when it cracked open.

"We'll need to think about training and teaching her some manners," Josh said as he disappeared down the back steps.

What the hell, thought Skye. The sun peeking through the clouds drew her outside. She crawled down off the ladder, abandoned her mission and took off running after man and dog. She caught up to them near the little ornamental pond. As they cruised past the hydrangeas, Skye watched Atka snub her nose at the flowers and squat between the sweet fern and pepperbush.

"Good girl."

"She's that, and smart," Josh said, easily enough. "You know she has wolf blood running through her, don't you? I can sense it."

Skye nodded. "I figured Kiya picked her out special for us for a reason. It never occurred to me that she would."

"It should have. The protector is on guard twenty-four seven."

"The bond we witnessed this morning is unconditional love, loyalty."

"Look up ahead. Kiya's teaching her until Atka finds her own way."

She followed his eyes, saw her wolf walking along the shore ahead of them, sniffing sand and surf. Atka trotted off to the same stretch of beach.

They followed the dog, drifting to the strand, hand in hand. Skye toed off her shoes, breaking the contact between them long enough to reach down and roll up the bottoms of her pant legs. She waded into the current with arms spread wide, spinning and turning.

Josh cupped his hands in the ice cold water and heaved it in her direction.

Darting just out of reach, she laughed and splashed him.

He was about to set off in pursuit when the wolf growled low in her throat. It got their attention about the same time the puppy began to bark loudly and distinctively.

"They share an ability to pick up on good versus evil."

"That's handy since you may want to take a look at what Atka's carrying in her mouth," Josh observed.

Skye stared down at Atka. "Oh my God. That's a bone. Atka, where did you find this?" But as Skye knelt down, scrubbed the pup's ears, she looked up at Josh. A realization beat a drum inside her. "He knows where we live."

"Yeah. And he left that bone—looks like a small rib bone to me—right where the dog would find it. He wants us to know there isn't a place we can run or hide, anywhere that he won't be able to find us."

"He was here while we were at the shelter." Skye stood up, steeled her spine. "We aren't running."

"No. And we damned sure aren't hiding."

"And because of that, we'll be the ones who'll end him."

After Harry had come and gone and taken his report, he'd left with one more souvenir destined for the coroner's office.

"It's like a puzzle. He's sending us these pieces of his first victim. He doesn't know we've ID'd her. Now we need to solve the mystery of this guy, what makes him tick, the why, the where of his other victims. How many are still out there?"

"We keep circling back to the military base. That has to mean something."

After they made dinner, the light of the full moon drew them outside onto the back porch. As they stood there locked up in each other's embrace, Skye cozied up against Josh's body. She looked out over the sparkling sea and felt as though her life had tilted perfect.

The only problem was she didn't trust perfect. Never had.

She'd looked into the eyes of evil before and she'd won. Now, she would do it again—for Trisha, for Vanessa, for Maggie and for young Willa.

Chapter Twenty-Three

Monday morning Skye faced the day with a newfound outlook. Maybe it was because she'd brought along the newest addition to the Ander household or the fact that she'd spent a relaxing couple of days resting her brain. Whatever it was, today she was ready to tackle the case from a new angle, a new perspective. And she had help.

At the rate volunteers were showing up to offer assistance at the Artemis Foundation, she might have to get a bigger place soon.

In addition to Velma Gentry and Karen Houston donating their time for a few hours each day, she could now add Travis and Tate to the mix. The two men had offered to come in three times a week as had Vanessa Farrington's parents, John and Doris. The state senator and his wife had written a generous check to help out the Foundation with expenses. Since there was still a string of other women unaccounted for, they'd also given Skye permission to use the money wherever she thought it would do the most good. Skye decided to do just that.

Today, she had dangled a fat cash incentive in front of three hardworking programmers, only to have each one tell her the same thing. Keep the money for getting the word out or use it to post a reward for information.

Leo, Reggie, and Winston had agreed to do whatever they had to do to stay as long as necessary until they found the man responsible for their coworker's death. They had only one request—food and drink—provide them with a steady stream of soda, burgers or pizza and they'd be her slaves for as long as Skye needed them.

And she needed all the help she could get. It wasn't just Maggie Bennett on everyone's mind or Willa Dover or Vanessa. Selma Tolliver was still missing. Her family hadn't heard a word from her and no one had found a body. Without a body, there was still hope.

That's one of the reasons so many people had shown up today. It made for a crowded work space. And because the clock kept ticking, they'd all gotten an early start.

Travis and Tate had showed up at seven a.m. to go through a stack of case binders that she and Josh had put together. The two men had gone page by page, making any notations with sticky notes about anything that law enforcement should check out a second time.

At the other end of the table the programmers sat elbow to elbow as they banged on their keyboards. It was nine a.m. and they'd picked up exactly where they'd left off the night before.

So when Winston came across a property tax record in Pierce County belonging to a man named Jason Berkenshaw, it was a big deal.

"I've been searching for all property owners in the specific area and zip code you and Josh suggested I look at. There aren't that many. It's fairly rural. But this Berkenshaw owns forty acres near the area you guys searched the other day. It fits because it's less than a mile from the military base. And since tax records are public, I didn't even have to hack anything to get the info," Winston said, a bit embarrassed by how unbelievably simple the process had been.

"You might want to look at this," Leo added, pointing to his laptop screen. "Berkenshaw is also a member of law enforcement. He's been a member of ICE for thirteen years now."

"ICE?" Skye asked, placed her hands on her hips. "You're telling me this guy works in Immigration and

Customs Enforcement, that he's one of the good guys who tries to stop human trafficking?"

"And a long list of other duties," Winston added.

"ICE agents do everything cops do but in the name of national security," Reggie stated.

Skye met the eyes of each programmer. She didn't want to rock the boat or toss water on their fire but... "What makes you guys so certain about this Berkenshaw guy? What about him sends up red flags?"

But in the amount of time it took her to spout the questions, a flash of memory kicked in.

"Wait. Wait a minute. Jason Berkenshaw. I've heard that name. I know that name," Skye repeated. Then it came to her. "That's the MP who questioned Daniel Cree after Ellen Schreiber went missing. I'm almost sure of it. You were there, Josh. Wasn't that the name Harry mentioned?"

Caught up in the amount of data Winston and Reggie had been able to grab on their suspect, Josh raised his head, peered over the computer. "Yeah, I'm almost certain that was the name. Leo, do me a favor and look that up," he directed. "Look to see if Berkenshaw was ever an MP at Fort Lewis. If he was, then he's our connection to the military base."

Leo began hitting keys on his Mac. Five minutes later, he turned the screen around. "He's an army veteran, all right." Leo rattled off his length of time in the military, his rank, his pay grade and his assigned duties while stationed at the nearby base.

Skye scanned through the details herself. "Berkenshaw started out as an MP when he was just eighteen, but got drummed out after nine years for having violent outbursts. And get this, he was stationed there during the time Trisha Danes and Ellen Schreiber disappeared two months apart."

Over Skye's shoulder, Josh read Berkenshaw's dossier. "None of this explains how he got a job in ICE—unless he found time to work in a college degree."

Skye turned to Reggie. "Switch gears. Try finding personal stuff, like education, any colleges he attended. And see if he has a criminal record."

"Dig back to juvenile records," Josh suggested. "This guy may have kept his nose squeaky clean for years but it doesn't mean he started out that way."

Skye nodded. "Let's go on the premise Berkenshaw managed to get his degree while in the army. A four-year degree is a requirement to even be considered for ICE. They tend to want recruits to present a professional demeanor, similar to the FBI."

"So at some point when Homeland Security is at startup, when the agency needs quality applicants, Berkenshaw sees his chance to go from army MP to a coveted position in law enforcement," Josh said.

"He applies and is accepted. After all, they think they're hiring a veteran, a good guy. Recruiting from the military had to help the newly created branch of government fill out its roster quickly. They no doubt hired Berkenshaw thinking they were getting a disciplined army guy," Skye posed.

"But how could they think he was such a good guy when he'd been kicked out of the army?" Leo asked.

"Maybe Berkenshaw slipped through the cracks somehow," Skye speculated.

"Did you say Berkenshaw?" Travis asked standing in the doorway between the office area and the kitchen holding a steaming cup of coffee.

"Yep. You know him?" Skye asked. But before he could answer she rolled on, "I just realized his name is very similar to what Tracy Schreiber gave me the other day. Obviously she couldn't remember it exactly. All Tracy recalled was that it was odd-sounding and reminded her of Birkenstocks. The shoes. Tracy's words. Birkenstock. Berkenshaw. That can't be a fluke."

Travis moved closer. "Berkenshaw is also the name of a guy who showed up at the ranch, said he was in the market for a horse. The man spent almost five hours on my property, in my house, before he wrote me a check for a broodmare. And yeah, I remember him but not because the name sticks in your head. He brought the horse back the next day, told me he'd changed his mind."

"What? Do people usually do that?"

"Hell no. In all the years I've been raising horses, it's the first time it ever happened to me. This jerk gave me some runaround about how he'd changed his mind about the color of the mare. The color. Like he'd bought a pair of pants and now wanted to bring them back to the department store because the shade didn't match his eyes or something."

Skye couldn't help it, she grinned at her dad's take on the incident, but then wanted to know, "When was this?"

"I'd have to go through my records but off the top of my head, I'd say sometime last summer. August maybe."

Skye and Josh exchanged long stares. "If that's true, Berkenshaw's been planning this—the murders of people close to us—for quite a while. But the man waited. He was patient. Why? He then took his sweet time digging up the bones and shipping them off to me for Christmas—his gift to me."

"If this was Ellen's boyfriend, do you think he came out to the ranch for the sole purpose of getting my DNA and slipping it into Ellen's evidence box?" Travis asked.

Skye frowned, shook her head. "I don't think that's what happened. Berkenshaw had no way of knowing your DNA was on the scarf and not Daniel's. There are only two people in the world who knew the truth, you and Daniel. And Daniel's gone. Besides, Ellen's box was locked up inside Seattle PD. I doubt even an ICE agent has access to evidence without signing in and out. But I'll follow up with Harry on it just to cover all our bases."

She paced back and forth in the little bit of space she had to walk. She went over to the window, stared out at the skyline. "But you can bet Berkenshaw had nefarious intent when he showed up at The Painted Crow. He could have followed me out there on any number of occasions that I made the trip." The idea of that gave her chills from head to toe.

Josh chewed on his jaw, directed his comments to the trio of hackers. "I want you guys to find out everything you can on Berkenshaw, federal income tax records, any social media account, credit check, background, get anything you can on property he owns for an address."

With three programmers digging dirt on one guy, it didn't take them long to find a slew of information.

"Cross-checking Berkenshaw's name, he's in the Jeep Cherokee database of owners we put together and were in the process of going through. We just hadn't gotten to his entry yet," Leo clarified.

"This is him," Josh said to Skye. "This is our guy. I can feel it."

"I think you're right. Come on guys, what's taking so long? Get us an address."

Reggie spoke up, "I have three. One's the property Winston already mentioned near the base but there's no house there. According to the power company, his main residence is a three-bedroom home in Lakewood."

"That's less than ten miles from the base."

"What's the third?" Josh wanted to know.

"A cabin on Silcox Island."

"Bingo."

"That's where we should start."

Josh looked at Leo. "How remote is the cabin?"

"According to Google Earth, very."

"Print out the area map."

"Then that's a go."

Chapter Twenty-Four

Across town, Jason Berkenshaw wasn't spending his day off on Silcox Island. No, he'd gone into what he called, ready mode.

Today was a kind of crossroads for him. He looked in the mirror at himself, stared at the image. For what he had in mind he needed to wear his field uniform today. It provided him with that extra edge of authority. He'd always liked the look, the blue shirt, the tan trousers, the navy lightweight jacket with the white lettering on the back.

It was a damn sight better than wearing army green.

He'd hated every minute of his nine-year stint as an army MP. The higher ups were always on his ass about something he'd done wrong, some line he'd crossed, some rule he'd broken. A guy gets tired of that kind of shit at work, day in and day out, he recalled now.

So when Homeland Security had created the Immigration and Customs Enforcement branch, also known as ICE, and sent out a call for recruits, he'd filled out his application the same day he read the notice.

Some people didn't think he'd ever make it through the testing, the rigorous training, the discipline at the academy, especially the mental evaluations, certainly not the background check. But he fooled them all. He'd shown them he could reinvent himself.

He'd always loved his time working the streets. As he stuffed his M9 into his jacket, he picked up the keys to his Jeep and headed out the door to find his next quarry. Since he already knew who it would be, he wasn't worried. Glancing at his watch, he realized he needed to get his ass in gear. He had just enough time to make it into Seattle before school let out.

<> <> <> <>

When Skye and Josh left the Foundation, they jumped in Skye's car and headed south. Driving down the I-5 toward American Lake, they went over the plan.

"Do you really think this is the guy?"

"It's gotta be." Josh ticked off the points. "He owns an isolated cabin *and* property near the military base. He was Ellen Schreiber's boyfriend at the time of her murder *and* he was stationed at Fort Lewis as an MP. Let's not forget that Berkenshaw interviewed Daniel Cree and even painted a picture to his superiors that Daniel had not been truthful about where he was the night Ellen went missing. We have so many indicators we should probably call Harry."

"Harry deals in hard facts. Let's wait and make sure we can give him something concrete that he won't be able to diss."

To get to Silcox Island they had to take a pontoon boat for the three-mile trip across the lake. Even though the water was choppy, it didn't take long. Thanks to the groundwork they'd done at the Foundation, when they stepped off the boat, they already had an address. Sort of. From Google Earth they knew the general area where Berkenshaw's cabin was located. What they didn't know was the exact directions on how to get there.

Once they disembarked, surveying the rustic setting of Silcox, it was easy to see why most residents had gone without electricity until 1967. Charming little European cottages blended with sturdy log houses used as second homes.

Heavily wooded, the terrain was intimidating. But not as much as the locals. Asking directions to the cabin got them blank stares along with several mind-your-own-business looks.

It soon became clear the little town was not stranger-friendly.

They finally found a man at the post office willing to tell them how to reach the place. The small house turned out to be more like a hut. There was no one home at the small eight-hundred-square-foot getaway. But Skye and Josh circled the perimeter anyway. It looked like Berkenshaw used the place mostly for a place to stash his fishing gear and hunting rifles, of which there were many.

It didn't go unnoticed that his nearest neighbor had to be a good half-mile down the road, providing him with a secluded spot to do whatever he wanted.

But despite the isolation, Skye commented, "This isn't what I expected. It looks more like a quaint retreat than a torture chamber used for murder."

"Looks can be deceiving."

When Josh removed a pick from his jacket pocket, Skye stared at him. "What are you doing?"

"What does it look like? I'm picking the lock."

"Another reason we didn't call Harry," Skye reasoned.

"Yeah, I know. But I can't very well kick the door in. What if he should come back? We don't want to let him know we've been here or that we're on to him."

Josh stuck the little wrench into the keyhole and when the tumbler clicked, they stepped inside.

If they were expecting blood and gore or at least traces of it, they were disappointed. What they found instead was a cabin that smelled like fish. The place was not only devoid of any signs of physical violence but there were no pictures on the walls. There were no personal effects, or possessions of any kind cluttering up space. Other than tacky, second-hand furniture, it sat empty. There was nothing there that could tell them who or what Jason Berkenshaw was all about.

Since there was no sign of carnage anywhere, no smell of death, and no signs that it had ever touched the four walls, they left the place as they'd found it.

Like every other fourteen-year-old at Hastings Middle School, Zoe heard the freedom bell ring at three-fifteen. She scooted out of last-period geography, ran to her locker, switched out her math book for her English text, and stuffed a copy of *Coraline* down into her already too-heavy backpack.

When her best friend, Molly, ran up to her in a breathless huff, Zoe prepared for the drama. Molly was always about the over-the-top rehashing of an ordinary event.

"Do you know what that stuck-up Suzie Meyers told Merry Ann Higginbotham about me?"

"What?"

"Suzie said I liked Tristan. You know that's not true. Tristan is one of those really snotty basketball players."

"I thought you liked Tristan and wanted him to ask you to the spring dance?" Zoe asked.

"What does that have to do with Suzie Meyers sticking her big fat nose into how I feel about Tristan?"

From there, Zoe gave up and listened to her friend. She didn't have much choice in the matter since she didn't seem to be able to ditch Molly or get her classmate to change the subject.

By the time the two girls reached the side door where the buses lined up, Molly still hadn't convinced Zoe that Tristan was such a bad guy. The girls kept up their steady stream of I-don't-really-like-Tristan chatter until Zoe tried, once again, to change the subject. "Are you going to the Spring Dance next month?"

"Well, sure."

"Then why don't you come over to Lena's house so we can get ready and go together?" Just as Zoe had hoped, that did the trick. Molly went into describing the dress she'd bought for the occasion.

"I was hoping Tristan would ask me to the dance."

Zoe sighed, rolled her eyes, knowing Molly was more than predictable.

"Come on, Molly, we have to hurry or we'll miss the bus." Zoe pushed open one of the heavy double doors and stepped out into another dull gray afternoon. Zoe bounded down the steps with Molly beside her until a man approached her. He was dressed in a uniform, wearing a pair of polarized Oakley sunglasses over his eyes. He flashed his badge at both teens, but directed his question to Zoe. "Are you Zoe Hollister?"

Zoe swallowed hard. She tried to remember if old Mrs. Faraday was so mean that the librarian would rat her out to a cop for not returning her copy of *A Separate Peace* on time. "Yes, I'm Zoe Hollister."

"Good. Is Lena Bowers your foster mother? "

"Sure, Lena's my foster mom. Is she okay?"

"I'm sorry to have to tell you this but Mrs. Bowers has been in a car accident. If you'll come with me, I'll take you to see her in the hospital."

⚓ ⚓ ⚓ ⚓

Skye and Josh left Silcox disheartened and moved on to Berkenshaw's main home in Lakewood. But they found no one there either. The little three-bedroom house appeared tidy and well maintained but like the cabin seemed completely without a personality.

By early afternoon, they realized the trip had been a complete waste of time. As they passed out of the city limits heading toward the I-5, they decided to try, once again, to locate the third property near the base.

"But there's no house there."

"The info's wrong. It has to be. Somewhere on this piece of property is where he takes his victims, his death house," Skye uttered in disgust. About that time, her cell phone dinged. She looked down, saw it was Leo.

"Something weird I thought you should know about."

"It seems to be the day for it. What happened?"

"Some guy left a bizarre message for you on the Foundation's website. The IP address tracks back to the Seattle Public Library downtown. You might want to take a look at it when you get a minute."

"Leo, you know I'm in the car right now, getting ready to check Berkenshaw's property near the army base. You'll have to read it to me."

"Okay, here goes. It says, 'Hey Skye, I promise this one's gonna hurt.' That's exactly word for word what it says."

The hairs on the back of Skye's neck stood up as she had Leo repeat it. When her phone rang signaling another call was coming in, she told Leo she'd call him back. Skye was surprised to see Lena's number on the display.

Sliding the bar across to answer, Skye discovered Lena frantic with hysteria. The words flowed out of the worried foster mom in one long breathless chain. "Molly Connelly, Zoe's best friend, saw a policeman take Zoe away. He had on a uniform and got her into his Jeep Cherokee this afternoon after school by telling her I had been in an accident. It's an obvious lie. He took off with her, Skye. She's gone. Zoe's gone."

"Okay. Okay. Calm down. We're on it, Lena. Josh and I are pretty sure we know where he's taking her. We're headed there now. Don't worry. I'll get her back."

But Josh was less certain. "The bastard took Zoe and you let Lena think we have a destination in mind. You know we don't. We only have the general vicinity and no specifics."

"Then we'll find specifics. I guess we know now why he wasn't at home or at his fishing cabin. He was kidnapping Zoe."

"Let's think about this rationally. He's in a vehicle we already know the description of. He can't get to his remote cabin without taking a boat. We either head back to Silcox Island or we try to find the property near the base. It's your call."

"Neither one of us picked up on anything at the cabin. But we both get the willies every time we get near the army base. My gut's telling me there's something about the property there."

"Then that's where we go. We do have an advantage."

"What's that?"

"We already did a trial run of this area before and know where it isn't."

Josh took out his portable GPS. "We're six minutes from the base. If the plan is to avoid where we've already looked, then we should approach from the north. Don't get on the 5. There's a back way in with an asphalt parking lot. It's about the only place to leave the car."

"Okay. But after that, we head deeper into the woods."

They maneuvered past traffic trying to get on the I-5 corridor and took a left heading east. The farther they went the more the landscape changed—less shopping and more of a rustic feel. To get to the paved parking lot, Skye followed Josh's directives from the GPS. That's when they spotted a Jeep Cherokee ahead of them. It was hurtling down the two-lane road at a high rate of speed.

Behind the wheel, Skye could make out two people in the car. About that time the driver spotted them. The Jeep took another left down a bumpy dirt road and disappeared from her line of sight.

Chapter Twenty-Five

Thunder rumbled in the distance. Thick drops of rain began to splat the windshield as Skye pulled up to the Jeep Cherokee parked on the side of the road. The driver's door stood open as though the occupants had fled in a hurry.

"He's ditched the car!" Skye shouted.

But Josh had already thrown open his door before she could come to a full stop. Jumping out, he began running, trying to pick up where the guy had taken Zoe.

All of a sudden, she could see Kiya sprinting ahead in the distance.

Shoving the gearshift into Park, she scrambled out of the car and took off after them doing her best to keep up.

She finally caught up with Kiya when the wolf stopped at a dry creek bed to sniff at the overgrown trail. The path forked left or right.

When Kiya started to head one way, abandoning the other path altogether, Skye suggested, "Maybe we should split up. That way we'll cover more ground."

"We stay together," Josh insisted.

"Josh, our priority right now is finding Zoe. Even though I only saw two people in the Jeep, you know as well as I do we might be dealing with two killers. Someone helped Jason Berkenshaw dump Willa's body in the park. You said so yourself. I'll take Kiya with me to the right. You follow your own nose to the left."

Josh still thought the idea of splitting up was a bad one, but there was no time to argue with her since Skye didn't wait around for agreement. She took off with Kiya in the lead.

On her own now, Skye looked up at the drizzling clouds, spotted a hawk floating overhead with a crow as part of its flock. She didn't like being separated from Josh. But it was good to know she was far from alone.

At a bend in the trail Kiya took a dog leg turn farther east into the forest of evergreens and aspen. They followed the ridgeline toward the military base, zigzagging at times to avoid boulders or stumps blocking the way.

She followed Kiya into a small clearing where horsetail and thistle were thriving in bunches. Skye heard gravel crunch behind her before Kiya snarled in warning.

But it was too late.

Berkenshaw was already on her from behind. She only had time to throw an elbow to his ribcage. But his momentum knocked Skye back a few steps. Off balance, she managed to block his first blow. There wasn't time to grab for the knife in her boot, only time to gather herself before he landed his next punch to her shoulder.

Instincts took over. She pivoted and swung her leg out. With a hard kick she aimed for his solar plexus and watched as the wind sailed out of him. It caused Berkenshaw to double over. He was forced to step back to get his breath.

Skye took advantage of his hesitation to slide out the knife from her boot. Anticipating his next move, she readied herself for what came next. Eyeing the fury on his face she knew it would be an all-out attack. When he launched himself with all the ferocity of a lion pouncing on his lesser prey, Skye landed the heel of her boot on his knee cap. She followed that by slashing her knife across his arm, causing Berkenshaw to stumble backward.

When she spotted Zoe out of the corner of her eye, Skye yelled, "Get out of here. Head back to the road. That way." Skye pointed to the west. "Run straight that way. The minute you get inside the car, lock the doors."

"But I don't want to leave you."

"I said go. Do what I say! Now!"

By that time, Berkenshaw had righted himself, but was still having trouble evening out his breathing. Skye caught a blur of movement. Berkenshaw tried to take something out of his jacket. She drove her boot into his wrist, knocking a Beretta M9 pistol out of his hand. The force of the blow had Berkenshaw back on his heels as Skye kicked the weapon into the sandy underbrush.

The move gave her time to assess Jason Berkenshaw. He had brown hair, green eyes and stood about five-eleven. But there was something about those cool green eyes that said no one was home.

"Well, come on, you big wimp, haven't you ever had a female fight back before?" Skye roared in challenge.

"Bitch," he spat out. "You'll pay for this. I knew I should've taken you down first."

"Not as smart as you thought you were, huh? You're such a dumb shit. You should've started with me. But you made a huge mistake. Trouble is I think you were scared, didn't think you could take me."

As she hoped, her insult brought him closer. Skye saw the hatred in his icy eyes as well as the violent way they reacted. He was so mad his green orbs darted about, unfocused.

"You killed your girlfriend, Ellen Schreiber, planted false evidence to frame my father for it when you were an MP."

"What the hell are you talking about? You're crazy. I don't know any Ellen Schreiber."

"Whatever you say." Skye figured she needed one more slam to push him over the edge. "After all the women you've killed, it's a female who has outsmarted you. That's got to chap your butt." Skye waited a beat for him to get within arm's reach.

"Fuck you," he shouted and spat in her face.

With the knife in her right hand, she jabbed him in the ribs, flicked her wrist ninety degrees, turning the blade for greater damage. With the heel of her left hand, she sent an uppercut to his nose. Although he staggered back for several seconds, the blow didn't take him down.

Skye swung her leg out in an arc, angled, and sent her boot into his face. But he still didn't go down. Instead, he decided to charge. Like a bull running toward a matador's cape, he tackled her and brought her to the ground.

Her back hit first with a thud. Berkenshaw jumped on her, doing his best to straddle her. Her sheer grit refused to let him take control. But with the blood oozing from his wounds it was enough to soak her gloves causing her to lose her solid grip on the knife. It slipped out of her grasp, landed somewhere next to them in the dirt.

She bucked hard and to the left, causing Berkenshaw to lose his balance and tip over. Momentum had her rolling until she prevailed on top.

From her sitting position, she brought her knee up, jammed it into his crotch. From a standing position with full thrust, the pain in his balls would've been a lot worse. But she had to settle for what she could dish out. That's why she didn't let up. With gloved fists, she pounded him and sent punch after punch to his belly, his face, his throat.

She spotted the knife about the same time he did. They grappled for it, but Skye got to it first. Wrapping her fist around the handle, they fought for control. While he pushed it away, she tried to angle it back toward his torso.

Gripping the handle as tight as she could, she brought it up, inches off the dirt. Strength to strength, she forced the blade until it hovered over his midsection. With a final burst of energy, she managed to cut a ribbon across his chest.

When he screamed out in pain, she changed directions, bringing the edge diagonally in a swath the other way. She raised the knife to stab him in the heart.

And then everything went black.

Josh might not have agreed with splitting up, but he couldn't deny there was someone behind him, dogging him, and circling back. He smelled blood right before he heard Kiya's mournful wail. He changed course and followed the abject moaning through a thick scrub of sagebrush and sedge.

Since he recognized what that sound meant, he knew Skye was in trouble. As soon as he reached a clear route, he took off running.

The minute he got to the little glade, he saw his wife lying on the ground, an open wound to the back of her head. Blood poured from the gash.

The silver wolf stood over her charge, her front paws resting on Skye's chest. Josh watched as Kiya licked the face of the woman he loved—and shimmered into an unconscious Skye.

Chapter Twenty-Six

Skye heard wheezing and someone gasping for air. She didn't realize she was the one having trouble breathing until she flicked open her eyes. She tried to focus. Unable to speak, she tried to block out the white bright light that wanted to blind her. As her eyes cleared, she saw two of Josh crouching above her. She watched as tears rolled down both his faces. Maybe it was the raging pain in her head that had her seeing double.

When the image finally merged together as one, everything inside her seared with heat. She felt a flash of energy as it spread throughout her body, organ to organ, limb to limb. Every nerve in her tingled.

She tried to sit up, swayed a little. "What happened to Berkenshaw?"

"You got the bastard."

"He's dead?"

"A knife buried up to its hilt through his heart generally does the trick every time. That's my girl."

Her head still buzzed with a dull pain. "Is Zoe all right?"

"I don't know. We need to find her."

"Go." She pushed at his chest. "I told her to head back to the car. You have to see if she's there."

"I'm not leaving you here alone, Skye."

"There's another killer here, Josh. Did you get the other one?"

"There's no denying somebody was here to bash your skull in."

"It felt like they used a baseball bat. You have to go find Zoe. I don't know how long I was unconscious."

"Not long."

"But by now, he could already have her. Go!"

"Come on, get up and go with me. Can you stand?" When she nodded, he pulled her to her feet even though she was far from steady or a hundred-percent. "We'll both go find her. Do you think you can walk?"

About that time, her eyes tracked to the spot where Kiya lay, spent. There, under a rocky mountain maple, with golden paintbrush all around, the silver wolf looked near death.

Skye's heart simply broke. She went over and kneeled to where Kiya struggled for breath. As the wolf's violet eyes fluttered closed, Skye ran a hand through the thick coat of silver fur. Her fingers gripped the medicine bag around her neck. She began to chant, asking for help from the Great Spirit.

"Fight like I fought and you'll be okay. You have to fight, Kiya. Don't die on me. Don't let go. You will not die."

Josh went down on one knee, stroked Kiya's head. "The merge took everything out of your wolf, Skye. Kiya's weak just as she was before when she did the same for me. But she'll be okay. You know she'll be okay. All she needs now is time to heal."

A sob caught in her throat. "I'll be back, Kiya, I have to go make sure Zoe's okay. You understand that, right?" When the wolf lifted her head to howl, Skye got to her feet, still wobbly.

"Come on, we need to go find Zoe." Josh grabbed Skye's hand, leading her through the underbrush, back through the creek bed.

Having been through the transformation himself, Josh knew about how long it would take for her to start feeling revitalized. It wasn't until half an hour later that he could tell that Skye began to gain her strength back twofold. He recognized the moment it happened. He saw a light come into her eyes—the aura around her brightened. Instead of sluggish steps, her pace quickened in the way she maneuvered around the vegetation.

As they made their way back to the road where they'd left the car, the two said nothing. It took them twenty minutes to reach the Subaru and when they did, they found it empty.

"Damn it! Zoe! Zoe!" Skye shouted as she hit the hood with her hand out of frustration. The force put a dent in the metal. In her dismay, Skye didn't even notice to what degree her strength had increased. "Maybe she's hiding. Zoe! Come on, Zoe! It's us. Where are you?"

When she started to storm off to search in what Josh termed was the wrong direction, he took her hand. "You're still disoriented. Remember things have changed. Use your instincts, Skye."

She leaned back on the vehicle, closed her eyes, thought of her protectors, the wolf, the hawk, the crow. Channeling those positive forces into a ball of light, she took several deep breaths and let her new abilities take over.

"Zoe's in complete darkness, a room without windows. Wherever it is, it's not that far away. We have to hurry though. Let's move out."

They headed east, talking as they went.

"Feeling better?"

"I would if Zoe had been where she was supposed to be. I never should've told her to go back."

"Not gonna work, Skye. Even if you had done that and Zoe had stayed planted where she was, the other guy would've come along and likely snatched her after taking you out."

"Okay. True."

"So how do you feel?"

"Energetic. Recharged. Like I could scramble up Mount Rainier in one climb. Now I know how you must've felt after it happened to you." She sighed. "But poor Kiya."

"Even though we talked about two killers, we never actually ran with it."

"It's one thing to theorize he had help in disposing of Willa and quite another to affirm he used another person. But you won't convince me Berkenshaw started out relying on a partner," Skye interjected. "He was a loner back then. I'm certain of it."

"I think that's true. He killed Trisha Danes and Ellen Schreiber, by himself without the help of anyone else. But Vanessa Farrington, Maggie Bennett, Willa Dover, Selma Tolliver, and God knows how many others, he had an accomplice, which means he had to take his time finding the right recruit."

"Working in tandem? It's not unheard of. There were the speed freak killers, Shermantine and Herzog, in California, and then Ng and Lake who worked together holding their victims captive for long periods of time. Then there was the pair of lovers, Coleman and Brown, who terrorized the Midwest in the eighties. And let's not forget the Hillside Stranglers who turned out to be cousins. Angelo Buono and Kenneth Bianchi worked together for three years, to name a few. I could go on but you get the picture. So it certainly isn't the first time."

He shouldn't have been surprised at the way she could rattle off a string of sick minds at the drop of a hat, and yet, he was. "You've done your research."

"I'm always doing research into the mind of savage killers. So who do you think we're dealing with here, Josh? Berkenshaw's son? His brother? A cousin? A BFF?"

Josh cocked a brow. "Whoever it is has lost their other half. That leaves them vulnerable. When we split up back there, I felt someone following me. I was pissed off at you for separating until I heard footsteps behind me. Before I could do anything about it, I heard Kiya howl and knew you were in trouble."

"You know what we have to do."

"Yeah, we have to do whatever it takes to locate the lair."

⋞⋟ ⋞⋟ ⋞⋟ ⋞⋟

As they plodded up another incline and down a ravine, they went over what they knew.

"We know the location is close to the base. We know there has to be a building around here somewhere that houses his dungeon."

"What about backtracking to that old train station? Maybe we missed something there," Skye wondered. "But you didn't pick up on anything when we were there last time."

"As you'll find out on your own, it isn't an exact science," Josh explained.

Suddenly she stopped walking. "The floorboards? The train station had a lopsided floor with space underneath. Could there have been—?"

"No. The train station is due west from here. We keep heading toward the military base."

"Right."

They slogged through a muddy marshland just as the sun peeked out behind another layer of pesky clouds. "It'll be dark soon," Skye noted.

"Don't worry. You should be able to see just fine with your new super powers."

Skye found that funny. "Really? I guess it'll be an excellent test. I hope Kiya is okay. Maybe we should've brought Atka."

Josh grinned imagining the pup's playful energy out here in the woods and her tendency to wander around curious about everything. "Atka would be all over this place. She needs seasoning before we turn her loose on the likes of Berkenshaw. And Kiya's slow recovery is the price of her valor. Our wolf will be fine, just as she was after giving me her bloodline. Now, she's given it to you. I hate to suggest this, but try to put Kiya out of your mind for now. Focus on the hunt, on Zoe. Keep your mind on the goal. You sure you're feeling okay? You aren't a hundred percent yet, are you?"

"A little fuzz-brained still but I'll be fine. Stop worrying about me."

Up ahead, an open field came into view, a meadow laden with blue-eyed grass and golden lady's slipper. They spotted a female hiker heading toward them from the opposite direction, the first person they'd encountered besides Berkenshaw. As the woman drew closer, in a friendly gesture, she sent them a casual wave of her hand as backpackers often do when they meet others on the trail.

After the hiker had passed them heading in the opposite direction, Josh looked over his shoulder, muttered, "That's strange. She's the first sign of life we've seen since tramping all over this place from the road in and back again."

"Except for Berkenshaw."

"She seemed surprised to see us, especially you," Josh decided.

"She did, didn't she?"

They both stared at each other until all at once they came to the same conclusion. "It's her!"

Turning on their heels, they took off running. The minute they did, the woman looked over her shoulder and began to sprint to reach the thicket of trees.

But Josh and Skye ran her down in a dozen long strides.

Out of breath, the hiker finally pulled up short of the woods. "Hey, what gives? If you plan to rob me, you've picked the wrong person. I don't have any money."

"Maybe you could tell us why you're out here in such an out-of-the-way spot. Alone."

"I don't know what you mean. I'm backpacking, found myself off the main trail in this place. Besides, two people start chasing me, I start trying to get away from them."

About that time, Skye noticed a series of blood droplets on the woman's sleeve. The spots seemed perfect for castoff from whatever the woman had used to bash Skye's skull in earlier. "Where did you ditch the baseball bat you hit me with?" Skye asked.

The woman's eyes went on guard. "I don't know what you're talking about. You guys are talking crazy."

About that time, Josh caught Skye staring at the woman's jacket and followed her eyes to the red drops. "Where'd you get the blood?"

"Huh?" The hiker looked down at her hoodie. "Oh that. I had a nose bleed earlier."

"Where's Zoe?" Skye asked matter-of-factly.

"Who? I don't know a Zoe. Ah, so you're out here looking for someone? This area's pretty secluded. If they got lost you may never find them."

"Don't count on it," Skye shot back. "We were just about to call the cops. I thought you said you wandered from the main trail, just happened upon the area. You talk as though you know it well. Where were you two hours ago?"

"Two hours?" The woman looked at her watch. "Not that it's any of your business but I was over by the creek."

"Cut the crap," Skye snapped. "Zoe isn't lost. A serial killer by the name of Jason Berkenshaw abducted her. I think you know where she is because you put her there. So I'll ask this one more time. Where is Zoe?"

This time the woman's calm, pretend demeanor changed. She became agitated. When she tried to reach inside her pocket, Skye pushed her back a step. "You're the one who hit me. Helluva swing you have there. What did you do with the bat? How long did you work with…let me guess…your boyfriend? Who are you exactly?"

In answer, the woman spat out, "Jason was my husband! And you killed him, you bitch! You were supposed to die back there. Why didn't you?"

Josh grabbed her arm right before she could lunge at Skye. He tightened his grip, put pressure on the woman's shoulder, making sure she calmed down. "Where's Zoe?"

Skye took the opening, began to go through the woman's pockets. When she found a Beretta that matched the one she'd knocked out of Berkenshaw's hand during the fight, she knew this was the killer's accomplice. The Washington State driver's license confirmed it.

"What do we have here? Looks like her name's Adela Berkenshaw. She's five-six, auburn hair, with deep brown eyes and this says she was forty years old on her last birthday." Skye sized Adela up. "Well, Mrs. Berkenshaw, I hope you don't have kids running around anywhere because you're going away for a long time. Now tell us where Zoe is."

Adela threw her head back and laughed. "You'll never find the little bitch. She'll starve to death before you guys even stumble upon anything. Jason and I have been in this area for years. We know it like the back of our hand. We've been at this for a long time. And we're good at what we do."

Josh took out his cell phone, dialed Harry. He went into a lengthy spiel about their suspect before giving him the bad news. "Berkenshaw's dead. But Jason had a wife who helped him." Josh listed all the particulars from Adela's driver's license before adding, "No, she won't be going anywhere, at least not until you guys get here. We still haven't found Zoe. So don't drag your ass taking the long way around."

With that, Josh gave him directions to their location while Skye kept needling and poking at Adela.

"You know, Jason had a girlfriend in the nineties who looked a lot like you."

"He did not."

"Oh yeah, he did. She ended up dead, murdered. Her name was Ellen Schreiber." Skye picked up a strand of Adele's hair. "Is this reddish color your natural shade or did you tint it—for Jason. Did he ask you to dye it this color?" By the look on Adela's face, Skye determined she'd hit a nerve. "Ellen's hair was gorgeous and natural. Yours isn't. Good ol' Jason probably talked you into dyeing yours to match Ellen's. He had a hard time letting Ellen go—a really hard time. That is, until he put a knife through her heart—sorta like I did his."

"Jason loved me. You don't know who you're messing with, little girl, I'll rip your heart out."

"I see that," Skye drawled, her tone calm as glass. "Where were you headed when you saw us? You were coming from deep in the woods, right, Adela?"

"Go to hell."

"You first." Skye took out her cell phone, scrolled through her contact list until she found the one belonging to her dad. "I need to put out a call to arms," Skye announced as she punched in the number. "We don't have a lot of time to waste."

As soon as Travis answered the phone back at the Foundation, Skye told him, "Round up the troops, anyone who can help, we need volunteers to search for Zoe." She gave him the specifics as she heard the wop wop wop of a chopper overhead.

Looking up, she spotted a helicopter circling them with the Pierce County logo on the side. "Looks like your ride is here, Adela. You be sure to have a great day."

Skye walked off to meet Harry at the Huey. After bringing him up to speed on Adela, she directed him to where they'd left Jason's body.

Once a sheriff's deputy slapped the cuffs on Adela, Josh and Skye decided to backtrack to where they'd first encountered the woman in the clearing. They didn't wait around for Harry or the search team. With darkness approaching, every minute counted.

Stepping through bunchberry and patches of bog rosemary, they searched for any disruption in the earth, any part of ground that looked as though it had been recently turned.

After trekking farther into lush backwoods, they fought the scrubland and the dense undergrowth, so thick it was like a jungle in some places. "We should've brought a machete to hack through this stuff," Skye grumbled when her hair got caught on a spray of brambles.

"Two of them," Josh added as he helped untangle the mass of strands from the bush. "No wonder we couldn't find this place."

While shafts of remaining daylight illuminated the way, they shuffled down into a gully filled with dead vines surrounding a surplus of old engine parts.

"Now we're talking," Josh stated. "This has a military feel to it. We're close."

They almost missed the rusted-out Quonset hut, complete with a corroded door, because it was overgrown with head-high weeds. Cordgrass and the shorter dagger-leaf rush guarded the area around it. Sitka spruce and noble fir grew in spotty patches as though someone had cut down a grove of trees to stake their claim.

Discarded metal ammo boxes had been used as a tiny porch and steps. But now, the containers were scattered about, littering the area. They moved several of the crates out of the way so they could peep inside. Decades of neglect had left it in disrepair. There was nothing much left except the shell. The back of the place had been gutted. But what they found there was another solid row of vegetation growing in overrun hedges.

"I'll hold it back for you to go through first," Skye offered as she picked up several prickly climbing plants. "How's that?"

"Look, there." Josh pointed to a carved-out section of hillside. Near the bottom of the grade hidden almost out of view was the entrance to the Berkenshaws' concrete bunker—an intimidating door built from steel.

"They spent a lot of time disguising the entryway," Skye decided as she took in the stack of evergreen branches tied together with a camouflage tarp across the top. About that time she looked up, spotted the crow and the hawk circling overhead. "No one could pick this out from the air. See how it blends into the surrounding hillside?"

Josh nodded. "It blends in perfectly with the topography."

He took one look at the heavy portal and uttered, "This door is from a shipping container. Looks like they used whatever supplies they could scavenge."

Eyeing the multiple locks used to deter trespassers from breaching the security, Skye whistled through her teeth. "This is gonna take some muscle."

She watched Josh try to force the door open with sheer strength and shook her head at his first effort. "You barely loosened that. How about we put our backs into it together?"

"Be careful you don't hurt yourself. This thing is massive."

Together they pulled on the metal until they were able to dislodge it from its hinges. Maneuvering it free, inch by inch they crawled through the opening.

There were steps leading down further underground. Once inside, it was obvious the main room had once been used as an old ammunition bunker. But in converting the narrow, rectangular space, the Berkenshaws had put their own personal touches to it. For one, the four walls reeked with the smell of urine and feces and death.

"This is where it all happened. No wonder this place gave us the creeps," Skye muttered as she scanned what was nothing more than a glorified cave. A crudely built bedframe held a dirty, ugly-looking mattress. But Zoe wasn't in it.

"Zoe!" Skye yelled. "Where are you, Zoe?" She tilted her head to listen, but heard nothing but a vaulted echo. "Josh."

"Not picking up anything yet."

Her eyes landed on a wooden bench, an altar that held all kinds of trinkets and keepsakes, earrings and necklaces, a few small handbags. "Look at all the trophies he kept. We might be able to use this stuff to solve a few missing person cases. What kind of sadistic people would purposely create something like this?"

"Berkenshaws. Bundys. Ridgways. Dahmers."

As they got deeper into the hollowed-out shell, Skye noted one section in the back had been cordoned off with steel reinforced rods to create a cage-like area. Several iron bolts and shackles had been hammered into the wall and floor. Heavy chains were attached. Filth covered the base. But there was no Zoe.

"It just keeps getting more disturbing with each step we take," Skye noted.

Josh came to a section where the concrete ran out. He stepped onto a hard-packed dirt floor. Beyond it, he spotted a three-foot open chasm. It became clear they might have to dig. "There's a drop-off here," he cautioned. "Watch your step."

At one time someone had chiseled out a steep set of stairs, either Berkenshaw or the military. Either one had aimed for keeping secrets here. "Let me go down first. It might be booby-trapped."

"It's like a crypt," Skye decided as she tried to make out the black pit Josh had agreed to explore first.

Josh took the lead and descended into an area without a flicker of light anywhere. It could only be described as what hell must look like.

His wolf's vision kicked in.

He spotted Zoe in a corner of the dungeon lying on a cot. She was fully clothed but her feet and wrists were manacled to a rusted restraint bolted into the cinder block wall, a filthy rag stuffed in her mouth. Dried tears had stained her cheeks. Her black hair was a mess of tangles.

"It's okay, Zoe. Don't be scared. It's me, Josh. Skye is right behind me."

At the sound of another voice in the blackness, Zoe tried to scream, but it came out muffled and weak.

Without hesitating any longer, he went over to her, gently removed the dirty cloth from between her teeth so she could talk.

"Is…it…really…you?" Zoe asked in between hitches in her breathing.

Knowing there was no way she could see him in the darkness, he waited a beat until Skye came up beside him, waited for Zoe to recognize Skye's voice.

"Zoe, we're getting those cuffs off your wrists," Skye pledged as she lightly touched the girl's jean-clad leg. She reached up and ripped the bolts out of the wall, pried the handcuffs off the girl's flesh.

Zoe flung herself in Skye's direction. "I was so scared. I was so sure I was going to die."

As Skye caught the girl up in her arms, she didn't want to admit she had been afraid of that too. "I know you were. But it's over now. We're getting you out of this hellhole."

Turning to Josh, Skye whispered, "The search party would never have found this place, not without a lot of luck."

He took out his phone. "Then I'd better give them detailed directions."

Together they marched Zoe out into the fresh air, took a seat on one of the old metal ammo boxes. By that time, the sun had gone down. Nightfall rallied around them, unsettling and silent.

"What is this awful place," Zoe wanted to know.

"A place that fourteen-year-olds should never have to see," Skye murmured softly. Even though Berkenshaw was dead and his wife was in custody, Skye didn't think she could ever forgive either one for exposing Zoe to this type of depravity at such a young age.

"Should we wait for the volunteers to catch up or use our night vision to get us out of here?" Josh asked.

"I vote we leave this place."

But about that time they heard voices in the distance. Skye recognized Harry's tone, followed by Travis's speech.

"We're over here," Josh shouted.

"Got you pinpointed," Travis yelled back. "The Foundation's group of volunteers is in the process of setting up floodlights around the perimeter so Zoe won't have to deal with the dark any longer than she has to."

"I love these people," Skye gushed in delight, her arms still wrapped around Zoe. The two sat where they were and watched in awe as the lights came on, one by dazzling one, washing the woods in a wave of brightness.

But even with the burst of illumination, this part of the woods still had a spooky feel to it in the dark. Tall trees, long shadows, twigs snapping made for an eerie backdrop.

In the dimness, Skye spotted Harry heading their way, noticed the slump of his shoulders, as if the cop dreaded what he had to do, what he had to ask the young teen, what he had to put Zoe through.

Knowing there were questions that needed answers, she leaned in, whispered in Zoe's ear to prepare her. "See that line of volunteers over there? So many people care about you, they united to make sure you were okay because they were worried about you. Right now, I need for you to listen to me. This is all over. But I want you to go with Harry. He'll take you to Lena first and then he'll want to ask you some questions, probably down at the station. I want you to tell Harry everything that happened to you from the time Berkenshaw picked you up from school, got you into his car, to when he dragged you into the woods. Are you okay with doing that?"

Zoe nodded. "I'll tell him how this woman prevented me from getting to the car when I tried to run like you told me to do."

"Good girl. Because I want you to tell Harry everything the guy said to you, everything his wife said to you when she took you down into that crypt and tied you up. Do you think you can remember everything?"

"I'll try. They were both crazy and mean, Skye," Zoe wanted her to know, still curled into Skye's side.

"Yes, they were crazy and mean, Zoe, a deadly combination. You saw me take the guy down though, right?"

"You were awesome. You kicked his ass."

From a few feet away, Skye noticed Josh's eyes twinkle with amusement.

"Skye Cree, an amazing warrior," he added for emphasis.

Grinning at them both, Skye went on, "I did what I had to do. Anyway, you know Berkenshaw's dead and will never hurt you. But the other one, the woman, is still alive." When she saw Zoe's alarmed reaction, she patted the girl's shoulder and quickly added, "She won't be able to touch you either. If you tell Harry everything, it will ensure that she stays locked up for a very long time. Do you understand?"

Skye wrapped her arms around the girl's shoulders, hugged her tight to get an answer. "It'll be okay, Zoe. You'll see."

"Promise?"

"I promise. Will you come see us at our new house? We're all settled in now. I want you to meet our new dog, Atka."

"I'd like that. I was hoping you'd ask me."

"You're welcome there any time. Now go, do what you have to do. The sooner it's done with, the sooner you can get on with your life."

Chapter Twenty-Seven

Over the next twenty-four hours, authorities discovered the Berkenshaws' dumping ground, a mere fifteen yards from the front door of the bunker. The final resting place for a multitude of bodies turned out to be a plot of earth that measured twenty by twenty feet.

County officials verified it was on federal land—which meant some of the murders could have occurred there. It also meant that Adela, if found guilty, could end up in a federal facility in Texas for death row inmates.

That ought to wipe that dumbass grin from yesterday off her face, thought Skye as she studied Harry and Dawson, deep in conversation overseeing the first attempt at excavating the vast number of remains.

When her phone chimed, she visibly jumped. It was just that kind of simple noise that could spook a person out in a place like this, even in broad daylight, even with a dozen people standing around. For the past couple of hours, if she didn't know better, she was almost certain it felt as if someone watched them. Old ghosts with a powerful history, Skye decided.

She shook off the feeling, read the display. When she saw Judy Howe's name and number appear, she did a double take. Sliding the bar across to answer the call, she wanted to know, "Is that really you, Judy?"

"Yes, it's me. Is it true what they're saying on the news? Is he dead? They said on the news you caught him. Is it true or did they just make it up?"

"It's true, Judy. You don't have to fear him showing up at your doorstep, not anymore. He's gone. He'll never be able to hurt another person."

"I want to work. I want to work for the Artemis Foundation. You haven't given away the job you promised me, have you?"

Skye laughed. "Nope. There are still phones to answer and envelopes to stuff. But you'll have to leave your apartment, Judy. Do you think you can handle that?"

"I'd like to try."

"Good. Then show up bright and early Monday morning. If you need help, call me."

By the time Skye ended the call, both Harry and Dawson had made their way over to where she and Josh were standing to the side, away from the digging.

"How's it going?" Josh asked.

"Can't complain," Harry replied. He stood there another minute before he could find the words he wanted to say. "A couple of things you might be interested in though. First, we found out Adela is a nurse, was working on a fifteen-year career at the same hospital. We think she used her position there as easy access to drugs, drugs the two of them used on their prey. That's why the drugs varied so much from victim to victim. Whatever Adela could get her hands on, that's what they used. One day it was rocuronium, the next, rohypnol or GHB."

"I'll be damned."

"Second, we may never know how the DNA that turned out to belong to Travis got on that scarf. Travis tells me he knew Ellen, so I'm thinking it might be one of those quirky things that pop up during investigations now and then. Third, we don't know what happened to the real Jason Berkenshaw."

"What? Excuse me?" Skye expressed in disbelief. "I know exactly what happened to him. I stabbed the bastard in the heart."

Harry tightened his lips, rocked back on his heels. "The man you took down was a killer, no doubt about that. But he was not born with the name Jason Berkenshaw."

"What? Are you absolutely certain of this, Harry?"

"The man you took down yesterday was not the real Jason Berkenshaw but someone who had used his name for years. The guy born with that name had a brother who has been looking for him for twenty-five years or more. The real Jason Berkenshaw was three inches shorter than the guy in the morgue, had brown eyes instead of green, and attained a degree from Portland State in 1967. That means he was born in 1945, a long damn time before the imposter came along and stole his identity to join the army.

"After that he used Jason's diploma from an accredited school, changed the dates on the paper and applied to ICE. When the media broke the story last night, I got a call from the brother, Sam Berkenshaw down in Eugene, Oregon. Sam told me his brother took a trip to Seattle back in 1989. He was never seen again. Checking out our perp's background, there were red flags all over the place. But we may never know who the guy actually was, where he was born or where he came from."

"Well, that sucks," Josh stated. "I wondered how he pulled off getting into ICE. What about fingerprints?"

"Nothing came back to tell us his true identity. The real Berkenshaw had to be dead by the time our guy entered the army."

"Why's that?" Skye wanted to know.

"Because the army fingerprints match our dead guy in the morgue."

Dawson shook his head. "It isn't all bad news, guys. There is hope. The imposter's DNA will be entered into CODIS. If he had a relative who has ever been picked up and jailed, we might one day get lucky. I doubt the mystery will go unanswered forever."

"I hope you're right, Dawson," Skye uttered. "What about Adela? What happens to her?"

"She'll likely plead out to avoid the death penalty," Harry stated. "That woman's a real piece of work though. She's already playing the Jason-made-me-do-it card. She was so dedicated to her hubby, so willing to do whatever he told her to do. I believe she used the words 'cult member' twenty-seven times during her first interview. She claims she doesn't have a mind of her own. For years, Jason told her how to dress, how to act, how to think."

"That's bullshit," Josh shot back. "I'm not buying it."

"Me either," Skye agreed. "You didn't see how defiant she was before you showed up. Although I do think Berkenshaw told her how he wanted her to *look*."

"Her complacency is an act. That woman has a temper on her. We saw it firsthand yesterday," Josh explained.

"If it's an act it'll eventually come out," Harry assured them. The cop turned to Dawson. "Tell them what you found."

"I'm able to confirm that the Berkenshaws, or whoever they were, over the course of their active years here, layered the bones we've found at various depths." He surveyed the burial ground and went on, "Eventually they ran out of room, started to put bodies on top of bodies. I've no doubt this mass grave has the potential to yield forty-plus victims. All I know at the moment is it's bigger than anything I've ever experienced. What I don't understand is where Berkenshaw kept the mummified body that the hand came from that he sent you, Skye."

"That's easy. It's in the crypt. Well, that's what Josh and I labeled it. That hollowed out piece of ground located under the bunker. It's creepy down there."

Josh turned to look at Skye. "I wasn't sure you'd seen that."

"Hard to miss a mummified body stuck in the corner. That victim must've been special to him."

"I see I'll have to send the lab down there. The good news is, thanks to the hard work your Foundation did ahead of this, we have a long list of the missing already categorized in a database. It'll make things go a lot smoother over the next several months as we try to put names to the remains."

Josh glanced at Harry. "You still haven't found any sign of Selma Tolliver though. Any luck with leaning on Adela to give up where they put Selma and any others that aren't here in this same spot."

"Not so far. But we will put pressure on her."

Skye blew out a ragged breath. "This has been such a long process. I've never been so tired of a case before until right this minute."

Josh picked up her hand, tugged her toward the car. "Then come on, Mrs. Ander, let's leave Dawson and Harry to their work. Let's get out of here and go home."

Dear Reader:

If you enjoyed *The Box of Bones*, please take the time
to leave a review.
A review shows others how you feel about my work.
By recommending it to your friends and family it helps
spread the word.
If you have the time, please let me know via Facebook
or my website.
I'd love to hear from you!

For a complete list of my other books visit my
website.
www.vickiemckeehan.com

Want to connect with me to leave a comment?
Go to Facebook
www.facebook.com/VickieMcKeehan

Don't miss these other exciting titles by bestselling author

Vickie McKeehan

The Pelican Pointe Series
PROMISE COVE
HIDDEN MOON BAY
DANCING TIDES
LIGHTHOUSE REEF
STARLIGHT DUNES
LAST CHANCE HARBOR
SEA GLASS COTTAGE
LAVENDER BEACH
SANDCASTLES UNDER THE CHRISTMAS MOON
BENEATH WINTER SAND
KEEPING CAPE SUMMER (2018)

The Evil Secrets Trilogy
JUST EVIL Book One
DEEPER EVIL Book Two
ENDING EVIL Book Three
EVIL SECRETS TRILOGY BOXED SET

The Skye Cree Novels
THE BONES OF OTHERS
THE BONES WILL TELL
THE BOX OF BONES
HIS GARDEN OF BONES
TRUTH IN THE BONES
SEA OF BONES (2018)

The Indigo Brothers Trilogy
INDIGO FIRE
INDIGO HEAT
INDIGO JUSTICE
INDIGO BROTHERS TRILOGY BOXED SET

Coyote Wells Mysteries
MYSTIC FALLS
SHADOW CANYON
SPIRIT LAKE (2018)

ABOUT THE AUTHOR

Vickie McKeehan has twenty-two novels to her credit and counting. Vickie's novels have consistently appeared on Amazon's Top 100 lists in Contemporary Romance, Romantic Suspense and Mystery / Thriller. She writes what she loves to read—heartwarming romance laced with suspense, heart-pounding thrillers, and riveting mysteries. Vickie loves to write about compelling and down-to-earth characters in settings that stay with her readers long after they've finished her books. She makes her home in Southern California.

You can visit the author at:
www.vickiemckeehan.com
www.facebook.com/VickieMcKeehan
http://vickiemckeehan.wordpress.com/
www.twitter.com/VickieMcKeehan